NOBODY'S GIRL

"WHY, IT'S BEAUTIFUL," SAID PERRINE, SOFTLY.

(See page 86)

NOBODY'S GIRL

(*En Famille*)

BY

HECTOR MALOT

TRANSLATED BY
FLORENCE CREWE-JONES

Illustrated by
THELMA GOOCH

NEW YORK   MCMXXII
CUPPLES & LEON COMPANY

CONTENTS

CONTENTS

LIST OF ILLUSTRATIONS

———o———

INTRODUCTION

―――――o―――――

" Nobody's Girl," published in France under the title " En Famille ", follows " Nobody's Boy " as a companion juvenile story, and takes place with it as one of the supreme juvenile stories of the world. Like " Nobody's Boy " it was also crowned by the Academy, and that literary judgment has also been verified by the test of time.

Nobody's Girl is not a human document, such as is Nobody's Boy, because it has more story plot, and the adventure is in a more restricted field, but it discloses no less the nobility of a right-minded child, and how loyalty wins the way to noble deeds and life. This is another beautiful literary creation of Hector Malot which every one can recommend as an ennobling book, of interest not only to childhood, page by page to the thrilling conclusion, but to every person who loves romance and character.

Only details, irrelevant for readers in America, have been eliminated. Little Perrine's loyal ideals, with their inspiring sentiments, are preserved by her through the most discouraging conditions, and are described with the simplicity for which Hector Malot is famous. The building up of a little girl's life is made a fine example for every child. Every reader of this story leaves it inspired for the better way.

THE PUBLISHERS.

NOBODY'S GIRL

CHAPTER I

PERRINE AND PALIKARE

IT WAS Saturday afternoon about 3 o'clock. There was the usual scene; outside the Gates of Bercy there was a crowd of people, and on the quays, four rows deep, carts and wagons were massed together. Coal carts, carts heaped with hay and straw, all were waiting in the clear, warm June sunshine for the examination from the custom official. All had been hurrying to reach Paris before Sunday.

Amongst the wagons, but at some little distance from the Gates, stood an odd looking cart, a sort of caravan. Over a light frame work which was erected on four wheels was stretched a heavy canvas; this was fastened to the light roof which covered the wagon. Once upon a time the canvas might have been blue, but it was so faded, so dirty and worn, that one could only guess what its original color had been. Neither was it possible to make out the inscriptions which were painted on the four sides. Most of the words were effaced. On one side there was a Greek word, the next side

1

bore part of a German word, on the third side were
the letters F I A, which was evidently Italian, and
on the last a newly painted French word stood out
boldly. This was *PHOTOGRAPHIE,* and was evidently the translation of all the others, indicating
the different countries through which the miserable
wagon had come before it had entered France and
finally arrived at the Gates of Paris.

Was it possible that the donkey that was harnessed to it had brought the cart all this distance?
At first glance it seemed impossible, but although
the animal was tired out, one could see upon a
closer view that it was very robust and much bigger
than the donkeys that one sees in Europe. Its coat
was a beautiful dark grey, the beauty of which could
be seen despite the dust which covered it. Its
slender legs were marked with jet black lines, and
worn out though the poor beast was, it still held
its head high. The harness, worthy of the caravan,
was fastened together with various colored strings,
short pieces, long pieces, just what was at hand at
the moment; the strings had been carefully hidden
under the flowers and branches which had been
gathered along the roads and used to protect the
animal from the sun and the flies.

Close by, seated on the edge of the curb, watching
the donkey, was a little girl of about thirteen years
of age. Her type was very unusual, but it was
quite apparent that there was a mixture of race.
The pale blond of her hair contrasted strangely with
the deep, rich coloring of her cheeks, and the sweet

expression of her face was accentuated by the dark, serious eyes. Her mouth also was very serious. Her figure, slim and full of grace, was garbed in an old, faded check dress, but the shabby old frock could not take away the child's distinguished air.

As the donkey had stopped just behind a large cart of straw, it would not have required much watching, but every now and again he pulled out the straw, in a cautious manner, like a very intelligent animal that knows quite well that it is doing wrong.

"Palikare! stop that!" said the girl for the third time.

The donkey again dropped his head in a guilty fashion, but as soon as he had eaten his wisps of straw he began to blink his eyes and agitate his ears, then again discreetly, but eagerly, tugged at what was ahead of him; this in a manner that testified to the poor beast's hunger.

While the little girl was scolding him, a voice from within the caravan called out:

"Perrine!"

Jumping to her feet, the child lifted up the canvas and passed inside, where a pale, thin woman was lying on a mattress.

"Do you need me, mama?"

"What is Palikare doing, dear?" asked the woman.

"He is eating the straw off the cart that's ahead of us."

"You must stop him."

"He's so hungry."

"Hunger is not an excuse for taking what does not belong to us. What will you say to the driver of that cart if he's angry?"

"I'll go and see that Palikare doesn't do it again," said the little girl.

"Shall we soon be in Paris?"

"Yes, we are waiting for the customs."

"Have we much longer to wait?"

"No, but are you in more pain, mother?"

"Don't worry, darling; it's because I'm closed in here," replied the woman, gasping. Then she smiled wanly, hoping to reassure her daughter.

The woman was in a pitiable plight. All her strength had gone and she could scarcely breathe. Although she was only about twenty-nine years of age, her life was ebbing away. There still remained traces of remarkable beauty: Her head and hair were lovely, and her eyes were soft and dark like her daughter's.

"Shall I give you something?" asked Perrine.

"What?"

"There are some shops near by. I can buy a lemon. I'll come back at once."

"No, keep the money. We have so little. Go back to Palikare and stop him from eating the straw."

"That's not easy," answered the little girl.

She went back to the donkey and pushed him on his haunches until he was out of reach of the straw in front of him.

At first the donkey was obstinate and tried to push forward again, but she spoke to him gently and stroked him, and kissed him on his nose; then he dropped his long ears with evident satisfaction and stood quite still.

There was no occasion to worry about him now, so she amused herself with watching what was going on around her.

A little boy about her own age, dressed up like a clown, and who evidently belonged to the circus caravans standing in the rear, had been strolling round her for ten long minutes, without being able to attract her attention.   At last he decided to speak to her.

" That's a fine donkey," he remarked.

She did not reply.

" It don't belong to this country.   If it does, I'm astonished."

She was looking at him, and thinking that after all he looked rather like a nice boy, she thought she would reply.

" He comes from Greece," she said.

" Greece ! " he echoed.

" That's why he's called Palikare."

" Ah ! that's why."

But in spite of his broad grin he was not at all sure why a donkey that came from Greece should be called Palikare.

" Is it far . . . Greece? "

" Very far."

" Farther than . . . China? "

" No, but it's a long way off."

" Then yer come from Greece, then? "

" No, farther than that."

" From China? "

" No, but Palikare's the only one that comes from Greece."

" Are you going to the Fair? "

" No."

" Where yer goin'? "

" Into Paris."

" I know that, but where yer goin' to put up that there cart? "

" We've been told that there are some free places round the fortifications."

The little clown slapped his thighs with his two hands.

" The fortifications: *Oh la la!* "

" Isn't there any place? "

" Yes."

" Well, then? "

" It ain't the place for you . . . round the fortifications! Have yer got any men with yer? Big strong men who are not afraid of a stab from a dagger. One who can give a jab as well as take one."

" There is only my mother and me, and mother is ill."

" Do you think much of that donkey? " he asked quickly.

" I should say so! "

" Well, the first thing he'll be stolen. He'll be

gone tomorrow. Then the rest 'll come after, and it's Fatty as tells yer so."

" Really? "

" Should say so! You've never been to Paris before? "

" No, never."

" That's easy to see. Some fools told you where to put your cart up, but you can't put it there. Why don't you go to Grain-of-Salt? "

" I don't know Grain-of-Salt."

" Why, he owns the Guillot Fields. You needn't be afraid of him, and he'd shoot anybody who tried to get in his place."

" Will it cost much to go there? "

" It costs a lot in winter, when everybody comes to Paris, but at this time I'm sure he won't make you pay more than forty sous a week. And your donkey can find its food in the field. Does he like thistles? "

" I should say he does like them! "

" Well, then, this is just the place for him, and Grain-of-Salt isn't a bad chap," said the little clown with a satisfied air.

" Is that his name . . . Grain of Salt? "

" They call him that 'cause he's always thirsty. He's only got one arm."

" Is his place far from here? "

" No, at Charonne; but I bet yer don't even know where Charonne is? "

" I've never been to Paris before."

"Well, then, it's over there." He waved his arms vaguely in a northerly direction.

"Once you have passed through the Gates, you turn straight to the right," he explained, "and you follow the road all along the fortifications for half an hour, then go down a wide avenue, then turn to your left, and then ask where the Guillot Field is. Everybody knows it."

"Thank you. I'll go and tell mama. If you'll stand beside Palikare for a minute, I'll go and tell her at once."

"Sure, I'll mind him for yer. I'll ask him to teach me Greek."

"And please don't let him eat that straw."

Perrine went inside the caravan and told her mother what the little clown had said.

"If that is so," said the sick woman, "we must not hesitate; we must go to Charonne. But can you find the way?"

"Yes, it's easy enough. Oh, mother," she added, as she was going out, "there are such a lot of wagons outside; they have printed on them 'Marau-court Factories,' and beneath that the name, 'Vul-fran Paindavoine.' There are all kinds of barrels and things in the carts. Such a number!"

"There is nothing remarkable in that, my child," said the woman.

"Yes, but it's strange to see so many wagons with the same name on them," replied the girl as she left the caravan.

Perrine found the donkey with his nose buried in the straw, which he was eating calmly.

"Why, you're letting him eat it!" she cried to the boy.

"Well, why not?" he retorted.

"And if the man is angry?"

"He'd better not be with me," said the small boy, putting himself in a position to fight and throwing his head back.

But his prowess was not to be brought into action, for at this moment the custom officer began to search the cart of straw, and then gave permission for it to pass on through the Gates of Paris.

"Now it's your turn," said the boy, "and I'll have to leave you. Goodbye, Mademoiselle. If you ever want news of me ask for Double Fat. Everybody knows me."

The employés who guard the entrances of Paris are accustomed to strange sights, yet the man who went into Perrine's caravan looked surprised when he found a young woman lying on a mattress, and even more surprised when his hasty glance revealed to him the extreme poverty of her surroundings.

"Have you anything to declare?" he asked, continuing his investigations.

"Nothing."

"No wine, no provisions?"

"Nothing."

This was only too true; apart from the mattress, the two cane chairs, a little table, a tiny stove, a camera and a few photographic supplies, there was nothing in this wagon; no trunks, no baskets, no clothes. . . . .

"All right; you can pass," said the man.

Once through the Gates, Perrine, holding Palikare by the bridle, followed the stretch of grass along the embankment.   In the brown, dirty grass she saw rough looking men lying on their backs or on their stomachs.   She saw now the class of people who frequent this spot.   From the very air of these men, with their bestial, criminal faces, she understood why it would be unsafe for them to be there at night.   She could well believe that their knives would be in ready use.

Looking towards the city, she saw nothing but dirty streets and filthy houses.   So this was Paris, the beautiful Paris of which her father had so often spoken.   With one word she made her donkey go faster, then turning to the left she inquired for the Guillot Field.

If everyone knew where it was situated, no two were of the same opinion as to which road she should take to get there, and several times, in trying to follow the various directions which were given to her, she lost her way.

At last she found the place for which she was looking.   This must be it!   Inside the field there was an old omnibus without wheels, and a railway car, also without wheels, was on the ground.   In addition, she saw a dozen little round pups rolling about.   Yes, this was the place!

Leaving Palikare in the street, she went into the

field.   The pups at once scrambled at her feet, barked, and snapped at her shoes.

" Who's there? " called a voice.

She looked around and saw a long, low building, which might have been a house, but which might serve for anything else.   The walls were made of bits of stone, wood and plaster.   Even tin boxes were used in its construction.   The roof was made of tarred canvas and cardboard, and most of the window panes were of paper, although in one or two instances there was some glass.   The man who designed it was another Robinson Crusoe, and his workman a man Friday.

A one-armed man with a shaggy beard was sorting out rags and throwing them into the baskets around him.

" Don't step on my dogs," he cried; " come nearer."

She did as she was told.

"Are you the owner of the Guillot Field?" she asked.

" That's me! " replied the man.

In a few words she told him what she wanted. So as not to waste his time while listening, he poured some red wine out of a bottle that stood on the ground and drank it down at a gulp.

" It can be arranged if you pay in advance," he said, sizing her up.

" How much? " she asked.

" Forty sous a week for the wagon and twenty for the donkey," he replied.

" That's a lot of money," she said, hesitatingly.

" That's my price."

" Your summer price? "

" Yes, my summer price."

" Can my donkey eat the thistles? "

" Yes, and the grass also if his teeth are strong enough."

" We can't pay for the whole week because we are only going to stay one day.   We are going through Paris on our way to Amiens, and we want to rest."

" Well, that's all right;   six sous a day for the cart and three for the donkey."

One by one she pulled out nine sous from the pocket in her skirt.

" That's for the first day," she said, handing them to the man.

" You can tell your people they can all come in," he said.   " How many are there?   If it's a whole company it's two sous extra for each person."

" I have only my mother."

" All right; but why didn't your mother come and settle this? "

" She is in the wagon, ill."

" Ill!   Well, this isn't a hospital."

Perrine was afraid that he would not let her sick mother come in.

" I mean she's a little bit tired.   We've come a long way."

" I never ask people where they come from," replied the man gruffly.   He pointed to a corner of the field, and added: " You can put your wagon

over there and tie up the donkey.   And if it
squashes one of my pups you'll pay me five francs,
one hundred sous . . . understand? "

As she was going he called out:

" Will you take a glass of wine? "

" No, thanks," she replied; " I never take wine."

" Good," he said; " I'll drink it for you."

He drained another glass, then returned to his
collection of rags.

As soon as she had installed Palikare in the place
that the man had pointed out to her, which was
accomplished not without some jolts, despite the
care which she took, Perrine climbed up into the
wagon.

" We've arrived at last, poor mama," she said,
bending over the woman.

" No more shaking, no more rolling about," said
the woman weakly.

" There, there; I'll make you some dinner," said
Perrine cheerfully.   " What would you like? "

" First, dear, unharness Palikare; he is very
tired also; and give him something to eat and
drink."

Perrine did as her mother told her, then returned
to the wagon and took out the small stove, some
pieces of coal and an old saucepan and some sticks.
Outside, she went down on her knees and made a
fire; at last, after blowing with all her might, she
had the satisfaction of seeing that it had taken.

" You'd like some rice, wouldn't you? " she asked,
leaning over her mother.

"I am not hungry."

"Is there anything else you would fancy?   I'll go and fetch anything you want.   What would you like, mama, dearie?"

"I think I prefer rice," said her mother.

Little Perrine threw a handful of rice into the saucepan that she had put on the fire and waited for the water to boil; then she stirred the rice with two white sticks that she had stripped of their bark. She only left her cooking once, to run over to Palikare to say a few loving words to him.   The donkey was eating the thistles with a satisfaction, the intensity of which was shown by the way his long ears stood up.

When the rice was cooked to perfection, Perrine filled a bowl and placed it at her mother's bedside, also two glasses, two plates and two forks.   Sitting down on the floor, with her legs tucked under her and her skirts spread out, she said, like a little girl who is playing with her doll: "Now we'll have a little din-din, mammy, dear, and I'll wait on you."

In spite of her gay tone, there was an anxious look in the child's eyes as she looked at her mother lying on the mattress, covered with an old shawl that had once been beautiful and costly, but was now only a faded rag.

The sick woman tried to swallow a mouthful of rice, then she looked at her daughter with a wan smile.

"It doesn't go down very well," she murmured.

"You must force yourself," said Perrine; "the

second will go down better, and the third better still."

"I cannot; no, I cannot, dear!"

"Oh, mama!"

The mother sank back on her mattress, gasping. But weak though she was, she thought of her little girl and smiled.

"The rice is delicious, dear," she said; "you eat it. As you do the work you must feed well. You must be very strong to be able to nurse me, so eat, darling, eat."

Keeping back her tears, Perrine made an effort to eat her dinner. Her mother continued to talk to her. Little by little she stopped crying and all the rice disappeared.

"Why don't you try to eat, mother?" she asked.

"I forced myself."

"But I'm ill, dear."

"I think I ought to go and fetch a doctor. We are in Paris now and there are good doctors here."

"Good doctors will not put themselves out unless they are paid."

"We'll pay."

"With what, my child?"

"With our money. You have seven francs in your pocket and a florin which we could change here. I've got 17 sous. Feel in your pocket."

The black dress, as worn as Perrine's skirt but not so dusty, for it had been brushed, was lying on the bed, and served for a cover. They found the seven francs and an Austrian coin.

"How much does that make in all?" asked Perrine; "I don't understand French money."

"I know very little more than you," replied her mother.

Counting the florin at two francs, they found they had nine francs and eighty-five centimes.

"You see we have more than what is needed for a doctor," insisted Perrine.

"He won't cure me with words; we shall have to buy medicine."

"I have an idea. You can imagine that all the time I was walking beside Palikare I did not waste my time just talking to him, although he likes that. I was also thinking of both of us, but mostly of you, mama, because you are sick. And I was thinking of our arrival at Maraucourt. Everybody has laughed at our wagon as we came along, and I am afraid if we go to Maraucourt with it we shall not get much of a welcome. If our relations are very proud, they'll be humiliated.

"So I thought," she added, wisely, "that as we don't need the wagon any more, we could sell it. Now that you are ill, no one will let me take their pictures, and even if they would we have not the money to buy the things for developing that we need. We must sell it."

"And how much can we get for it?"

"We can get something; then there is the camera and the mattress."

"Everything," said the sick woman.

"But you don't mind, do you, mother, dear? . . . "

"We have lived in this wagon for more than a year," said her mother; "your father died here, and although it's a poor thing, it makes me sad to part with it. . . . It is all that remains of him . . . there is not one of these old things here that does not remind us of him . . ."

She stopped, gasping; the tears were rolling down her cheeks.

"Oh, forgive me, mother, for speaking about it," cried Perrine.

"My darling, you are right. You are only a child, but you have thought of the things that I should have. I shall not be better tomorrow nor the next day, and we must sell these things, and we must decide to sell . . ."

The mother hesitated. There was a painful silence.

"Palikare," said Perrine at last.

"You have thought that also?" asked the mother.

"Yes," said Perrine, "and I have been so unhappy about it, and sometimes I did not dare look at him for fear he would guess that we were going to part with him instead of taking him to Maraucourt with us. He would have been so happy there after such a long journey."

"If we were only sure of a welcome, but they may turn us away. If they do, all we can do then is to lie down by the roadside and die, but no matter what it costs, we must get to Maraucourt, and we must present ourselves as well as we can so that they will not shut their doors upon us . . ."

"Would that be possible, mama? . . . The memory of papa . . . he was so good. Could they be angry with him now he is dead?"

"I am speaking as your father would have spoken, dear . . . so we will sell Palikare. With the money that we get for him we will have a doctor, so that I can get stronger; then, when I am well enough, we will buy a nice dress for you and one for me, and then we'll start. We will take the train as far as we can and walk the rest of the way."

"That boy who spoke to me at the Gates told me that Palikare was a fine donkey, and he knows, for he is in a circus. It was because he thought Palikare was so beautiful that he spoke to me."

"I don't know how much an Eastern donkey would bring in Paris, but we'll see as soon as we can," said the sick woman.

Leaving her mother to rest, Perrine got together their soiled clothing and decided to do some washing. Adding her own waist to a bundle consisting of three handkerchiefs, two pairs of stockings and two combinations, she put them all into a basin, and with her washboard and a piece of soap she went outside. She had ready some boiling water which she had put on the fire after cooking the rice; this she poured over the things. Kneeling on the grass, she soaped and rubbed until all were clean; then she rinsed them and hung them on a line to dry.

While she worked, Palikare, who was tied up at a short distance from her, had glanced her way several times. When he saw that she had finished her task he stretched his neck towards her and sent forth five or six brays . . . an imperative call.

" Did you think I had forgotten you? " she called out. She went to him, changed his place, gave him some water to drink from her saucepan, which she had carefully rinsed, for if he was satisfied with all the food that they gave him, he was very particular about what he drank. He would only drink pure water from a clean vessel, or red wine . . . this he liked better than anything.

She stroked him and talked to him lovingly, like a kind nurse would to a little child, and the donkey, who had thrown himself down on the grass the moment he was free, placed his head against her shoulder. He loved his young mistress, and every now and again he looked up at her and shook his long ears in sign of utter content.

All was quiet in the field and the streets close by were now deserted. From the distance came the dim roar of the great city, deep, powerful, mysterious; the breath and life of Paris, active and incessant, seemed like the roar of a mighty ocean going on and on, in spite of the night that falls.

Then, in the softness of the coming night, little Perrine seemed to feel more impressed with the talk that she had had with her mother, and leaning her head against her donkey's, she let the tears, which she had kept back so long, flow silently, and Palikare, in mute sympathy, bent his head and licked her hands.

CHAPTER II

GRAIN-OF-SALT IS KIND

MANY times that night Perrine, lying beside her mother, had jumped up and run to the well for water so as to have it fresh. In spite of her desire to fetch the doctor as early as possible the next morning, she had to wait until Grain-of-Salt had risen, for she did not know what doctor to call in. She asked him.

Certainly he knew of a good doctor! and a famous one, too! who made his rounds in a carriage, not on foot, like doctors of no account. Dr. Centrier, rue Rublet, near the Church; he was the man! To find the street she had only to follow the railway tracks as far as the station.

When he spoke of such a great doctor who made his rounds in a carriage, Perrine was afraid that she would not have enough money to pay him, and timidly she questioned Grain-of-Salt, not daring to ask outright what she wanted to know. Finally he understood.

"What you'd have to pay?" he asked. "It's a lot, but it won't be more than forty sous, and so as to make sure, you'll have to pay him in advance."

Following the directions that Grain-of-Salt gave her, she easily found the house, but the doctor had

not yet risen, so she had to wait.   She sat down on
a bench in the street, outside a stable door, behind
which a coachman was harnessing a horse to a carriage.   She thought if she waited there she would
be sure to catch the doctor as he left the house, and
if she gave him her forty sous he would consent to
come.   She was quite sure that he would not if she
had simply asked him to visit a patient who was
staying in the Guillot Field.

She waited a long time; her suspense increased
at the thought that her mother would be wondering
what kept her away so long.

At last an old-fashioned carriage and a clumsy
horse came out of the stables and stood before the
doctor's house.   Almost immediately the doctor
appeared, big, fat, with a grey beard.

Before he could step into his carriage Perrine was
beside him.   She put her question tremblingly.

" The Guillot Field? " he said.   " Has there been
a fight? "

" No, sir; it's my mother who is ill."

" Who is your mother? "

" We are photographers."

He put his foot on the step.   She offered him her
forty sous quickly.

" We can pay you," she hastened to say.

" Then it's sixty sous," said he.

She added twenty sous more.   He took the money
and slipped it into his waistcoat pocket.

" I'll be with your mother in about fifteen minutes." he said.

She ran all the way back, happy, to take the good news.

"He'll cure you, mama; he's a real, real doctor!" she said, breathlessly.

She quickly busied herself with her mother, washing her hands and face and arranging her hair, which was beautiful, black and silky; then she tidied up the "room," which only had the result of making it look emptier and poorer still.

She had not long to wait. Hearing the carriage in the road, she ran out to meet the doctor. As he was walking towards the house she pointed to the wagon.

"We live there in our wagon," she said.

He did not seem surprised; he was accustomed to the extreme poverty of his patients; but Perrine, who was looking at him, noticed that he frowned when he saw the sick woman lying on the mattress in the miserable cart.

"Put out your tongue and give me your hand," he said.

Those who pay forty or a hundred francs for a visit from a doctor have no idea of the brevity with which the poor people's cases are diagnosed. In less than a minute his examination was made.

"A case for the hospital," he said.

Simultaneously, little Perrine and her mother uttered a cry.

"Now, child, leave me alone with your mother," he said in a tone of command.

For a moment Perrine hesitated, but at a sign

from her mother she left the wagon and stood just outside.

"I am going to die," said the woman in a low voice.

"Who says that? What you need is nursing, and you can't get that here."

"Could I have my daughter at the hospital?"

"She can see you Thursdays and Sundays."

"What will become of her without me," murmured the mother, "alone in Paris? If I have to die I want to go holding her hand in mine."

"Well, anyway, you can't be left in this cart. The cold nights would be fatal for you. You must take a room. Can you?"

"If it is not for long, perhaps."

"Grain-of-Salt can rent you one, and won't charge much; but the room is not all. You must have medicine and good food and care, all of which you would get at the hospital."

"Doctor, that is impossible," said the sick woman. "I cannot leave my little girl. What would become of her?"

"Well, it's as you like; it's your own affair. I have told you what I think."

"You can come in, little girl, now," he called out. Then taking a leaf from his note pad, he wrote out a prescription.

"Take that to the druggist, near the Church," he said, handing it to Perrine. "No other, mind you. The packet marked *No. 1* give to your mother. Then give her the potion every hour. Give her the

Quinquina wine when she eats, for she must eat anything she wants, especially eggs. I'll drop in again this evening."

She ran out after him.

" Is my mama very ill?" she asked.

" Well . . . try and get her to go to the hospital."

" Can't you cure her? "

" I hope so, but I can't give her what she'll get at the hospital. It is foolish for her not to go. She won't go because she has to leave you. Nothing will happen to you, for you look like a girl who can take care of yourself."

Striding on, he reached his carriage. Perrine wanted him to say more, but he jumped in quickly, and was driven off. She returned to the wagon.

" Go quickly to the druggist; then get some eggs. Take all the money; I must get well," said the mother.

" The doctor said he could cure you," said Perrine. " I'll go quickly for the things."

But all the money she took was not enough. When the druggist had read the prescription he looked at Perrine.

" Have you the money to pay for this? " he asked.

She opened her hand.

" This will come to seven francs, fifty," said the man who had already made his calculation.

She counted what she had in her hand and found that she had six francs eighty-five centimes, in counting the Austrian florin as two francs. She needed thirteen sous more.

"I have only six francs eighty-five centimes. Would you take this florin? I have counted that," she said.

"Oh, no; I should say not!" replied the man.

What was to be done? She stood in the middle of the store with her hand open. She was in despair.

"If you'll take the florin there will be only thirteen sous lacking," she said at last, "and I'll bring them this afternoon."

But the druggist would not agree to this arrangement. He would neither give her credit for thirteen sous nor accept the florin.

"As there is no hurry for the wine," he said, "you can come and fetch it this afternoon. I'll prepare the other things at once and they'll only cost you three francs fifty."

With the money that remained she bought some eggs, a little Vienna loaf which she thought might tempt her mother's appetite, and then she returned to the Field, running as fast as she could all the way.

"The eggs are fresh," she said. "I held them up to the light. And look at the bread! Isn't it a beautiful loaf, mama? You'll eat it, won't you?"

"Yes, darling."

Both were full of hope. Perrine had absolute faith in the doctor, and was certain that he would perform the miracle. Why should he deceive them? When one asks the doctor to tell the truth, doesn't he do so?

Hope had given the sick woman an appetite. She

had eaten nothing for two days; now she ate a half of the roll.

" You see," said Perrine, gleefully.

" Everything will be all right soon," answered her mother with a smile.

Perrine went to the house to inquire of Grain-of-Salt what steps she should take to sell the wagon and dear Palikare.

As for the wagon, nothing was easier. Grain-of-Salt would buy it himself; he bought everything, furniture, clothes, tools, musical instruments . . . but a donkey! That was another thing. He did not buy animals, except pups, and his advice was that they should wait for a day and sell it at the Horse Market. That would be on Wednesday.

Wednesday seemed a long way off, for in her excitement, and filled with hope, Perrine had thought that by Wednesday her mother would be strong enough to start for Maraucourt. But to have to wait like this! There was one thing, though: With what she got for the wagon she could buy the two dresses and the railway tickets, and if Grain-of-Salt paid them enough, then they need not sell Palikare. He could stay at the Guillot Field and she could send for him after they arrived at Maraucourt. Dear Palikare! How contented he would be to have a beautiful stable to live in and go out every day in the green fields.

But alas! Grain-of-Salt would not give one sou over fifteen francs for the wagon.

" Only fifteen francs!" she murmured.

" Yes, and I am only doing that to oblige you. What do you think I can do with it? " he said. He struck the wheels and the shafts with an iron bar; then shrugged his shoulders in disgust.

After a great deal of bargaining all she could get was two francs fifty on the price he had offered, and the promise that he would not take it until after they had gone, so that they could stay in it all day, which she thought would be much better for her mother than closed up in the house.

After she had looked at the room that Grain-of-Salt was willing to rent, she realized how much the wagon meant to them, for in spite of the pride in which he spoke of his " Apartments," and the contempt in which he spoke of the wagon, Perrine was heartbroken at the thought that she must bring her dear mother to this dirty smelling house.

As she hesitated, wondering if her mother would not be poisoned from the odor which came from the heaps of things outside, Grain-of-Salt said impatiently :

" Hurry up! The rag pickers will be here in a moment and I'll have to get busy."

" Does the doctor know what these rooms are like? " she asked.

" Sure! He came to this one lots of times to see the Baroness."

That decided her. If the doctor had seen the rooms he knew what he was doing in advising them to take one, and then if a Baroness lived in one, her mother could very well live in the other.

" You'll have to pay one week in advance," said the landlord, " and three sous for the donkey and six for the wagon."

" But you've bought the wagon," she said in surprise.

" Yes, but as you're using it, it's only fair that you should pay."

She had no reply to make to this. It was not the first time that she had been cheated. It had happened so often on their long journey.

" Very well," said the poor little girl.

She employed the greater part of the day in cleaning their room, washing the floor, wiping down the walls, the ceiling, the windows. Such a scrubbing had never been seen in that house since the place had been built!

During the numerous trips that she made from the house to the pump she saw that not only did grass and thistles grow in the Field, but there were flowers. Evidently some neighbors had thrown some plants over the fence and the seeds had sprung up here and there. Scattered about she saw a few roots of wall-flowers, pinks and even some violets!

What a lovely idea! She would pick some and put them in their room. They would drive away the bad odor, and at the same time make the place look gay.

It seemed that the flowers belonged to no one, for Palikare was allowed to eat them if he wished, yet she was afraid to pick the tiniest one without first asking Grain-of-Salt.

" Do you want to sell them? " he asked.

" No, just to put a few in our room," she replied.

" Oh, if that's it you may take as many as you like, but if you are going to sell them, I might do that myself. As it's for your room, help yourself, little one. You like the smell of flowers. I like the smell of wine. That's the only thing I can smell."

She picked the flowers, and searching amongst the heap of broken glass she found an old vase and some tumblers.

The miserable room was soon filled with the sweet perfume of wall-flowers, pinks and violets, which kept out the bad odors of the rest of the house, and at the same time the fresh, bright colors lent a beauty to the dark walls.

While working, she had made the acquaintance of her neighbors. On one side of their room lived an old woman whose gray head was adorned with a bonnet decorated with the tri-color ribbon of the French flag. On the other side lived a big man, almost bent double. He wore a leather apron, so long and so large that it seemed to be his only garment. The woman with the tri-color ribbons was a street singer, so the big man told her, and no less a person than the Baroness of whom Grain-of-Salt had spoken. Every day she left the Guillot Field with a great red umbrella and a big stick which she stuck in the ground at the crossroads or at the end of a bridge. She would shelter herself from the sun or the rain under her red umbrella and sing, and then sell to the passersby copies of the songs she sang.

As to the big man with the apron, he was a cobbler, so she learned from the Baroness, and he worked from morning to night.   He was always silent, like a fish, and for this reason everybody called him Father Carp.   But although he did little talking he made enough noise with his hammer.

At sunset Perrine's room was ready.   Her mother, as she was helped in, looked at the flowers with surprise and pleasure.

" How good you are to your mama, darling," she murmured as she clung to Perrine's arm.

" How good I am to myself," Perrine cried gayly, " because if I do anything that pleases you, I am so happy."

At night they had to put the flowers outside. Then the odors of the old house rose up terribly strong, but the sick woman did not dare complain. What would be the use, for she could not leave the Guillot Field to go elsewhere?

Her sleep was restless, and when the doctor came the next morning he found her worse, which made him change the treatment, and Perrine was obliged to go again to the druggist.   This time he asked five francs to fill out the prescription.   She did not flinch, but paid bravely, although she could scarcely breathe when she got outside the store.   If the expenses continued to increase at this rate poor Palikare would have to be sold on Wednesday.   He would have to go now anyway.   And if the doctor prescribed something else the next day, costing five francs or more, where would she find the money?

When, with her mother and father, she had tramped over the mountains, they had often been hungry, and more than once since they had left Greece on their way to France they had been without food. But hunger in the mountains and in the country was another thing — there was always the chance that they would find some wild fruit or vegetables. But in Paris there was no hope for those who had no money in their pockets.

What would become of them? And the terrible thing was that she must take the responsibility. Her mother was too ill now to think or plan, and Perrine, although only a child, realized that she must now be the mother.

On Tuesday morning her fears were realized. After a brief examination, the doctor took from his pocket that terrible notebook that Perrine dreaded to see and began to write. She had the courage to stop him.

" Doctor, if the medicines which you are ordering are not all of the same importance," she said, " will you please write out those which are needed the most? "

" What do you mean? " he asked angrily.

She trembled but continued bravely:

" I mean that we have not much money today, and we shall not get any perhaps until tomorrow . . . so . . ."

He looked at her, then glanced round the room,

as though for the first time remarking their poverty;
then he put his notebook back in his pocket.

"We won't change the treatment until tomorrow,
then," he said.   "There is no hurry for this.   Continue the same today."

"No hurry!"   Perrine repeated the words to
herself.   There was no hurry then . . . her mother
was not so ill as she had feared; they had just to
wait and hope . . .

Wednesday was the day for which she was waiting, yet at the same time how she dreaded it.   Dear,
dear Palikare. . . . Whenever her mother did not
need her she would run out into the field and kiss
his nose and talk to him, and as he had no work to
do, and all the thistles to eat that he wanted and his
little mistress' love, he was the happiest donkey in
the world.

"Ah, if you only knew," murmured Perrine, as
she caressed him.

But he did not know.   All he knew was that she
loved him and that the thistles were good.   So, as
she kissed and kissed, he brayed in contentment
and shook his long ears as he looked at her from
the corner of his eyes.

Besides, he had made friends with Grain-of-Salt
and had received a proof of his friendship in a way
that flattered his greed.   On Monday, having broken
loose, he had trotted up to Grain-of-Salt, who was
occupied in sorting out the rags and bones that had
just arrived, and he stood beside him.   The man
was about to pour out a drink from the bottle that

was always beside him when he saw Palikare, his eyes fixed on him, his neck stretched out.

" What are you doing here? " he asked. As the words were not said in anger, the donkey knew, and he did not move.

" Want a drink . . . a glass of wine? " he asked mockingly.   The glass that he was about to put to his lips he offered in a joke to the donkey.   Palikare, taking the offer seriously, came a step nearer and pushing out his lips to make them as thin and as long as possible, drank a good half of the glass which had been filled to the brim.

" *Oh la la! la la!* " cried Grain-of-Salt, bursting with laughter.   " Baroness! Carp! Come here! "

At his calls, the Baroness and Carp, also a rag picker who came into the field at that moment and a man with a push-cart who sold red and yellow and blue sugar sticks, ran up.

" What's the matter? " demanded the Baroness.

He filled the glass again and held it out to the donkey, who, as before, absorbed half of the contents amidst the laughter and shouts of those who looked on.

" I heard that donkeys liked wine, but I never believed it," said the candy man.

" You ought to buy him; he'd be a good companion for you," said the Baroness.

" A fine pair," said another.

But Grain-of-Salt did not buy him, although he took a great liking to him, and told Perrine that he would go with her on Wednesday to the Horse

Market. This was a great relief for Perrine, for
she had wondered how she would ever be able to find
the place; neither did she know how to discuss
prices, and she was very much afraid that she would
be robbed. She had heard so many stories about
Paris thieves, and what could she have done to
protect herself? . . .

Wednesday morning came. At an early hour she
busied herself with brushing Palikare and making
his beautiful coat shine so that he would look his
best. How she kissed him! How she stroked him
while her tears fell!

When Palikare saw that instead of being hitched
to the wagon, a rope was put round his neck, his
surprise was great; and still more surprised was
he when Grain-of-Salt, who did not want to walk all
the way from Charonne to the Horse Market,
climbed up on a chair and from the chair onto his
back. But as Perrine held him and spoke to him,
he offered no resistance. Besides, was not Grain-
of-Salt his friend?

They started thus. Palikare, still surprised,
walked gravely along, led by Perrine. On through
the streets they went. At first they met but few
vehicles, and soon they arrived at a bridge which
jutted into a large garden.

"That's the Zoo," said Grain-of-Salt, "and I'm
sure that they haven't got a donkey there like
yours."

"Then perhaps we can sell him to the Zoo,"
exclaimed Perrine, thinking that in a zoological

garden all the animals have to do is to walk about and be looked at. That would be very nice for dear Palikare!

" An affair with the Government," said Grain-of-Salt; " better not, 'cause the Government . . . "

From his expression it was evident that Grain-of-Salt had no faith in the Government.

From now on the traffic was intense. Perrine needed all her wits and eyes about her. After what seemed a long time they arrived at the Market and Grain-of-Salt jumped off the donkey. But while he was getting down Palikare had time to gaze about him, and when Perrine tried to make him go through the iron gate at the entrance he refused to budge.

He seemed to know by instinct that this was a market where horses and donkeys were sold. He was afraid. Perrine coaxed him, commanded him, begged him, but he still refused to move. Grain-of-Salt thought that if he pushed him from behind he would go forward, but Palikare, who would not permit such familiarity, backed and reared, dragging Perrine with him.

There was already a small circle of onlookers around them. In the first row, as usual, there were messenger boys and errand boys, each giving his word of advice as to what means to use to force the donkey through the gate.

" That there donkey is going to give some trouble to the fool who buys him," cried one.

These were dangerous words that might effect the

sale, so Grain-of-Salt thought he ought to say something.

"He's the cleverest donkey that ever was!" he cried. "He knows he's going to be sold, and he's doin' this 'cause he loves us and don't want ter leave us!"

"Are you so sure of that, Grain-of-Salt?" called out a voice in the crowd.

"Zooks! who knows my name here?" cried the one addressed.

"Don't you recognize La Rouquerie?"

"My faith, that's so," he cried, as the speaker came forward. They shook hands.

"That donkey yours?"

"No; it belongs to this little gal."

"Do you know anything about it?"

"We've had more than one glass together, and if you want a good donkey I'll speak for him."

"I need one and yet I don't need one," said La Rouquerie.

"Well, come and take a drink. T'aint worth while to pay for a place in the Market . . ."

"Especially if he won't budge!"

"I told you he was a smart one; he's that intelligent."

"If I buy him it's not for his tricks nor 'cause he can take a drink with one, but he must work."

"He can work, sure! He's come all the way from Greece without stopping."

"From Greece!"

Grain-of-Salt made a sign to Perrine to follow

him, and Palikare, now that he knew that he was not going into the market, trotted beside her docilely. She did not even have to pull his rope.

Who was this prospective buyer? A man? A woman? From the general appearance and the hairless face it might be a woman of about fifty, but from the clothes, which consisted of a workingman's blouse and trousers and a tall leather hat like a coachman wears, and from the short, black pipe which the individual was smoking, it surely was a man. But whatever it was, Perrine decided that the person looked kind. The expression was not hard or wicked.

Grain-of-Salt and the stranger turned down a narrow street and stopped at a wine shop. They sat down at one of the tables outside on the pavement and ordered a bottle of wine and two glasses. Perrine remained by the curb, still holding her donkey.

"You'll see if he isn't cunning," said Grain-of-Salt, holding out his full glass.

Palikare stretched out his neck, thinned his lips and quickly drank the half glass of wine.

But this feat did not give La Rouquerie any particular satisfaction.

"I don't want him to drink my wine, but to drag my cart with the rabbit skins," she said.

"Didn't I just tell you that he came from Greece, draggin' a wagon the whole way?"

"Ah, that's another thing!"

The strange looking woman carefully examined the animal; then she gave the greatest attention to every detail; then asked Perrine how much she wanted for him. The price which Perrine had arranged with her landlord beforehand was one hundred francs. This was the sum that she asked.

La Rouquerie gave a cry of amazement. One hundred francs! Sell a donkey without any guarantee for that sum! Were they crazy? Then she began to find all kind of faults with the unfortunate Palikare.

"Oh, very well," said Grain-of-Salt, after a lengthy discussion; "we'll take him to the Market."

Perrine breathed. The thought of only getting twenty francs had stunned her. In their terrible distress what would twenty francs be? A hundred francs even was not sufficient for their pressing needs.

"Let's see if he'll go in any more now than he did then," cried La Rouquerie.

Palikare followed Perrine up to the Market gates obediently, but once there he stopped short. She insisted, and talked, and pulled at the rope, but it was no use. Finally he sat down in the middle of the street.

"Palikare, do come! Do come, dear Palikare," Perrine said, imploringly.

But he sat there as though he did not understand a word of what she was saying. A crowd gathered round and began to jeer.

"Set fire to his tail," cried one.

Grain-of-Salt was furious, Perrine in despair.

"You see he won't go in," cried La Rouquerie. "I'll give thirty francs, that's ten more'n I said, 'cause his cunning shows that this donkey is a good boy, but hurry up and take the money or I'll buy another."

"Grain-of-Salt consulted Perrine with a glance; he made her a sign that she ought to accept the offer. But she seemed stunned at such a fraud. She was standing there undecided when a policeman told her roughly that she was blocking up the street and that she must move on.

"Go forward, or go back, but don't stand there," he ordered.

She could not go forward, for Palikare had no intention of doing so. As soon as he understood that she had given up all hope of getting him into the Market, he got up and followed her docilely, agitating his long ears with satisfaction.

"Now," said La Rouquerie, after she had put thirty francs into poor Perrine's hand, "you must take him to my place, for I'm beginning to know him and he's quite capable of refusing to come with me. I don't live far from here."

But Grain-of-Salt would not consent to do this; he declared that the distance was too far for him.

"You go with the lady alone," he said to Perrine, "and don't be too cut up about your donkey. He'll be all right with her. She's a good woman."

"But how shall I find my way back to Charonne?" asked Perrine, bewildered. She dreaded to be lost in the great city.

"You follow the fortifications . . . nothing easier."

As it happened, the street where La Rouquerie lived was not far from the Horse Market, and it did not take them long to get there. There were heaps of garbage before her place, just like in Guillot Field.

The moment of parting had come. As she tied Palikare up in a little stable, her tears fell on his head.

"Don't take on so," said the woman; "I'll take care of him, I promise you."

"We loved him so much," said little Perrine. Then she went on her way.

CHAPTER III

" POOR LITTLE GIRL "

WHAT was she to do with thirty francs when she had calculated that they must at least have one hundred. She turned this question over in her mind sadly as she walked along by the fortifications. She found her way back easily. She put the money into her mother's hand, for she did not know how to spend it. It was her mother who decided what to do.

" We must go at once to Maraucourt," she said.

" But are you strong enough? " Perrine asked doubtfully.

" I must be. We have waited too long in the hope that I should get better. And while we wait our money is going. What poor Palikare has brought us will go also. I did not want to go in this miserable state . . . "

" When must we go? Today? " asked Perrine.

" No; it's too late today. We must go tomorrow morning. You go and find out the hours of the train and the price of the tickets. It is the Gare du Nord station, and the place where we get out is Picquigny."

Perrine anxiously sought Grain-of-Salt. He told her it was better for her to consult a time table

41

than to go to the station, which was a long way off.
From the time table they learned that there were
two trains in the morning, one at six o'clock and
one at ten, and that the fare to Picquigny, third
class, was nine francs twenty-five centimes.

" We'll take the ten o'clock train," said her
mother, " and we will take a cab, for I certainly
cannot walk to the station."

And yet when nine o'clock the next day came she
could not even get to the cab that Perrine had waiting for her. She attempted the few steps from her
room to the cab, but would have fallen to the ground
had not Perrine held her.

" I must go back," she said weakly. " Don't be
anxious . . . . it will pass."

But it did not pass, and the Baroness, who was
watching them depart, had to bring a chair. The
moment she dropped into the seat she fainted.

" She must go back and lie down," said the
Baroness, rubbing her cold hands. " It is nothing,
girl; don't look so scared . . . just go and find
Carp. The two of us can carry her to her room.
You can't go . . . not just now."

The Baroness soon had the sick woman in her
bed, where she regained consciousness.

" Now you must just stay there in your bed," said
the Baroness, kindly. " You can go just as well
tomorrow. I'll get Carp to give you a nice cup of
bouillon. He loves soup as much as the landlord
loves wine; winter and summer he gets up at five

o'clock and makes his soup; good stuff it is, too.
Few can make better."

Without waiting for a reply, she went to Carp,
who was again at his work.

"Will you give me a cup of your bouillon for our
patient?" she asked.

He replied with a smile only, but he quickly took
the lid from a saucepan and filled a cup with the
savory soup.

The Baroness returned with it, carrying it carefully, so as not to spill a drop.

"Take that, my dear lady," she said, kneeling
down beside the bed.   "Don't move, but just open
your lips."

A spoonful was put to the sick woman's lips, but
she could not swallow it.   Again she fainted, and
this time she remained unconscious for a longer
time.   The Baroness saw that the soup was not
needed, and so as not to waste it, she made Perrine
take it.

A day passed.   The doctor came, but there was
nothing he could do.

Perrine was in despair. She wondered how long
the thirty francs that La Rouquerie had given her
would last. Although their expenses were not
great, there was first one thing, then another, that
was needed.   When the last sous were spent, where
would they go?   What would become of them if
they could get no more money?

She was seated beside her mother's bedside, her
beautiful little face white and drawn with anxiety.

Suddenly she felt her mother's hand, which she held in hers, clasp her fingers more tightly.

" You want something? " she asked quickly, bending her head.

" I want to speak to you . . . the hour has come for my last words to you, darling," said her mother.

" Oh, mama! mama!" cried Perrine.

" Don't interrupt, darling, and let us both try to control ourselves.   I did not want to frighten you, and that is the reason why, until now, I have said nothing that would add to your grief.   But what I have to say must be said, although it hurts us both. We are going to part . . . "

In spite of her efforts, Perrine could not keep back her sobs.

" Yes, it is terrible, dear child, and yet I am wondering if, after all, it is not for the best . . . that you will be an orphan.   It may be better for you to go alone than to be taken to them by a mother whom they have scorned.   Well, God's will is that you should be left alone . . . in a few hours . . . tomorrow, perhaps . . . "

For a moment she stopped, overcome with emotion.

" When I . . . am gone . . . there will be things for you to do.   In my pocket you will find a large envelope which contains my marriage certificate. The certificate bears my name and your father's. You will be asked to show it, but make them give it back to you.   You might need it later on to prove your parentage.   Take great care of it, dear.   How-

ever, you might lose it, so I want you to learn it by
heart, so that you will never forget it. Then, when
a day comes and you need it, you must get another
copy. You understand? Remember all that I tell
you."

"Yes, mama; yes."

"You will be very unhappy, but you must not
give way to despair. When you have nothing more
to do in Paris . . . when you are left alone . . .
then you must go off at once to Maraucourt . . . by
train if you have enough money . . . on foot, if you
have not. Better to sleep by the roadside and have
nothing to eat than to stay in Paris. You promise
to leave Paris at once, Perrine?"

"I promise, mama," sobbed the little girl.

The sick woman made a sign that she wanted to
say more, but that she must rest for a moment.
Little Perrine waited, her eyes fixed on her mother's
face.

"You will go to Maraucourt?" said the dying
woman after a few moments had passed. "You
have no right to claim anything . . . what you get
must be for yourself alone . . . be good, and make
yourself loved. All is there . . . for you. I have
hope . . . you will be loved for yourself . . . they
cannot help loving you . . . and then your troubles
will be over, my darling."

She clasped her hands in prayer. Then a look of
heavenly rapture came over her face.

"I see," she cried; "I see . . . my darling will
be loved! She will be happy . . . she will be cared

for. I can die in peace now with this thought . . . Perrine, my Perrine, keep a place in your heart for me always, child . . . "

These words, which seemed like an exaltation to Heaven, had exhausted her; she sank back on the mattress and sighed. Perrine waited . . . waited. Her mother did not speak. She was dead. Then the child left the bedside and went out of the house. In the field she threw herself down on the grass and broke into sobs. It seemed as though her little heart would break.

It was a long time before she could calm herself. Then her breath came in hiccoughs. Vaguely she thought that she ought not to leave her mother alone. Some one should watch over her.

The field was now filled with shadows; the night was falling. She wandered about, not knowing where she went, still sobbing.

She passed the wagon for the tenth time. The candy man, who had watched her come out of the house, went towards her with two sugar sticks in his hand.

" Poor little girl," he said, pityingly.

" Oh! . . . " she sobbed.

" There, there! Take these," he said, offering her the candy. " Sweetness is good for sorrow."

CHAPTER IV

A HARD ROAD TO TRAVEL

THE last prayers had been uttered. Perrine still stood before the grave. The Baroness, who had not left her, gently took her arm.

"Come," she said; "you must come away," she added more firmly as Perrine attempted to resist her.

Holding her tightly by the arm, she drew her away. They walked on for some moments, Perrine not knowing what was passing around her, nor understanding where they were leading her. Her thoughts, her spirit, her heart, were with her mother.

At last they stopped in one of the side paths; then she saw standing round her the Baroness, who had now let go of her arm, Grain-of-Salt and the candy man, but she saw them only vaguely. The Baroness had black ribbons on her bonnet; Grain-of-Salt was dressed like a gentleman and wore a high silk hat; Carp had replaced his leather apron by a black Prince Albert which came down to his feet, and the candy man had cast aside his white blouse for a cloth coat. For, like the real Parisian who practises the cult of the dead, they had dressed themselves up in their best to pay respect to the one they had just buried.

"I want to tell you, little one," commenced Grain-

47

of-Salt, who thought that he should speak first, being the most important person present; " I want to tell you that you can stay as long as you like in Guillot Fields without paying."

" If you'd like to sing with me," said the Baroness, " you can earn enough to live on.   It's a nice profession."

" If you'd like to go into the candy business, I'll teach you; that's a real trade and a nice one," said the candy man.

Carp said nothing, but with a smile and a gesture he let her understand that she could always find a bowl of soup at his place . . . and good soup, too!

Perrine's eyes filled with fresh tears, soft tears which washed away the bitterness of the burning ones which for two days had flowed from her eyes.

" How good you all are to me," she murmured.

" One does what one can," said Grain-of-Salt.

" One should not leave an honest little girl like you on the streets of Paris," said the Baroness.

" I must not stay in Paris," replied Perrine; "I must go at once to my relations."

"You have relations?" exclaimed Grain-of-Salt, looking at the others with an air which said that he did not think that those relations could be worth much.   " Where are your relations? "

" Near Amiens."

" And how can you go to Amiens?   Have you got money? "

" Not enough to take the train, but I'm going to walk there,"

"Do you know the way?"

"I have a map in my pocket . . . "

"Yes, but does that tell you which road you have to take from here, here in Paris?"

"No, but if you will tell me . . . "

They all were eager to give her this information, but it was all so confused and contradictory that Grain-of-Salt cut the talk short.

"If you want to lose yourself in Paris, just listen to what they are saying," he said. "Now, this is the way you must go," and he explained to her which road she should take. "Now, when do you want to go?"

"At once; I promised my mother," said Perrine.

"You must obey her," said the Baroness, solemnly, "but not before I've kissed you; you're a good girl."

The men shook hands with her.

She knew she must leave the cemetery, yet she hesitated and turned once more towards the grave that she had just left, but the Baroness stopped her.

"As you are obliged to go, go at once; it is best," she said.

"Yes, go," said Grain-of-Salt.

When she had climbed into the car on the belt line she took an old map of France from her pocket which she had consulted many times alone since they left Italy. From Paris to Amiens the road was easy; she had only to take the Calais road; this was indicated on her map by a little black line. From Amiens she would go to Boulogne, and as she

had learned also to calculate distances, she thought
that to Maraucourt it ought to be about one hundred
and fifty-eight miles.

But could she do all those miles, regularly . . .
go on day after day?   She knew that to walk four
or five miles by chance on one day was a very different matter to taking a long, continuous journey
like she was contemplating.   There would be bad
days . . . rainy days . . . and how long would her
money last?   She had only five francs thirty-five
centimes left.   The train pulled up at the station
at which she had to get out.   Now she had to turn
to the right, and as the sun would not go down for
two or three hours she hoped to be far away from
Paris by night, and find a place in the open country
where she could sleep.

Yet as far as her eyes could see there was nothing
but houses and factories, factories with great tall
chimneys sending forth clouds of thick, black smoke,
and all along the road wagons, tramways and carts.
Again she saw a lot of trucks bearing the name that
she had noticed while waiting to pass through the
Gates: "Maraucourt Factories, Vulfran Paindavoine."

Would Paris ever end?   Would she ever get out
of this great city?   She was not afraid of the lonely
fields, nor the silence of the country at night, nor
the mysterious shadows, but of Paris, the crowd,
the lights.   She was now on the outskirts of the
city.   Before leaving it (although she had no appetite), she thought she would buy a piece of bread

so that she would have something to eat before going to sleep.   She went into a baker shop.

"I want some bread, please," she said.

"Have you any money?" demanded the woman, who did not seem to put much confidence in Perrine's appearance.

"Yes, and I want one pound, please.   Here is five francs.   Will you give me the change?"

Before cutting the bread the woman took up the five franc piece and examined it.

"What! that!" she exclaimed, making it ring on the marble slab.

"It's a five franc piece," said Perrine.

"Who told you to try and pass that off on me?" asked the woman, angrily.

"No one, and I am asking you for a pound of bread for my supper."

"Well, then, you won't get any bread, and you'd better get out of here as quickly as you can before I have you arrested."

"Arrested!   Why?" she stammered in surprise.

"Because you're a thief!"

"Oh! . . ."

"You want to pass counterfeit money on me. You vagabond . . . you thief!   Be off!   No, wait; I'll get a policeman."

Perrine knew that she was not a thief, whether the money was real or false, but vagabond she was. She had no home, no parents.   What would she answer the policeman?   They would arrest her for being a vagabond.

She put this question to herself very quickly, but although her fear was great, she thought of her money.

" If you don't wish to sell me the bread, at least you can give me back my money," she said, holding out her hand.

"So that you can pass it on someone else, eh? I'll keep your money. If you want it, go and fetch the police," cried the woman, furiously. " Be off, you thief."

The woman's loud cries could be heard in the street, and several people by now had gathered round the door.

" What's the matter? " someone cried.

" Why, this girl here is trying to rob my till," shouted the woman. " There never is a cop when one wants one."

Terrified, Perrine wondered how she could get out, but they let her pass as she made for the door, hissing her and calling her names as she ran. She ran on and on, too afraid to turn round to see if anyone was following her.

After a few minutes, which to her seemed hours, she found herself in the country, and was able to stop and breathe. No one was calling after her; no one following her.

After her fears had calmed down she realized that she had nothing to eat and no money. What should she do? Instinctively she glanced at the fields by the wayside. She saw beets, onions, cabbages, but there was nothing there ready to eat, and besides, even if there had been ripe melons and trees laden with fruit, what good would they have been to her; she could not stretch out her hand to pick the fruit any more than she could stretch it out to beg of the passersby. No, little Perrine was not a thief, nor a beggar, nor a vagabond.

She felt very depressed. It was eventide, and in the quietness of the twilight she realized how utterly alone she was; but she knew that she must not give way; she felt that while there was still light she must walk on, and by the time night fell perhaps she would have found a spot where she could sleep in safety.

She had not gone far before she found what she thought would be the very place. As she came to a field of artichokes she saw a man and woman picking artichoke heads and packing them in baskets, which they piled up in a cart that stood by the roadside. She stopped to look at them at their work. A moment later another cart driven by a girl came up.

"So you're getting yours all in?" called out the girl.

"Should say so, and it's none too soon," replied the man. "It's no fun sleeping here all night to watch for those rogues. I at least shall sleep in my bed tonight."

"And what about Monneau's lot?" grinned the girl.

"Oh, Monneau's a sly dog," answered the man; "he counts on us others watching out for his. He's not going to be here tonight. Serve him right if he finds all his gone!"

All three laughed heartily. They were not over-anxious that Monneau should prosper. Didn't he profit by their watch to take his own slumbers in peace?

"That'll be a joke, eh?"

"Wait for me," said the girl. "I won't be a jiffy; then we'll go together."

The man and the woman waited, and in a few minutes the girl had finished her task and the two carts, laden with artichokes, went towards the village. Perrine stood in the deserted road looking at the two fields, which presented such a difference in appearance. One was completely stripped of its vegetables; the other was filled with a splendid crop. At the end of the field was a little hut made of branches where the man who watched the field had slept. Perrine decided that she would stay there for the night, now that she knew it would not be occupied by the watch. She did not fear that she would be disturbed, yet she dared not take possession of the place until it was quite dark. She sat down by a ditch and waited, thankful that she had found what she wanted. Then at last, when it was quite dark and all was quiet, she picked her way carefully over the beds of artichokes and slipped into the hut. It was better inside than she had hoped, for the ground was covered with straw and there was a wooden box that would serve her for a pillow.

Ever since she had run from the baker's shop it had seemed to her that she was like a tracked animal, and more than once she had looked behind her with fear, half expecting to see the police on her heels.

She felt now in the hut that she was safe. Her nerves relaxed. After a few minutes she realized that she had another cause for anxiety. She was hungry, very hungry. While she was tramping along the roads, overwhelmed by her great loss, it had seemed to her that she would never want to eat or drink again. She felt the pangs of hunger now and she had only one sou left. How could she live on one sou for five or six days? This was a very serious question. But then, had she not found shelter for the night; perhaps she would find food for the morrow.

She closed her eyes, her long black lashes heavy with tears. The last thing at night she had always thought of her dead father; now it was the spirits of both her father and her mother that seemed to hover around her. Again and again she stretched out her arms in the darkness to them, and then, worn out with fatigue, with a sob she dropped off to sleep.

But although she was tired out, her slumbers were broken. She turned and tossed on the straw. Every now and again the rumbling of a cart on the road would wake her, and sometimes some mysterious noise, which in the silence of the night made her heart beat quickly. Then it seemed to her that she

heard a cart stop near the hut on the road.   She
raised herself on her elbow to listen.

She had not made a mistake; she heard some
whispering.   She sprang to her feet and looked
through the cracks of the hut.   A cart had stopped
at the end of the field, and by the pale light from
the stars she could dimly see the form of a man or
woman throwing out baskets to two others, who
carried them into the field.   This was Monneau's
lot.   What did it mean at such an hour?   Had
Monneau come so late to cut his artichokes?

Then she understood!   These were the thieves!
They had come to strip Monneau's field!   They
quickly cut the artichoke heads and heaped them
up in the baskets.   The woman had taken the cart
away; evidently they did not want it to stay on the
road while they worked for fear of attracting the
attention of anyone passing by.

What would happen to her if the thieves saw her?
She had heard that thieves sometimes killed a person who caught them at their work.   There was the
chance that they would not discover her.   For they
certainly knew that the hut would not be occupied
on this night that they had planned to strip the
field.   But if they caught her? And then . . .
if they were arrested, she would be taken with
them!

At this thought cold beads of perspiration broke
out on her forehead.   Thieves work quickly; they
would soon have finished!

But presently they were disturbed. From the

distance could be heard the noise of a cart on the paved road.   As it drew nearer they hid themselves, lying down flat between the artichoke beds.

The cart passed.   Then they went on with their work even more quickly.   In spite of their feverish haste it seemed to little Perrine that they would never be finished.   Every moment she feared that someone would come and catch them and she be arrested with them.

If she could only get away.   She looked about her to see if it were possible for her to leave the hut. This could easily be done, but then they would be sure to see her once she was on the road.   It would be better to remain where she was.

She lay down again and pretended to sleep.   As it was impossible for her to go out without being seen, it was wiser to pretend that she had not seen anything if they should come into the hut.

For some time they went on cutting the artichokes.   Then there was another noise on the road. It was their cart coming back.   It stopped at the end of the field.   In a few minutes the baskets were all stowed in the cart and the thieves jumped in and drove off hurriedly in the direction of Paris.

If she had known the hour she could have slept until dawn, but not knowing how long she had been there, she thought that it would be better if she went on her way.   In the country people are about at an early hour.   If, when day broke, the laborers going to work saw her coming out of the hut, or even if they saw her round about the field, they might suspect her of having been with the thieves and arrest her.

So she slipped out of the hut, ears on the alert for the slightest noise, eyes glancing in every direction.

She reached the main road, then hurried off. The stars in the skies above were disappearing, and from the east a faint streak of light lit the shadows of the night and announced the approach of day.

CHAPTER V

S HE had not walked far before she saw in the distance a black mass silhouetted against the dawning light in the grey sky.   Chimneys, houses and steeples rose up in the coming dawn, leaving the rest of the landscape obscure in the shadows.

She reached the first straggling cottages of the village.   Instinctively she trod more softly on the paved road.   This was a useless precaution, for with the exception of the cats which ran about the streets, everyone slept, and her little footsteps only awoke a few dogs who barked at her behind closed gates.

She was famished; she was weak and faint with hunger.

What would become of her if she dropped unconscious?   She was afraid she might soon.   So that this would not happen, she thought it better to rest a minute, and as she was now passing before a barn full of hay, she went in quietly and threw herself down on the soft bed.   The rest, the warmth, and also the sweet smell of the hay, soothed her and soon she slept.

When she awoke the sun was already high in the heavens and was casting its rays over the fields where men and women were busily at work.

59

The pangs of hunger were now more acute than ever. Her head whirled; she was so giddy that she could scarcely see where she went as she staggered on. She had just reached the top of a hill, and before her, close by, was the village with its shops. She would spend her last sou for a piece of bread! She had heard of people finding money on the road; perhaps she would find a coin tomorrow; anyhow, she must have a piece of bread now.

She looked carefully at the last sou she possessed. Poor little girl, she did not know the difference between real money and false, and although she thought this sou looked real, she was very nervous when she entered the first baker shop that she came across.

"Will you cut me a sou's worth of bread?" she asked, timidly.

The man behind the counter took from the basket a little penny roll and handed it to her.   Instead of stretching out her hand, she hesitated.

"If you'll cut a piece for me," she said, "it doesn't matter if it is not today's bread."

The baker gave her a large piece of bread that had been on the counter for two or three days.

What did that matter?   The great thing was that it was larger than the little penny roll.   It was worth two rolls.

As soon as it was in her hand her mouth filled with water.   But she would not eat it until she had got out of the village.   This she did very quickly. As soon as she had passed the last house, she took her little knife from her pocket and made a cross on the piece of bread so as to be able to cut it into four equal parts. She took one piece, keeping the three others for the three following days, hoping that it might last her until she reached Amiens.

She had calculated this as she had hurried through the village, and it had seemed such as easy matter. But scarcely had she swallowed a mouthful of her little piece of bread than she felt that the strongest arguments had no power against hunger. She was famished! She must eat! The second piece followed the first, the third followed the second. Never had her will power been so weak. She was hungry; she must have it . . . all . . . all. Her only excuse was that the pieces were so tiny. When all four were put together, the whole only weighed a half a pound. And a whole pound would not have been enough for her in her ravenous condition. The day before she had only had a little cup of soup that Carp had given her. She devoured the fourth piece.

She went on her way. Although she had only just eaten her piece of bread, a terrible thought obsessed her. Where would she next get a mouthful? She now knew what torture she would have to go through . . . the pangs of hunger were terrible to endure. Where should she get her next meal? She walked through two more villages. She was getting thirsty now, very thirsty. Her tongue was dry, her lips parched. She came to the

last house in the village, but she did not dare ask
for a glass of water.   She had noticed that the
people looked at her curiously, and even the dogs
seemed to show their teeth at the ragged picture
she presented.

She must walk on.   The sun was very hot now,
and her thirst became more intense as she tramped
along the white road.   There was not a tree along
the road, and little clouds of dust rose around her
every instant, making her lips more parched.   Oh,
for a drink of water!   The palate of her mouth
seemed hard, like a corn.

The fact that she was thirsty had not worried her
at first.   One did not have to go into a shop to buy
water.   Anybody could have it.   When she saw a
brook or a river she had only to make a cup of her
hands and drink all she wanted.   But she had
walked miles in the dust and could see no sign of
water.   At last she picked up some little round
stones and put them in her mouth.   Her tongue
seemed to be moister while she kept them there.
She changed them from time to time, hoping that
she would soon come to a brook.

Then suddenly the atmosphere changed, and
although the heat was still suffocating, the sun was
hidden.   Thick black clouds filled the sky.   A
storm was coming on, there would be rain, and she
would be able to hold her mouth up to it, or she
could stoop down to the puddles that it made and
drink!

The wind came up.   A terrific swirl, carrying

clouds of dust and leaves, swept over the country and battered down the crops, uprooting plants and shrubs in its mad fracas. Perrine could not withstand this whirlwind. As she was lifted off her feet, a deafening crash of thunder shook the earth. Throwing herself down in the ditch, she laid flat on her stomach, covering her mouth and her eyes with her two small hands. The thunder rolled heavily on.

A moment ago she had been mad with thirst and had prayed that the storm would break quickly; now she realized that the storm would not only bring thunder and rain, but lightning — terrible flashes of lightning that almost blinded her.

And there would be torrents of rain and hail! Where could she go? Her dress would be soaked, and how could she dry it?

She clambered out of the ditch. In the distance she saw a wood. She thought that she might find a nook there where she could take shelter.

She had no time to lose. It was very dark. The claps of thunder became more frequent and louder, and the vivid lightning played fantastically on the black sky.

Would she be able to reach the wood before the storm broke? She ran as quickly as her panting breath would allow, now and again casting a look behind her at the black clouds which seemed to be sweeping down upon her.

She had seen terrible storms in the mountains when travelling with her father and mother, but

they were with her then; now she was alone.   Not
a soul near her in this desolate country.   Fortunately the wind was behind her; it blew her along,
at times carrying her off her feet.   If she could only
keep up this pace; the storm had not caught up
with her yet.

Holding her elbows against her little body and
bending forward, she ran on . . . but the storm also
made greater strides.

At this moment came a crash, louder and heavier.
The storm was just over her now and the ground
around her was cleaved with blue flames.   It was
better to stop running now; far better be drenched
than struck down by lightning.

Soon a few drops of rain fell.   Fortunately she
was nearing the wood, and now she could distin-
guish clearly the great trees.   A little more courage.   Many times her father had told her that if
one kept one's courage in times of danger one stood
a better chance of being saved.   She kept on.

When at last she entered the forest it was all so
black and dark she could scarcely make out anything.   Then suddenly a flash of lightning dazzled
her, and in the vivid glare she thought she saw a
little cabin not far away to which led a bad road
hollowed with deep ruts.   Again the lightning
flashed across the darkness, and she saw that she
had not made a mistake.   About fifty steps farther
on there was a little hut made of faggots, that the
woodcutters had built.

She made a final dash; then, at the end of her

strength, worn out and breathless, she sank down
on the underbrush that covered the floor.

She had not regained her breath when a terrible
noise filled the forest. The crash, mingled with the
splintering of wood, was so terrific that she thought
her end had come. The trees bent their trunks,
twisting and writhing, and the dead branches fell
everywhere with a dull, crackling sound.

Could her hut withstand this fury? She crawled
to the opening. She had no time to think — a blue
flame, followed by a frightful crash, threw her over,
blinded and dazed. When she came to herself,
astonished to find that she was still alive, she looked
out and saw that a giant oak that stood near the
hut had been struck by lightning. In falling its
length the trunk had been stripped of its bark from
top to bottom, and two of the biggest branches were
twisted round its roots.

She crept back, trembling, terrified at the thought
that Death had been so near her, so near that its
terrible breath had laid her low. As she stood
there, pale and shaking, she heard an extraordinary
rolling sound, more powerful than that of an express
train. It was the rain and the hail which was
beating down on the forest. The cabin cracked
from top to bottom; the roof bent under the fury
of the tempest, but it did not fall in. No house,
however solid, could be to her what this little hut
was at this moment, and she was mistress of it.

She grew calm; she would wait here until the
storm had passed. A sense of well-being stole over

her, and although the thunder continued to rumble
and the rain came down in a deluge, and the wind
whistled through the trees, and the unchained tempest went on its mad way through the air and on
the earth, she felt safe in her little hut. Then she
made a pillow for her head from the underbrush,
and stretching herself out, she fell asleep.

When she awoke the thunder had stopped, but the
rain was still falling in a fine drizzle. The forest,
with its solitude and silence, did not terrify her.
She was refreshed from her long sleep and she liked
her little cabin so much that she thought she would
spend the night there. She at least had a roof over
her head and a dry bed.

She did not know how long she had slept, but
that did not matter; she would know when night
came.

She had not washed herself since she had left
Paris, and the dust which had covered her from
head to foot made her skin smart. Now she was
alone, and there was plenty of water in the ditch
outside and she would profit by it.

In her pocket she had, beside her map and her
mother's certificate, a few little things tied up in a
rag. There was a piece of soap, a small comb, a
thimble, and a spool of thread, in which she had
stuck two needles. She undid her packet; then
taking off her vest, her shoes, and her stockings,
she leaned over the ditch, in which the water flowed
clear, and soaped her face, shoulders and feet. For
a towel she had only the rag she had used to tie up

her belongings, and it was neither big nor thick, but it was better than nothing.

This toilette did her almost as much good as her sleep. She combed her golden hair in two big braids and let them hang over her shoulders. If it were not for the little pain in her stomach, and the few torn places in her shoes, which had been the cause of her sore feet, she would have been quite at ease in mind and body.

She was hungry, but there was nothing she could do. She could not find a bit of nourishment in this cabin, and as it was still raining, she felt that she ought not to leave this shelter until the next day.

Then when night came her hunger became more intense, till finally she began to cut some twigs and nibble on them, but they were hard and bitter, and after chewing on them for a few minutes she threw them away. She tried the leaves; they went down easier.

While she ate her meal and darned her stockings, night came on. Soon all was dark and silent. She could hear no other sound than that of the rain-drops falling from the branches.

Although she had made up her mind to spend the night there, she experienced a feeling of fright at being all alone in this black forest. True, she had spent a part of the day in the same place, running no other danger than that of being struck, but the woods in the daytime are not like the woods at night, with the solemn silence and the mysterious

shadows, which make one conjure up the vision of
so many weird things.

What was in the woods? she wondered.   Wolves,
perhaps!

At this thought she became wide awake, and
jumping up, she found a big stick, which she cut to
a point with her knife; then she strewed branches
and fagots all around her, piling them high.   She
could at least defend herself behind her rampart.

Reassured, she laid down again, and it was not
long before she was asleep.

The song of a bird awoke her.   She recognized at
once the sweet, shrill notes of a blackbird.   Day
was breaking.   She began to shake, for she was
chilled to the bone.   The dampness of the night had
made her clothes as wet as though she had been
through a shower.

She jumped to her feet and shook herself violently
like a dog.   She felt that she ought to move about,
but she did not want to go on her way yet, for it
was not yet light enough for her to study the sky
to see if it were going to rain again.   To pass the
time, and still more with the wish to be on the move,
she arranged the fagots which she had disturbed
the night before.   Then she combed her hair and
washed herself in the ditch, which was full of water.

When she had finished the sun had risen, and the
sky gleamed blue through the branches of the trees.
There was not the slightest cloud to be seen.   She
must go.

Although she had darned her stockings well

which had worn away through the holes in her shoes, the continual tramp, tramp, tramp, made her little feet ache. After a time, however, she stepped out with a regular step on the road, which had been softened by the rain, and the rays from the beautiful sun fell upon her back and warmed her.

Never had she seen such a lovely morning. The storm, which had washed the roads and the fields, had given new life to the plants. Surely this was a good omen. She was full of hope.

Her imagination began to soar on wings. She hoped that somebody had had a hole in their pockets and had lost some money, and that she could find it on the road. She hoped she might find something, not a purse full, because she would have to try to find the owner, but just a little coin, one penny, or perhaps ten cents. She even thought that she might find some work to do, something that could bring her in a few cents.

She needed so little to be able to live for three or four days.

She trudged along with her eyes fixed on the ground, but neither a copper nor a silver coin did she see, and neither did she meet anybody who could give her work.

Oh, for something to eat! She was famished. Again and again she had to sit down by the wayside, she was so weak from lack of food.

She wondered if she found nothing would she have to sit down by the road and die.

Finally she came to a field and saw four young

girls picking peas. A peasant woman seemed to be in charge.

Gathering courage, she crossed over the road and walked towards the woman. But the woman stopped her before she could reach her.

" What cher want? " she shouted.

" I want to know if I can help, too," answered Perrine.

" We don't want no one! "

" You can give me just what you wish."

" Where d'ye come from? "

" From Paris."

One of the girls raised her head and cast her an angry look.

" The galavanter! " she cried, " she comes from Paris to try to get our job."

" I told yer we don't want nobody," said the woman again.

There was nothing to do but to go on her way, which she did with a heavy heart.

" Look out! A cop's comin'! " cried one of the girls.

Perrine turned her head quickly, and they all burst out laughing, amused at the joke.

She had not gone far before she had to stop. She could not see the road for the tears which filled her eyes. What had she done to those girls that they should be so mean to her?

Evidently it was as difficult for tramps to get work as it was for them to find pennies. She did not dare ask again for a job. She dragged her feet along, only hurrying when she was passing through the villages so that she could escape the stares.

She was almost prostrated when she reached a wood. It was mid-day and the sun was scorching; there was not a breath of air. She was exhausted and dripping with perspiration. Then her heart seemed to stop and she fell to the ground, unable to move or think.

A wagon coming up behind her passed by.

"This heat'll kill one," shouted the driver.

In a half conscious state she caught his words. They came to her like in a dream; it was as though sentence had been passed upon her.

So she was to die? She had thought so herself, but now a messenger of Death was saying so.

Well, she would die. She could keep up no longer. Her father was dead, and her mother was dead, now she was going to die. A cruel thought flitted through her dull brain. She wondered why she could not have died with them rather than in a ditch like a poor animal.

She tried to make a last effort to get to the wood where she could find a spot to lie down for her last sleep, somewhere away from the road. She managed to drag herself into the wood, and there she found a little grassy spot where violets were growing. She laid down under a large tree, her head on her arm, just as she did at night when she went to sleep.

CHAPTER VI

THE RESCUE

SOMETHING warm passing over her face made her open her eyes. Dimly she saw a large velvety head bending over her. In terror she tried to throw herself on one side, but a big tongue licked her cheek and held her to the grass. So quickly had this happened that she had not had time to recognize the big velvety head which belonged to a donkey, but while the great tongue continued to lick her face and hands she was able to look up at it.

Palikare! It was dear, dear Palikare! She threw her arms around her donkey's neck and burst into tears.

"My darling, dear, darling Palikare," she murmured.

When he heard his name he stopped licking her and lifting his head he sent forth five or six triumphant brays of happiness. Then, as though that was not enough to express his contentment, he let out five or six more, but not quite so loud.

Perrine then noticed that he was without a harness or a rope.

While she stroked him with her hand and he bent his long ears down to her, she heard a hoarse voice calling:

SOMETHING WARM PASSING OVER HER FACE MADE HER
OPEN HER EYES.

"What yer found, old chap? I'll be there in a minute. I'm comin', old boy."

There was a quick step on the road, and Perrine saw what appeared to be a man dressed in a smock and wearing a leather hat and with a pipe in his mouth.

"Hi, kid, what yer doin' with my donkey?" he cried, without taking the pipe from his lip.

Then Perrine saw that it was the rag woman to whom she had sold Palikare at the Horse Market. The woman did not recognize her at first. She stared hard at her for a moment.

"Sure I've seen yer somewhere," she said at last.

"It was I who sold you Palikare," said Perrine.

"Why, sure it's you, little one, but what in Heaven's name are you doin' here?"

Perrine could not reply. She was so giddy her head whirled. She had been sitting up, but now she was obliged to lie down again, and her pallor and tears spoke for her.

"What's the matter? Are you sick?" demanded La Rouquerie.

Although Perrine moved her lips as though to speak, no sound came. Again she was sinking into unconsciousness, partly from emotion, partly from weakness.

But La Rouquerie was a woman of experience; she had seen all miseries.

"The kid's dying of hunger," she muttered to herself.

She hurried over the road to a little truck over

the sides of which were spread out some dried rabbit skins. The woman quickly opened a box and took out a slice of bread, a piece of cheese and a bottle. She carried it back on the run.

Perrine was still in the same condition.

" One little minute, girlie; one little minute," she said encouragingly.

Kneeling down beside little Perrine, she put the bottle to her lips.

" Take a good drink; that'll keep you up," she said.

True, the good drink brought the blood back to her cheeks.

" Are you hungry? "

" Yes," murmured Perrine.

" Well, now you must eat, but gently; wait a minute."

She broke off a piece of bread and cheese and offered it to her.

" Eat it slowly," she said, advisedly, for already Perrine had devoured the half of what was handed to her. " I'll eat with you, then you won't eat so fast."

Palikare had been standing quietly looking on with his big soft eyes. When he saw La Rouquerie sit down on the grass beside Perrine, he also knelt down beside them.

" The old rogue, he wants a bite, too," said the woman.

" May I give him a piece? " asked Perrine.

" Yes, you can give him a piece or two. When

we've eaten this there is more in the cart. Give him some; he is so pleased to see you again, good old boy. You know he *is* a good boy."

" Yes, isn't he a dear? " said Perrine, softly.

" Now when you've eaten that you can tell me how you come to be in these woods pretty near starved to death. Sure it'd be a pity for you to kick the bucket yet awhile."

After she had eaten as much as was good for her, Perrine told her story, commencing with the death of her mother. When she came to the scene she had had with the baker woman at St. Denis, the woman took her pipe from her mouth and called the baker woman some very bad names.

" She's a thief, a thief! " she cried. " I've never given bad money to no one, 'cause I never take any from nobody. Be easy! She'll give that back to me next time I pass by her shop, or I'll put the whole neighborhood against her. I've friends at St. Denis, and we'll set her store on fire if she don't give it up! "

Perrine finished her story.

" You was just about goin' to die," said La Rouquerie; " what was the feelin' like? "

" At first I felt very sad," said Perrine, " and I think I must have cried like one cries in the night when one is suffocating; then I dreamed of Heaven and of the good food I should have there. Mama, who was waiting for me, had made me some milk chocolate; I could smell it."

" It's funny that this heat wave, which was going

to kill you, really was the cause of yer bein' saved.
If it hadn't been for this darned heat I never should
have stopped to let that donkey rest in this wood,
and then he wouldn't have found yer. What cher
goin' to do now?"

"Go on my way."

"And tomorrow? What yer got to eat? One's
got to be young like you to take such a trip as this."

"But what could I do?"

La Rouquerie gravely took two or three puffs at
her pipe. She was thoughtful for a moment; then
she said:

"See here, I'm goin' as far as Creil, no farther.
I'm buyin' odds and ends in the villages as I go
along. It's on the way to Chantilly, so you come
along with me. Now yell out a bit if you've got the
strength: "Rabbit skins! Rags and bones to sell!""

Perrine straightened herself and cried out as she
was told.

"That's fine! You've got a good, clear voice.
As I've got a sore throat, you can do the calling out
for me, so like that you'll earn your grub. When
we get to Creil I know a farmer there who goes as
far as Amiens to get eggs and things. I'll ask him
to take you in his cart. When you get to Amiens
you can take the train to where yer relations hang
out."

"But what with? How can I take a train?"

"I'll advance you the five francs that I'm goin'
to get back from that baker. I'll get it! So I'll
give yer five francs for your fare."

CHAPTER VII

MARAUCOURT AT LAST

THINGS came to pass as La Rouquerie had arranged. For eight days Perrine ran through the streets of the villages and towns crying out: "Rabbit skins! Rags! Bones!"

"You've got a voice that would make yer famous for this here business," said La Rouquerie admiringly, as Perrine's clear treble was heard in the streets. If yer'd stay with me you'd be doin' me a service and yer wouldn't be unhappy. You'd make a livin'. Is it a go?"

"Oh, thank you, but it's not possible," replied Perrine.

Finding that the reasons she advanced were not sufficient to induce Perrine to stay with her, La Rouquerie put forth another:

"And yer wouldn't have to leave Palikare."

This was a great grief, but Perrine had made up her mind.

"I must go to my relations; I really must," she said.

"Did your relatives save yer life, like that there donkey?" insisted La Rouquerie.

"But I promised my mother."

"Go, then, but you see one fine day you'll be sorry yer didn't take what I offered yer p'raps."

"You are very kind and I shall always remember you."

When they reached Creil, La Rouquerie hunted up her friend, the farmer, and asked him to give Perrine a lift in his cart as far as Amiens. He was quite willing, and for one whole day Perrine enjoyed the comfort of lying stretched out on the straw behind two good trotting horses. At Essentaux she slept in a barn.

The next day was Sunday, and she was up bright and early and quickly made her way to the railway station. Handing her five francs to the ticket seller she asked for a ticket to Picquigny. This time she had the satisfaction of seeing that her five francs was accepted. She received her ticket and seventy-five cents in change.

It was 12 o'clock when the train pulled in at the station at Picquigny. It was a beautiful, sunny morning, the air was soft and warm, far different from the scorching heat which had prostrated her in the woods, and she . . . how unlike she was from that miserable little girl who had fallen by the wayside. And she was clean, too. During the days she had spent with La Rouquerie she had been able to mend her waist and her skirt, and had washed her linen and shined her shoes. Her past experience was a lesson: she must never give up hope at the darkest moment; she must always remember that there was a silver cloud, if she would only persevere.

She had a long walk after she got out of the train

at Picquigny.   But she walked along lightly past
the meadows bordered with poplars and limes, past
the river where the villagers in their Sunday clothes
were fishing, past the windmills which, despite the
fact that the day was calm, were slowly moving
round, blown by the breeze from the sea which
could be felt even there.

She walked through the pretty village of St. Pipoy
with its red roofs and quaint church, and over the
railway tracks which unites the towns wherein
Vulfran Paindavoine has his factories, and which
joins the main line to Boulogne.

As Perrine passed the pretty church the people
were coming out from mass.   Listening to them as
they talked in groups she heard again the sing-
song manner of talking that her father had often
imitated so as to amuse her.

On the country road she saw a young girl walking slowly ahead of her carrying a very heavy
basket on her arm.

" Is this the way to Maraucourt? " Perrine asked.

" Yes, this road . . .   quite straight."

" Quite straight," said Perrine laughing, " it isn't
so very straight after all."

" If you are going to Maraucourt, I'm going there
too, and we could go together," suggested the girl.

" I will if you'll let me help you carry your basket," said Perrine with a smile.

" I won't say no to that, for it's sure heavy! "

The girl put her basket on the ground and
breathed a sigh of relief.

"You don't belong to Maraucourt, do you?" asked the girl.

"No, do you?"

"Sure I do."

"Do you work in the factories?"

"Should say so, everybody does here."

"How much do they pay?"

"Ten sous."

"And is it hard work?"

"Not very; but you have to have a sharp eye and not waste time. Do you want to get in there?"

"Yes, if they'd have me."

"Should say they would have you; they take anybody. If they didn't how do you think they'd get the seven thousand hands they've got. Just be there tomorrow morning at 6 o'clock at the gate. We must hurry now or I'll be late. Come on."

She took the handle of the basket on one side and Perrine took it on the other side and they set out on the road, keeping in step down the middle.

Here was an opportunity for Perrine to learn what held interest for her. It was too good for her not to seize it. But she was afraid to question this girl openly. She must put the questions she wanted answered in a way that would not arouse her suspicions.

"Were you born at Maraucourt?" she began.

"Sure, I'm a native and my mother was too, my father came from Picquigny."

"Have you lost them?"

"Yes, I live with my grandmother who keeps a

grocer store and restaurant.   She's Madame Francoise."

"Ah! Madame Francoise."

"What! do you know her?"

"No, I just said, 'Ah, Madame Francoise.'"

"She's known everywhere for her 'eats' and 'cause she was nurse to Monsieur Edmond Paindavoine.   Whenever the men want to ask the boss, Monsieur Vulfran Paindavoine, for anything, they get my grandmother to ask for them."

"Does she always get what they want?"

"Sometimes yes, sometimes no; Monsieur Vulfran ain't always obliging."

"If your grandmother was nurse to Monsieur Edmond why doesn't she ask him?"

"M. Edmond? he's the boss' son, and he went away from here before I was born, no one's seen him since. He had a quarrel with his father, and his father sent him to India to buy jute. The boss has made his fortune out of jute. He's rich, as rich as . . ."

She could not think how rich M. Vulfan was so she said abruptly: "Now shall we change arms?"

"If you like.   What is your name?"

"Rosalie.   What's yours?"

Perrine did not want to give her real name, so she chanced on one.

"Aurelie," she said.

They rested for a while, then went on again at their regular step.

"You say that the son had a quarrel with his father," said Perrine, "then went away?"

"Yes, and the old gentleman got madder still with him 'cause he married a Hindoo girl, and a marriage like that doesn't count. His father wanted him to marry a young lady who came of a very fine family, the best in Picardy. It was because he wanted his son to marry this other girl that he built the beautiful mansion he's got. It cost millions and millions of francs. But M. Edmond wouldn't part with the wife he's got over there to take up with the young lady here, so the quarrel got worse and worse, and now they don't even know if the son is dead or alive. They haven't had news of him for years, so they say. Monsieur Vulfran doesn't speak to anyone about it, neither do the two nephews."

"Oh, he has nephews?"

"Yes, Monsieur Theodore Paindavoine, his brother's son, and Monsieur Casimir Bretonneux, his sister's son, who help him in the business. If M. Edmond doesn't come back the fortune and all the factories will go to his two nephews."

"Oh, really!"

"Yes, and that'll be a sad thing, sad for the whole town. Them nephews ain't no good for the business . . . and so many people have to get their living from it. Sure, it'll be a sad day when they get it, and they will if poor M. Edmond doesn't come back. On Sundays, when I serve the meals, I hear all sorts of things."

" About his nephews? "

" Yes, about them two and others also.   But it's none of our business; let's talk of something else."

" Yes, why not? "

As Perrine did not want to appear too inquisitive, she walked on silently, but Rosalie's tongue could not be still for very long.

" Did you come along with your parents to Maraucourt? " she asked.

" I have no parents."

" No father, no mother! "

" No."

" You're like me, but I've got a grandmother who's very good, and she'd be still better if it wasn't for my uncles and aunts; she has to please them. If it wasn't for them I should not have to work in the factories; I should stay at home and help in the store, but grandmother can't do as she wants always.   So you're all alone? "

" Yes, all alone."

" Was it your own idea to leave Paris and come to Maraucourt? "

" I was told that I might find work at Maraucourt, so instead of going further on to some relations, I stopped here.   If you don't know your relations, and they don't know you, you're not sure if you're going to get a welcome."

" That's true.   If there are kind ones, there are some mighty unkind ones in this world."

" Yes, that is so," Perrine said, nodding her pretty head.

"Well, don't worry; you'll find work in the factories. Ten sous a day is not much, but it's something, and you can get as much as twenty-two sous. I'm going to ask you a question; you can answer or not, as you like. Have you got any money?"

"A little."

"Well, if you'd like to lodge at my grandmother's, that'll cost you twenty-eight sous a week, pay in advance."

"I can pay twenty-eight sous."

"Now, I don't promise you a fine room all to yourself at that price; there'll be six in the same room, but you'll have a bed, some sheets and a coverlet. Everybody ain't got that."

"I'd like it and thank you very much."

"My grandmother don't only take in lodgers who can only pay twenty-eight sous. We've got some very fine rooms in our house. Our boarders are employed at the factories. There's Monsieur Fabry, the engineer of the building; Monsieur Mombleau, the head clerk, and Mr. Bendit, who has charge of the foreign correspondence. If you ever speak to him always call him Mr. Benndite. He's an Englishman, and he gets mad if you pronounce his name 'Bendit.' He thinks that one wants to insult him, just as though one was calling him 'Thief'!"

"I won't forget; besides, I know English."

"You know English! You!"

"My mother was English."

"So, so! Well, that'll be fine for Mr. Bendit, but he'd be more pleased if you knew every lan-

guage.   His great stunt on Sunday is to read
prayers that are printed in twenty-five languages.
When he's gone through them once, he goes over
them again and again.   Every Sunday he does the
same thing.   All the same, he's a very fine man."

CHAPTER VIII

GRANDFATHER VULFRAN

THROUGH the great trees which framed the road on either side, Perrine could see beyond the hill the tops of some high chimneys and buildings.

"We're coming to Maraucourt," said Rosalie; "you'll see Monsieur Paindavoine's mansion soon, then the factories. We shan't see the village until we get down the other side of the hill. Over by the river there's the church and cemetery."

Then, as they neared the spot where the poplars were swaying, there came into view a beautiful chateau towering grandly above the trees, with its façade of stone gabled roofs and chimneys standing out magnificently in a park planted with trees and shrubs which stretched out as far as the meadows.

Perrine stopped short in amazement, whilst Rosalie continue to step out. This made them jolt the basket, whereupon Rosalie plumped it down on the ground and stretched herself.

"Ah, you think that fine, don't you?" said Rosalie, following Perrine's glance.

"Why, it's beautiful," said Perrine, softly.

"Well, old Monsieur Vulfran lives there all alone. He's got a dozen servants to wait on him, without counting the gardeners and stablemen who live in those quarters over there at the end of the park. That place over there is the electric power house for lighting up the chateau. Fine, ain't it? And you should see the inside! There's gold everywhere, and velvets, and such carpets! ˈThem nephews want to live there with him, but he won't have 'em. He even eats his meals all alone."

They took up the basket and went on again. Soon they saw a general view of the works. But to Perrine's eyes there seemed only a confusion of buildings, some old, some new, just a great gray mass with big, tall chimneys everywhere. Then they came to the first houses of the village, with apple trees and pear trees growing in the gardens. Here was the village of which her father had spoken so often.

What struck her most was the number of people she saw. Groups of men, women and children dressed up in their Sunday clothes stood chatting before the houses or sat in the low rooms, the windows of which were thrown wide open. A mass of people, people everywhere. In the low-ceiling rooms, where those from outside could see all that was passing within, some were drinking bright colored drinks, others had jugs of cider, while others had on the tables before them black coffee or whisky. And what a tapping of glasses and voices raised in angry dispute!

" What a lot of people there seem to be drinking," said Perrine.

"That's because it's Sunday. They got two weeks' pay yesterday. They can't always drink like this; you'll see."

What was characteristic of most of the houses was that nearly all, although old and badly built of brick or wood, affected an air of coquetry, at least in the painting that embellished the doors and windows. This attracted the eye like a sign. And in truth it was a sign, for in default of other preparations, the bright paint gave a promise of cleanliness which a glance at the inside of the place belied at once.

"We've arrived," said Rosalie, pointing with her free hand to a small red brick house which stood a little way from the road, behind a ragged hedge. Adjoining the house was a store where general provisions were sold, and also liquor. The floors above were rented to the best lodgers, and behind the house was a building which was rented out to the factory hands. A little gate in the hedge led to a small garden planted with apple trees and to a gravel walk leading to the house.

As soon as Rosalie and Perrine entered the yard, a woman, still young, called out from the doorway: "Hurry up, you slow coach! Say, you take a time to go to Picquigny, don't you?"

"That's my Aunt Zenobie," whispered Rosalie; "she's none too nice."

"What yer whispering there?" yelled the disagreeable woman.

"I said that if somebody hadn't been there to help

carry this basket I wouldn't be here by now," retorted Rosalie.

"You'd better hold your tongue!"

These words were uttered in such a shrill tone
that they brought a tall old woman to the door.

"Who are you going on at now, Zenobie?" she
asked, calmly.

"She's mad 'cause I'm late, grandmother; but
the basket's awful heavy," said Rosalie.

"There, there!" said the grandmother, placidly;
"put it down and go and get your supper; you'll
find it kept warm on the stove."

"You wait for me here in the yard," said Rosalie
to Perrine; "I'll be out in a minute and we'll have
supper together.   You go and buy your bread.
You'll find the baker in the third house on the left.
Hurry up."

When Perrine returned she found Rosalie seated
at a table under a big apple tree.   On the table were
two plates full of meat stew and potatoes.

"Sit down and share my stew," said Rosalie.

"But . . . " hesitated Perrine.

"You don't like to take it; you can.   I asked my
grandmother, and it's all right."

In that case Perrine thought that she should
accept this hospitality, so she sat down at the table
opposite her new friend.

"And it's all arranged about your lodging here,"
said Rosalie, with her mouth full of stew.   "You've
only to give your twenty-eight sous to grandmother.
That's where you'll be."

Rosalie pointed to a house a part of which could be seen at the end of the yard; the rest of it was hidden by the brick house. It looked such a dilapidated old place that one wondered how it still held together.

"My grandmother lived there before she built this house," explained Rosalie. "She did it with the money that she got when she was nurse for Monsieur Edmond. You won't be comfortable down there as you would in this house, but factory hands can't live like rich people, can they?"

Perrine agreed that they could not.

At another table, standing a little distance from theirs, a man about forty years of age, grave, stiff, wearing a coat buttoned up and a high hat, was reading a small book with great attention.

"That's Mr. Bendit; he's reading his Bible," whispered Rosalie.

Then suddenly, with no respect for the gentleman's occupation, she said: "Monsieur Bendit, here's a girl who speaks English."

"Ah!" he said, without raising his eyes from his Bible.

Two minutes elapsed before he lifted his eyes and turned them to Perrine.

"Are you an English girl?" he asked in English.

"No, but my mother was," replied Perrine in the same language.

Without another word he went on with his reading.

They were just finishing their supper when a carriage coming along the road stopped at the gate.

"Why, it's Monsieur Vulfran in his carriage!" cried Rosalie, getting up from her seat and running to the gate.

Perrine did not dare leave her place, but she looked towards the road.

Two people were in the buggy. A young man was driving for an old man with white hair, who, although seated, seemed to be very tall. It was M. Paindavoine.

Rosalie went up to the buggy.

"Here is someone," said the young man, who was about to get out.

"Who is it?" demanded M. Paindavoine.

It was Rosalie who replied to this question.

"It's Rosalie, monsieur," she said.

"Tell your grandmother to come and speak to me," said the gentleman.

Rosalie ran to the house and came hurrying back with her grandmother.

"Good day, Monsieur Vulfran," said the old woman.

"Good day, Francoise."

"What can I do for you, sir; I'm at your service."

"I've come about your brother Omer. I've just come from his place. His drunken wife was the only person there and she could not understand anything."

"Omer's gone to Amiens; he comes back to-night."

" Tell him that I have heard that he has rented
his hall to some rascals to hold a public meeting
and . . . I don't wish that meeting to take place."

" But if they've rented it, sir? "

" He can compromise.   If he doesn't, the very
next day I'll put him out.   That's one of the conditions that I made.   I'll do what I say.   I don't
want any meeting of that sort here."

" There have been some at Flexelles."

" Flexelles is not Maraucourt.   I do not want
the people of my village to become like those at
Flexelle.   It's my duty to guard against that.   You
understand?   Tell Omer what I say.   Good day,
Francoise."

" Good day, Monsieur Vulfran."

He fumbled in his vest pocket.

" Where is Rosalie? "

" Here I am, Monsieur Vulfran."

He held out a ten cent piece.

" This is for you," he said.

" Oh, thank you, Monsieur Vulfran," said Rosalie,
taking the money with a smile.

The buggy went off.

Perrine had not lost a word of what had been
said, but what impressed her more than the actual
words was the tone of authority in which they had
been spoken.   " I don't wish that meeting to take
place."   She had never heard anyone speak like
that before.   The tone alone bespoke how firm was
the will, but the old gentleman's uncertain, hesitating gestures did not seem to accord with his words.

Rosalie returned to her seat, delighted.

"Monsieur Paindavoine gave me ten cents," she said.

"Yes, I saw him," replied Perrine.

"Let's hope Aunt Zenobie won't know, or she'll take it to keep it for me."

"Monsieur Paindavoine did not seem as though he knew you," said Perrine.

"Not know me?   Why, he's my godfather!" exclaimed Rosalie.

"But he said 'Where is Rosalie?' when you were standing quite near him."

"That's because he's blind," answered Rosalie, placidly.

"Blind!" cried Perrine.

She repeated the word quite softly to herself two or three times.

"Has he been blind long?" she asked, in the same awed voice.

"For a long time his sight was failing," replied Rosalie, "but no one paid any attention; they thought that he was fretting over his son being away.   Then he got pneumonia, and that left him with a bad cough, and then one day he couldn't see to read, then he went quite blind.   Think what it would have meant to the town if he had been obliged to give up his factories!   But no; he wasn't going to give them up; not he!   He goes to business just the same as though he had his sight.   Those who counted on being the master there, 'cause he fell ill, have been put in their places."   She lowered her

voice.   " His nephews and Talouel; they're the
ones I mean."

Aunt Zenobie came to the door.

" Say, Rosalie, have you finished, you young
loafer? " she called.

" I've only just this minute got through,"
answered Rosalie, defiantly.

" Well, there are some customers to wait on . . .
come on."

" I'll have to go," said Rosalie, regretfully.
" Sorry I can't stay with you."

" Oh, don't mind me," said little Perrine, politely.
" See you tonight."

With a slow, reluctant step Rosalie got up and
dragged herself to the house.

CHAPTER IX

ONE SLEEPLESS NIGHT

AFTER her new friend had left, Perrine would like to have still sat at the table as though she were in her own place, but it was precisely because she was not in the place where she belonged that she felt she could not. She had learned that the little garden was reserved for the boarders and that the factory hands were not priviledged to sit there. She could not see any seats near the old tumble-down house where she was to lodge, so she left the table and sauntered down the village street.

Although she went at a slow step, she had soon walked down all the streets, and as everyone stared at her, being a stranger, this had prevented her from stopping when she had wanted to.

On the top of the hill opposite the factories she had noticed a wood. Perhaps she would be alone there and could sit down without anyone paying attention to her.

She climbed the hill, then stretched herself out on the grass and looked down over the village . . . her father's birthplace, which he had described so often to her mother and herself.

She had arrived at Maraucourt! This name, which she had repeated so often since she had trod

on French soil, the name she had seen on the big
vans standing outside the Gates of Paris. This
was not a country of dreams. She was in Maraucourt; before her she could see the vast works which
belonged to her grandfather. He had made his
fortune here, bit by bit, sous by sous, until now he
was worth millions.

Her eyes wandered from the great chimneys to
the railway tracks, where all was quiet on this Sabbath day, to the winding streets and the quaint
houses with their tiled or thatched roofs. Amongst
the very old houses there was one which seemed
more pretentious than the others. It stood in a
large garden in which there were great trees and a
terrace, and at the remote corner of the garden a
wash-house.

That house had been described to her so many
times, she recognized it. It was the one in which
her grandfather had lived before he had built the
beautiful chateau. How many hours her father,
when a boy, had spent in that wash-house on washing days, listening to the washerwomen's chatter
and to the stories they told, quaint old legends.
He had remembered them all those years, and later
on had told them to his little daughter. There was
the " Fairy of the Cascade," " The Whirling Dwarf,"
and lots of others. She remembered them all, and
her dead father had listened to the old women telling them at that very spot down there by the river.

The sun was in her eyes now, so she changed her
place. She found another grassy nook and sat

down again, very thoughtful. She was thinking of her future, poor little girl.

She was sure of getting work now, and bread and a place in which to sleep, but that was not all. How would she ever be able to realize her dead mother's hopes? She trembled; it all seemed so difficult; but at least she had accomplished one great thing in having reached Maraucourt.

She must never despair, never give up hope, and now that she had a roof over her head and ten sous a day, although not much, it was far better now for her than a few days ago, when she had been penniless, famished, and had had no place where to lay her head.

She thought it would be wise, as she was beginning a new life on the morrow, that she should make a plan of what she should and what she should not say. But she was so ignorant of everything, and she soon realized that this was a task beyond her. If her mother had reached Maraucourt she would have known just what to have done. But she, poor little girl, had had no experience; she had not the wisdom nor the intelligence of a grown-up person; she was but a child, and alone.

This thought and the memory of her mother brought tears to her eyes. She began to cry unrestrainedly.

"Mother, dear mother," she sobbed.

Then her mother's last words came to her: "I see . . . I know that you will be happy!"

Her mother's words might come true. Those who

are at Death's door, their souls hovering between Heaven and earth, may have sometimes a divine knowledge of things which are not revealed to the living.

This burst of emotion, instead of making her more despondent, did her good.   After she had wiped her tears away she was more hopeful, and it seemed to her that the light evening breeze which fanned her cheek from time to time brought her a kiss from her mother, touching her wet cheeks and whispering to her her last words: "I see . . . I know you will be happy."

And why should it not be so?   Why should her mother not be near her, leaning over her at this moment like a guardian angel?   For a long time she sat deep in thought.   Her beautiful little face was very grave.   She wondered, would everything come out all right for her in the end?

Then mechanically her eye fell on a large cluster of marguerites.   She got up quickly and picked a few, closing her eyes so as not to choose.

She came back to her place and, taking up one with a hand that shook, she commenced to pick off the petals, one at a time, saying: "I shall succeed; a little; a lot; completely; not at all."   She repeated this very carefully until there were only a few petals left on the last flower.

How many, she did not want to count, for their number would have told her the answer.   So, with a heart beating rapidly, she quickly pulled off the last petals.

" I shall succeed; a little; a lot; completely . . . "

At the same moment a warm breeze passed over her hair, over her lips.   It was surely her mother's reply in a kiss, the tenderest that she had ever given her.

The night fell.   She decided to go.   Already down the straight road as far as the river white vapors were rising, floating lightly around the great trees.   Here and there little lights from behind the windows of the houses pierced the gathering darkness, and vague sounds broke the silence of the peaceful Sabbath evening.

There was no need for her to stay out late now, for she had a roof to cover her and a bed to sleep in; besides, as she was to get up early the next day to go to work, it would be better to go to bed early.

As she walked through the village she recognized that the noises that she had heard came from the cabarets.   They were full.   Men and women were seated at the tables drinking.   From the open door the odor of coffee, hot alcohol and tobacco filled the street as though it were a vast sink.

She passed one cabaret after another.   There were so many that to every three houses there was at least one in which liquor was sold.   On her tramps along the high roads and through the various towns she had seen many drinking places, but nowhere had she heard such words, so clear and shrill, as those which came confusedly from the low rooms.

When she reached Mother Francoise's garden she saw Mr. Bendit still reading. Before him was a lighted candle, a piece of newspaper protecting the light, around which the moths and mosquitoes flew. But he paid no attention to them, so absorbed was he in his reading.

Yet, as she was passing him, he raised his head and recognized her. For the pleasure of speaking in his own language, he spoke to her in English.

"I hope you'll have a good night's rest," he said.

"Thank you," she replied. "Good night, sir."

"Where have you been?" he continued in English.

"I took a walk as far as the woods," she replied in the same language.

"All alone?"

"Yes; I do not know anyone here."

"Then why don't you stay in and read. There is nothing better to do on Sunday than read."

"I have no books."

"Oh! Well, I'll lend you. Good night."

"Good night, sir."

Rosalie was seated in the doorway taking the fresh air.

"Do you want to go to bed now?" she asked.

"Yes, I'd like to," replied Perrine.

"I'll take you up there then, but first you'll have to arrange with grandmother. Go to the café; she's there."

The matter, having been arranged by Rosalie and her grandmother beforehand, was quickly settled.

Perrine laid her twenty-eight sous on the table and two sous extra for lighting for the week.

"So you are going to stay in our village, little one?" asked Mother Francoise, with a kindly, placid air.

"Yes, if it is possible."

"You can do it if you'll work."

"That is all I ask," replied Perrine.

"Well, that's all right.   You won't stop at ten sous; you'll soon get a franc or perhaps two, then later on you'll marry a good workingman who'll earn three.   Between you, that'll be five francs a day.   With that you're rich . . . if you don't drink; but one mustn't drink.   It's a good thing that M. Vulfran can give employment to the whole county. There is the lands, to be sure, but tilling ground can't provide a living to all who have to be fed."

Whilst the old nurse babbled this advice with the importance and the authority of a woman accustomed to having her word respected, Rosalie was getting some linen from a closet, and Perrine, who, while listening, had been looking at her, saw that the sheets were made of a thick yellow canvas.   It was so long since she had slept in sheets that she ought to think herself fortunate to get even these, hard though they were.   La Rouquerie on her tramps had never spent money for a bed, and a long time ago the sheets they had in the wagon, with the exception of those kept for her mother, had been sold or worn to rags.

She went with Rosalie across the yard where

about twenty men, women and children were seated on a clump of wood or standing about, talking and smoking, waiting for the hour to retire. How could all these people live in the old house, which seemed far from large?

At the sight of the attic, after Rosalie had lit a candle stuck behind a wire trellis, Perrine understood. In a space of six yards long and a little more than three wide, six beds were placed along the length of the walls, and the passage between the beds was only one yard wide. Six people, then, had to spend the night in a place where there was scarcely room for two. Although a little window opened on the yard opposite the door, there was a rank, sharp odor which made Perrine gasp. But she said nothing.

"Well," said Rosalie, "you think it's a bit small, eh?"

"Yes, it is, rather," was all she said.

"Four sous a night is not one hundred sous, you know," remarked Rosalie.

"That is true," answered Perrine, with a smothered sigh.

After all, it was better for her to have a place in this tiny room than be out in the woods and fields. If she had been able to endure the odor in Grain-of-Salt's shack, she would probably be able to bear it here.

"There's your bed," said Rosalie, pointing to one placed near the window.

What she called a bed was a straw mattress

placed on four feet and held together by two boards. Instead of a pillow there was a sack.

"You know," said Rosalie, "this is fresh straw; they never give old straw to anyone to sleep on. In the hotels they do that sort of thing, but we don't here."

Although there were too many beds in the little room, there was not one chair.

"There are some nails on the walls," said Rosalie, in reply to Perrine's questioning look; "you can hang your clothes up there."

There were also some boxes and baskets under the bed. If the lodgers had any underwear they could make use of these, but as Perrine had only what she was wearing, the nail at the head of the bed was sufficient.

"They're all honest here," remarked Rosalie, "and if La Noyelle talks in the night it's 'cause she's been drinking; she's a chatterbox. Tomorrow you get up with the others. I'll tell you where you have to go to wash. Good night."

"Good night, and thank you," replied Perrine.

She hurriedly undressed, thankful that she was alone and would not have to submit to the inquisitive regards of the other occupants of the room. But when she was between the sheets she did not feel so comfortable as she had hoped, for they were very rough and hard. But then the ground had seemed very hard the first time she had slept on it, and she had quickly grown accustomed to it.

It was not long before the door was opened and

a young girl about fifteen came in and commenced
to get undressed.   From time to time she glanced
at Perrine, but without saying a word.   As she was
in her Sunday clothes, her disrobing took longer
than usual, for she had to put away her best dress
in a small box and hang her working clothes on the
nail for the next day.

A second girl came in, then a third, then a fourth.
There was a babble of tongues, all talking at the
same time, each relating what had happened during
the day.   In the narrow space between the beds
they pulled out and pushed back their boxes or
baskets, and with each effort came an outburst of
impatience and furious upbraidings against the
landlady.

" What a hole ! "

" She'll be putting another bed in here soon."

" Sure!   But I won't stay ! "

" Where would yer go?   It ain't no better nowhere else."

The complaining, mixed with a desultory chatter,
continued.   At length, however, when the two who
had first arrived were in bed, a little order was
established.   Soon all the beds were occupied but
one.

But even then the conversation did not cease.
They had discussed the doings of the day just
passed, so now they went on to the next day, to the
work at the factories, the quarrels, the doings of
the heads of the concern — M. Vulfran Paindavoine
and his nephews, whom they called " the kids," and

the foreman, Talouel.   They spoke of this man by name only once, but the names they called him bespoke better than words what they thought of him.

Perrine experienced a strange contradictory feeling which surprised her.   She wanted to hear everything, for this information might be of great importance to her, yet on the other hand she felt embarrassed, almost ashamed, to listen to such talk.

Most of the talk was rather vague to Perrine, not knowing the persons to whom it applied, but she soon gathered that " Skinny," " Judas," and " Sneak " were all one and the same man, and that man was Talouel, the foreman.   The factory hands evidently considered him a bully; they all hated him, yet feared him.

" Let's go to sleep," at last said one.

" Yes, why not? "

" La Noyelle hasn't come in yet."

" I saw her outside when I came in."

" How was she? "

" Full.   She couldn't stand up."

" Ugh! d'ye think she can get upstairs? "

" Not sure about that."

" Suppose we lock the door? "

" Yes, and what a row she'd make! "

" Like last Sunday; maybe worse."

They groaned.   At this moment the sound of heavy shambling footsteps was heard on the stairs.

" Here she is."

The steps stopped, then there was a fall, followed by a moan.

"She's fallen down!"

"Suppose she can't get up?"

"She'd sleep as well on the stairs as here."

"And we'd sleep better."

The moaning continued, interrupted by calls for help.

"Come, Laide," called out a thick voice; "give us a hand, my child."

But Laide did not move. After a time the calls ceased.

"She's gone to sleep. That's luck."

But the drunken girl had not gone to sleep at all; on the contrary, she was using every effort to get up the stairs again.

"Laide, come and give me a hand, child. Laide, Laide," she cried.

She evidently made no progress, for the calls still came from the bottom of the stairs, and became more and more persistent. Finally she began to cry.

"Little Laide, little Laide, come to me," she wailed. "Oh! oh! the stairs are slipping; where am I?"

A burst of laughter came from each bed.

"It's cause yer ain't come in yet, Laide; that's why yer don't come. I'll go and find yer."

"Now she's gone and we'll have some peace," said one.

"No, she'll go to look for Laide and won't find

her, and it'll all begin over again.   We'll never get
to sleep."

" Go and give her a hand, Laide," advised one.

" Go yerself," retorted Laide.

" But she wants you."

Laide decided to go, and slipping on her skirt, she
went down the stairs.

" Oh, my child, my child," cried La Noyelle, brokenly, when she caught sight of her.

The joy of seeing Laide drove all thoughts of getting upstairs safely away.

" Come with me, little one, and I'll treat you to
a glass; come on," urged the drunken creature.

But Laide would not be tempted.

" No, come on to bed," she said.

The woman continued to insist.

They argued for a long time, La Noyelle repeating the words, " a little glass."

" I want to go to sleep," said one of the girls in
bed.   " How long is this going to keep up?   And
we got to be up early tomorrow."

" Oh, Lord! and it's like this every Sunday,"
sighed another.

And little Perrine had thought that if she only
had a roof over her head she would be able to sleep
in peace!   The open fields, with their dark shadows
and the chances of bad weather, was far better than
this crowded room, reeking with odors that were
almost suffocating her.   She wondered if she would
be able to pass the night in this dreadful room.

The argument was still going on at the foot of

the stairs. La Noyelle's voice could be heard repeating "a little glass."

"I'm goin' to help Laide," said one, "or this'll last till tomorrow. The woman got up and went down the narrow stairs. Then came the sound of angry voices, heavy footsteps and blows. The people on the ground floor came out to see what was the matter, and finally everyone in the house was awake.

At last La Noyelle was dragged into the room, crying out in despair.

"What have I done to you that you should be so unkind to me?"

Ignoring her complaints, they undressed her and put her into bed, but even then she did not sleep, but continued to moan and cry.

"What have I done to you girls that you should treat me so badly. I'm very unhappy, and I'm thirsty."

She continued to complain until everyone was so exasperated that they one and all shouted out in anger.

However, she went on all the same. She carried on a conversation with an imaginary person till the occupants of the room were driven to distraction. Now and again her voice dropped as though she were going off to sleep, then suddenly she cried out in a shriller voice, and those who had dropped off into a slumber awoke with a start and frightened her badly, but despite their anger she would not stop.

Perrine wondered if it really was to be like that

every Sunday. How could they put up with her? Was there no place in Maraucourt where one could sleep peacefully?

It was not alone the noise that disturbed her, but the air was now so stifling that she could scarcely breathe.

At last La Noyelle was quiet, or rather it was only a prolonged snore that came from her lips.

But although all was silent Perrine could not sleep. She was oppressed. It seemed as though a hammer was beating on her forehead, and she was perspiring from head to foot.

It was not to be wondered at. She was suffocating for want of air; and if the other girls in the room were not stifled like her, it was because they were accustomed to this atmosphere, which to one who was in the habit of sleeping in the open air was unbearable.

But she thought that if they could endure it she should. But unfortunately one does not breathe as one wishes, nor when one wishes. If she closed her mouth she could not get enough air into her lungs.

What was going to happen to her? She struggled up in bed, tearing at the paper which replaced the window pane against which her bed was placed. She tore away the paper, doing so as quietly as possible so as not to wake the girls beside her. Then putting her mouth to the opening she leaned her tired little head on the window sill. Finally in sheer weariness she fell asleep.

CHAPTER X

THE HUT ON THE ISLAND

WHEN she awoke a pale streak of light fell across the window, but it was so feeble that it did not lighten the room. Outside the cocks were crowing. Day was breaking.

A chill, damp air was penetrating through the opening she had made in the window, but in spite of that the bad odor in the room still remained. It was dreadful!

Yet all the girls slept a deep slumber, only broken now and again with a stifled moan.

Very quietly she got up and dressed. Then taking her shoes in her hands she crept down the stairs to the door. She put on her shoes and went out.

Oh! the fresh, delicious air! Never had she taken a breath with such thankfulness. She went through the little yard with her mouth wide open, her nostrils quivering, her head thrown back. The sound of her footsteps awoke a dog, which commenced to bark; then several other dogs joined in.

But what did that matter? She was no longer a little tramp at whom dogs were at liberty to bark. If she wished to leave her bed she had a perfect right to do so; she had paid out money for it.

The yard was too small for her present mood;

she felt she must move about. She went out onto the road and walked straight ahead without knowing where.

The shades of night still filled the roads, but above her head she saw the dawn already whitening the tops of the trees and the roofs of the houses. In a few minutes it would be day. At this moment the clang of a bell broke the deep silence. It was the factory clock striking three. She still had three more hours before going to work.

How should she pass the time? She could not keep walking until six, she would be too tired; so she would find a place where she could sit down and wait.

The sky was gradually getting brighter, and round about her various forms were taking a concrete shape.

At the end of a glade she could see a small hut made of branches and twigs which was used by the game keepers during the winter. She thought that if she could get to the hut she would be hidden there and no one would see her and inquire what she was doing out in the fields at that early hour.

She found a small trail, barely traced, which seemed to lead to the hut. She took it, and although it led her straight in the direction of the little cabin, she had not reached it when the path ended, for it was built upon a small island upon which grew three weeping willows. Around it was a ditch full of water. Fortunately, the trunk of a tree had been thrown across the ditch. Although it was not very straight, and was wet with the morning dew, which made it very slippery, Perrine was not deterred from crossing.

She managed to get across, and soon found herself before the door of the little hut, which she only had to push to open.

Oh, what a pretty nest! The hut was square, and from roof to floor was lined inside with ferns. There was a little opening on each of the four sides, which from without was invisible, but from within one could gain a good view of the surrounding country. On the ground was a thick bed of ferns, and in one of the corners a bench made from the trunk of a tree.

How delightful! And how little it resembled the room she had just left! How much better it would be for her if she could sleep here in the fresh air, sleeping in peace amongst the ferns, with no other noise but the rustling of the leaves and the ripple of the water.

How much better to be here than lying between Mother Francoise's hard sheets, listening to the complaints of La Noyelle and her friends in that dreadful atmosphere which even now seemed to assail her nostrils.

She laid down on the ferms, curled up in a corner against the soft walls covered with reeds, then closed her eyes. Before long she felt a soft numbness creeping over her. She jumped to her feet, fearing that she might drop off to sleep and not awake before it was time for her to go to the factory.

The sun had now risen, and through the aperture facing east a streak of gold entered the hut. Outside the birds were singing, and all over the tiny island, on the pond, on the branches of the weeping willows, was heard a confusion of sounds, twittering and little shrill cries which announced an awakening to life. Looking out of the window, she could see the birds picking at the humid earth with their beaks, snapping at the worms. Over the pond floated a light mist. A wild duck, far prettier than the tame ducks, was swimming on the water, surrounded with her young. She tried to keep them beside her with continual little quacks, but she found it impossible to do so. The ducklings escaped from the mother duck, scurrying off amongst the reeds to search for the insects which came within their reach.

Suddenly a quick blue streak, like lightning, flashed before Perrine's eyes. It was not until it had disappeared that she realized that it was a kingfisher which had just crossed the pond. For a long time, standing quite still for fear a movement might betray her presence and cause the birds to fly away, she stood at the opening looking out at them. How pretty it all was in the morning light, gay, alive, amusing, something new to look upon.

Now and again she saw dark shadows pass capriciously over the pond. The shadows grew larger without apparent cause, covering the pond. She could not understand this, for the sun, which had risen above the horizon, was shining in the sky without a cloud. How did these shadows come?

She went to the door and saw a thick black smoke coming from the factory chimneys.

Work would commence very soon; it was time to leave the hut. As she was about to go she picked up a newspaper from the seat that she had not noticed before in the dim light. The newspaper was dated February 2. Then this thought came to her: This newspaper was on the only spot in the place where one could sit down, and the date of it was several months previous, so then this proved that the hut had been abandoned and no one had passed through the door since last February.

CHAPTER XI

WORK IN THE FACTORY

WHEN she reached the road a loud whistle was heard, shrill and powerful. Almost immediately other whistles replied from the distance. This was the call for the factory hands who lived in Maraucourt, and the other whistles repeated the summons to work from village to village, St. Pipoy, Harcheux, Racour, Flexelles, in all the Paindavoine factories, announcing to the owner of the vast works that everywhere, at the same time, his factories were calling to his employés to be ready for the day's work.

Fearing she might be late she ran as far as the village. There she found all the doors of the houses open. On the thresholds the men were eating their soups or leaning against the walls; others were in the cabarets drinking wine; others were washing at the pump in the yard. No one seemed to be going to work, so evidently it was not time yet, so Perrine thought that there was no occasion for her to hurry.

But before long a louder whistle was blown, and then there was a general movement everywhere; from houses, yards and taverns came a dense crowd, filling the street. Men, women and children went towards the factories, some smoking their pipes, others munching a crust of bread, the greater number chattering loudly.   In one of the groups Perrine caught sight of Rosalie in company with La Noyelle.   She joined them.

"Why, where have you been?" asked Rosalie in surprise.

"I got up early so as to take a walk," Perrine replied.

"You did?   I went to look for you."

"Oh, thank you; but never do that, for I get up very early," said Perrine.

Upon arriving at the factory the crowd went into the various workshops under the watchful eye of a tall thin man who stood near the iron gates, his hand in the pocket of his coat, his straw hat stuck on the back of his head.   His sharp eyes scanned everyone who passed.

"That's Skinny," informed Rosalie in a whisper.

Perrine did not need to be told this.   She seemed to know at once that this was the foreman Talouel.

"Do I come in with you?" asked Perrine.

"Sure!"

This was a decisive moment for little Perrine, but she controlled her nervousness and drew herself up to her full height.   Why should they not take her if they took everyone?

Rosalie drew Perrine out of the crowd, then went up to Talouel.

"Monsieur," she said, "here's a friend of mine who wants a job."

Talouel glanced sharply at the friend.

" In a moment . . . we'll see," he replied curtly.

Rosalie, who knew what to do, signed to Perrine to stand aside and wait. At this moment there was a slight commotion at the gates, and the crowd drew aside respectfully to allow Monsieur Paindavoine's carriage to pass. The same young man who had driven him the evening before was now driving. Although everyone knew that their chief, Vulfran Paindavoine, was blind, all the men took off their hats as he passed and the women curtseyed.

" You see he's not the last one to come," said Rosalie, as the phaeton passed through the gates, " but his nephews likely will be late."

The clock struck, then a few late comers came running up. A young man came hurrying along, arranging his tie as he ran.

" Good morning, Talouel," he said; "is uncle here yet? "

" Yes, Monsieur Theodore," said the foreman, " he got here a good five minutes ago."

" Oh ! "

" You're not the last, though. Monsieur Casimir is late also. I can see him coming now."

As Theodore went towards the offices his cousin Casimir came up hurriedly.

The two cousins were not at all alike, either in their looks or ways. Casimir gave the foreman a short nod, but did not say a word.

" What can your friend do? " asked Talouel, turning to Rosalie, his hands still in his pockets.

Perrine herself replied to this question.

" I have not worked in a factory before," she said in a voice that she tried to control.

Talouel gave her a sharp look, then turned again to Rosalie.

" Tell Oneux to put her with the trucks.   Now be off.   Hurry up! "

Thus dismissed, Rosalie hurried Perrine away.

" What are the trucks? " asked little Perrine as she followed her friend through the big courtyard. She wondered, poor child, if she had the strength and the intelligence to do what was required of her.

" Oh, it's easy enough," replied Rosalie, lightly. " Don't be afraid; you've only got to load the trucks."

" Oh! . . . "

" And when it's full," continued Rosalie, "you push it along to the place where they empty it. You give a good shove to begin with, then it'll go all alone."

As they passed down the corridors they could scarcely hear each other speak for the noise of the machinery.   Rosalie pushed open the door of one of the workshops and took Perrine into a long room. There was a deafening roar from the thousand tiny machines, yet above the noise they could hear a man calling out: " Ah, there you are, you loafer! "

" Who's a loafer, pray? " retorted Rosalie. " That ain't me, just understand that, Father Nine-pins."

" What have you been doin'? "

"Skinny told me to bring my friend to you to work on the trucks."

The one whom she had addressed in this amiable manner was an old man with a wooden leg. He had lost his leg in the factory twelve years previous, hence his nickname, "Ninepins." He now had charge of a number of girls whom he treated rudely, shouting and swearing at them. The working of these machines needed as much attention of the eye as deftness of hand in lifting up the full spools and replacing them with empty ones, and fastening the broken thread. He was convinced that if he did not shout and swear at them incessantly, emphasizing each curse with a stout bang of his wooden leg on the floor, he would see his machines stop, which to him was intolerable. But as he was a good man at heart, no one paid much attention to him, and besides, the greater part of his cursing was lost in the noise of the machinery.

"Yes, and with it all, your machine has stopped," cried Rosalie triumphantly, shaking her fist at him.

"Go on with you," he shouted back; "that ain't my fault."

"What's your name?" he added, addressing Perrine.

This request, which she ought to have foreseen, for only the night before Rosalie had asked the same question, made her start. As she did not wish to give her real name, she stood hesitating. Old Ninepins thought that she had not heard, and bang-ing his wooden leg on the floor again, he cried:

"I asked you what your name was, didn't I? Eh?"

She had time to collect herself and to recall the one that she had already given to Rosalie.

"Aurelie," she said.

"Aurelie what?" he demanded.

"That is all . . . just Aurelie," she replied.

"All right, Aurelie; come on with me," he said.

He took her to a small truck stationed in a far corner and explained what she had to do, the same as Rosalie had.

"Do you understand?" he shouted several times. She nodded.

And really what she had to do was so simple that she would indeed have been stupid if she had been unable to do it.   She gave all her attention to the task, but every now and again old Ninepins called after her:

"Now, don't play on the way."   But this was more to warn than to scold her.

She had no thought of playing, but as she pushed her truck with a good regular speed, while not stopping, she was able to see what was going on on the way.   One push started the truck, and all she had to do was to see that there were no obstacles in its way.

At luncheon time each girl hurried to her home. Perrine went to the baker's and got the baker to cut her a half a pound of bread, which she ate as she walked the streets, smelling the while the good odor of the soup which came from the open doors before which she passed. She walked slowly when she smelled a soup that she liked. She was rather hungry, and a half a pound of bread is not much, so it disappeared quickly.

Long before the time for her to go back to work she was at the gates. She sat down on a bench in the shade of a tree and waited for the whistle, watching the boys and girls playing, running and jumping. She was too timid to join in their games, although she would like to have done so.

When Rosalie came she went back to her work with her.

Before the day was ended she was so tired that she did indeed merit Ninepins' sharp rebuke.

"Go on! Can't you go faster than that?" he cried.

Startled by the bang from his wooden leg which accompanied his words, she stepped out like a horse under the lash of a whip, but only to slow up the moment she was out of his sight. Her shoulders ached, her arms ached, her head ached. At first it had seemed so easy to push the truck, but to have to keep at it all day was too much for her. All she wanted now was for the day to end. Why could she not do as much as the others? Some of them were not so old as she, and yet they did not appear tired. Perhaps when she was accustomed to the work she would not feel so exhausted.

She reasoned thus as she wearily pushed her loaded truck, glancing at the others with envy as

they briskly went on with their work.   Suddenly
she saw Rosalie, who was fastening some threads,
fall down beside the girl who was next to her.   At
the same time a girlish cry of anguish was heard.

The machinery was stopped at once.   All was
silent now, the silence only broken by a moan.
Boys and girls, in fact everyone, hurried towards
Rosalie, despite the sharp words from old Ninepins.
"Thunder in Heaven, the machines have stopped.
What's the matter?" he cried.

The girls crowded around Rosalie and lifted her
to her feet.

"What's the matter?" they asked.

"It's my hand," she murmured; "I caught it in
the machine.   Oh! . . ."

Her face was very pale, her lips bloodless.   Drops
of blood were falling from her crushed hand.   But
upon examining it it was found that only two fingers
were hurt, one probably broken.

Ninepins, who at first had felt pity for the girl,
now began pushing those who surrounded her back
to their places.

"Be off; go back to your work," he cried.   "A
lot of fuss about nothing."

"Yes; it was a lot of fuss for nothing when you
broke your leg, wasn't it?" cried out a voice.

He glanced about to see who had spoken, but it
was impossible to find out in the crowd.   Then he
shouted again:

"Get back to your work.   Hurry up!"

Slowly they dispersed, and Perrine, like the

others, was on her way back to her truck, when Ninepins called to her:

"Here, you new one, there; come here! Come on, quicker than that."

She came back timidly, wondering why she was more guilty than the others who had also left their work. But she found that he did not wish to punish her.

"Take that young fool there to the foreman," he said.

"What do you call me a fool for?" cried Rosalie, raising her voice, for already the machines were in motion. "It wasn't my fault, was it?"

"Sure, it was your fault, clumsy." Then he added in a softer tone:

"Does it hurt?"

"Not so very much," replied Rosalie bravely.

"Well, go on home; be off now."

Rosalie and Perrine went out together, Rosalie holding her wounded hand, which was the left, in her right hand.

"Won't you lean on me, Rosalie?" asked little Perrine anxiously. "I am sure it must be dreadful."

"No, I'm all right; thank you," said Rosalie. "At least I can walk."

"Well, then, it isn't much then, is it?" asked Perrine.

"One can't tell the first day. It's later that one suffers. I slipped, that's how it happened."

"You must have been getting tired," said Perrine, thinking of her own feelings.

"Sure, it's always when one is tired that one is caught," said Rosalie. "We are quick and sharp first thing in the morning. I wonder what Aunt Zenobie will say!"

"But it wasn't your fault," insisted Perrine.

"I know that," said Rosalie, ruefully. "Grandmother will believe that, but Aunt Zenobie won't. She'll say it's 'cause I don't want to work."

On their way through the building several men stopped them to ask what was the matter. Some pitied Rosalie, but most of them listened indifferently, as though they were used to such accidents. They said that it was always so: one gets hurt the same as one falls sick; just a matter of chance, each in his turn, you today, and me tomorrow. But there were some who showed anger that such an accident could have occurred.

They came to a small outside building which was used for offices. They had to mount some wide steps which led to a porch. Talouel was standing on the porch, walking up and down with his hands in his pockets, his hat on his head. He seemed to be taking a general survey, like a captain on the bridge.

"What's the matter now?" he cried, angrily, when he saw the two girls.

Rosalie showed him her bleeding hand.

"Wrap your paw up in your handkerchief then," he said, roughly.

With Perrine's aid she got her handkerchief out of her pocket. Talouel strode up and down the

"WHAT'S THE MATTER NOW?" HE CRIED ANGRILY.

porch.   After the handkerchief had been twisted around the wounded hand he came over to poor Rosalie and stood towering above her.

"Empty your pockets," he ordered.   She looked at him, not understanding.

"I say, take everything out of your pockets," he said again.

She did what she was told, and drew from her pockets an assortment of things—a whistle made from a nut, some bones, a thimble, a stick of liquorice, three cents, and a little mirror.

The bully at once seized the mirror.

"Ah, I was sure of it," he cried.   "While you were looking at yourself in the glass a thread broke and your spool stopped.   You tried to catch the time lost and that's how it happened."

"I did not look in my glass," said Rosalie.

"Bah! you're all the same.   I know you.   Now what's the trouble?"

"I don't know, but my hand is crushed," said poor Rosalie, trying to keep back her tears.

"Well, and what do you want me to do?"

"Father Ninepins told me to come to you," said Rosalie.

"And you . . . what's the matter with you?" he asked, turning to Perrine.

"Nothing," she replied, disconcerted.

"Well?"

"Father Ninepins told her to bring me here," said Rosalie.

"Well, she can take you to Dr. Ruchon and let

him see it. But I'm going to look into this matter and find out if it is your fault, and if it is . . . . look out!"

He spoke in a loud, bullying voice which could be heard throughout the offices.

As the two girls were about to go M. Vulfran Paindavoine appeared, guiding himself with his hand along the wall.

"What's it all about, Talouel? What's the matter here?"

"Nothing much, sir," replied the foreman. "One of the girls has hurt her hand."

"Where is she?"

"Here I am, Monsieur Vulfran," said Rosalie, going up to him.

"Why, it's Mother Francoise's granddaughter, Rosalie, isn't it?" asked the blind man.

"Yes, it's me, Monsieur Vulfran," said Rosalie, beginning to cry. Harsh words had hardened her heart, but this tone of pity was too much for poor Rosalie.

"What is the matter with your hand, my poor girl?" asked the blind man.

"Oh, sir, I think my two fingers are broken," she said, "although I am not in much pain."

"Well, why are you crying?" asked M. Vulfran, tenderly.

"Because you speak so kindly to me."

Talouel shrugged his shoulders.

"Now go home at once," said M. Vulfran, "and I'll send the doctor to you."

" Write a note to Dr. Ruchon," he said, turning to Talouel, " and tell him to call at Mother Francoise's house; say that the matter is urgent and he must go there at once."

" Do you want anyone to go with you? " he asked, addressing Rosalie.

" Oh, thank you, Monsieur Vulfran; I have a friend here with me," she replied.

" She can go with you then, and tell your grand-mother that you will be paid while you are away."

It was Perrine now who felt like crying, but catching Talouel's glance, she stiffened. It was not until they had passed out of the yard that she betrayed her emotion.

" Isn't Monsieur Vulfran kind? " she said.

" Yes," replied Rosalie; " he would be all right if he were alone, but with Skinny he can't be; he hasn't the time and he has a lot to think about."

" Well, he seemed very kind to you," said little Perrine.

" Oh, yes," Rosalie said, drawing herself up; " I make him think of his son. My mother was Monsieur Edmond's foster sister."

" Does he think of his son? "

" He thinks of nothing else."

Everybody came to their doors as Rosalie and Perrine passed. Rosalie's handkerchief was cov-ered with blood. Most of the people were merely curious, others felt sorry, others were angry, know-ing that what had happened to this girl that day might happen the next day, at any moment, to their fathers, husbands, and children. Was not everyone in Maraucourt employed at the factory?

"You come on in with me," said Rosalie, when they reached the house; "then perhaps Aunt Zenobie won't say much."

But Perrine's presence had no effect upon the terrible aunt. Seeing Rosalie arrive at such an unusual hour, and noticing that her hand was wrapped up, she cried out shrilly: "Now, then, you've gone and hurt yourself, you lazy bones. I bet you did it on purpose."

"Oh, I'm goin' to be paid," retorted Rosalie, scornfully.

"You think so, do you?"

"Monsieur Vulfran told me that I should."

But this information did not appease Aunt Zenobie. She continued to scold until Mother Françoise, leaving her store, came to see what was the matter. But the old grandmother, instead of showing anger, put her arms about Rosalie and said: "Oh, my dearie; you've gone and got hurt."

"Just a little, grandmother . . . it's my fingers . . . but it ain't much."

"We must have Dr. Ruchon."

"Monsieur Vulfran is going to send him here."

Perrine was about to follow them into the house when Aunt Zenobie turned upon her and stopped her.

"What are you coming for?" she asked. "Do you think we need you to look after her?"

" Thank you for coming," called out Rosalie to Perrine.

Perrine had nothing to do but to return to the factory, which she did.   But just as she reached the gates a whistle announced that it was closing time.

CHAPTER XII

NEW SHOES

A DOZEN times during the day she had asked herself how she could possibly sleep in that room where she had been almost suffocated. She was sure that she would not be able to sleep any better that night, or the next, or the next.

And if she could not find rest after a hard day's work, whatever would happen to her?

In her little mind she weighed all the consequences of this terrible question. If she had not the strength to do her work she would be sent away from the factory, and that would be the end of all her hopes. She would be ill and there would be no one to help her, and she would have to lie down at the foot of a tree and die.

It is true that unless she wished she was not obliged to occupy the bed that she had paid for, but where would she find another, and what would she say to Rosalie? How could she say in a nice way that what was good for others was not good for her, and when they knew how disgusted she had been, how would they treat her? She might create such ill feeling that she would be forced to leave the factory.

The day had passed without her having come to a decision.

But now that Rosalie had hurt her hand the situation was changed. Poor Rosalie would probably have to stay in bed for several days, and she would not know what happened in the house at the end of the yard. She would not know who slept in the room or who did not; consequently she need fear no questions. And, on the other hand, as none of the girls in the room knew who the new lodger for the night had been, neither would they bother about her; it might very well be some one who had decided to find a lodging elsewhere.

Reasoning thus, she decided quickly that she would go and sleep in her new little home. How good it would be to sleep there — nothing to fear from anyone, a roof to cover her head, without counting the enjoyment of living in a house of one's own.

The matter was quite decided, and after having been to the baker's to buy another half a pound of bread for her supper, instead of returning to Mother Francoise's she again took the road that she had taken early that morning.

She slipped behind the hedge as the factory hands who lived outside Maraucourt came tramping along the road on their way home. She did not wish to be seen by them. While she waited for them to pass she gathered a quantity of rushes and ferns and made a broom. Her new home was clean and comfortable, but with a little attention it could be

made more so, and she would pick a lot of dried
ferns and make a good soft bed to lie upon.

Forgetting her fatigue, she quickly tied the broom
together with some wisps of straw and fastened it to
a stick.   No less quickly a bunch of ferns was arranged in a mass so that she could easily carry them
to her hut.

The road was now deserted as far as she could see.
Hoisting the bed of ferns on her back and taking the
broom in her hands, she ran down the hill and
across the road.   When she came to the narrow
path she had to slacken her speed, for the ferns
caught in the branches and she could not pass without going down on her knees.

Upon arriving at the island, she began at once to
do her housework.   She threw away the old ferns,
then commenced to sweep everywhere, the roof, the
walls and the ground.

As she looked out over the pond and saw the
reeds growing thickly, a bright idea came to her.
She needed some shoes.   One does not go about a
deserted island in leather shoes.   She knew how to
plait, and she would make a pair of soles with the
reeds and get a little canvas for the tops and tie
them on with ribbon.

As soon as she had finished her sweeping she ran
out to the pond and picked a quantity of the most
flexible reeds and carried them back to the door of
her hut and commenced to work.   But after she
had made a plait of reeds about a yard long she
found that this sole that she was making would be

too light; because it was too hollow, there would be no solidity, and that before plaiting the reeds they would have to undergo a preparation which in crushing the fibres would transform them into coarse strings.

However, this did not stop her. Now she needed a hammer of course she could not find one, but what she did find was a big round stone, which served her purpose very well indeed. Then she commenced to beat the reeds. Night came on while she was still at work, and she went to sleep dreaming of the beautiful sandals tied with blue ribbons which she would have, for she did not doubt but that she would succeed with what she had undertaken . . . if not the first time, well, then the second or the third . . . or the tenth.

By the next evening she had plaited enough to begin the soles, and the following day, having bought a curved awl for the price of one sou, some thread for one sou, a piece of ribbon for the same price, a small piece of rough canvas for four sous, in all seven sous, which was all that she could spend if she did not wish to go without bread on the Saturday, she tried to make a sole like those worn on shoes. The first one that she made was almost round. This was not exactly the shape of the foot. The second one, to which she gave much more attention, seemed to resemble nothing at all; the third was a little better, but finally the fourth, which, with some practice, she had managed to tighten in the center and draw in at the heel, could pass for a sole.

Once more she had proved that with a little perseverance, a little will, one can do what one wants, even if at first it seems impossible. And she had done this with scarcely anything, a few sous, with no tools, with hardly anything at her command. She was really very happy and she considered that her work was very successful.

Now what she needed most to finish her sandals were scissors. They would cost so much to buy she would have to manage without them. Fortunately she had her knife, and with the help of a stone to sharpen the point she could make it fine enough to trim the canvas.

But the cutting of the pieces of canvas she found quite a difficult matter. Finally she accomplished it, and on the following Saturday morning she had the satisfaction of going forth shod in a nice pair of gray canvas shoes, tied with blue ribbons crossed over her stockings.

While she had been working on her shoes (the work had taken four evenings and three mornings beginning at the break of day), she had wondered what she should do with her leather shoes while she was away from the hut. She had no fear that they would be stolen by anyone, for no one came to the place, but then the rats might eat them. So as to prevent this she would put them in a place where the rats could not get at them.

This was a rather difficult matter, for the rats

seemed to be everywhere.   She had no closet, no
box to put them away in.   Finally she tied them to
the roof with some wisps of straw.

CHAPTER XIII

ALTHOUGH she was very proud of her shoes, she was rather anxious as to how she would conduct herself while wearing them at work. While she loaded her truck or pushed it alone she was continually looking down at her feet.

By doing so she would probably attract the attention of the other girls. This is exactly what did happen. Several of her comrades noticed them and complimented her.

" Where did you buy those shoes? " one asked.

" They are not shoes; they are sandals," corrected Perrine.

" No, they are not; they are shoes," said the girl; " but whatever they are they sure are pretty. Where did you buy them? "

" I made them myself with plaited reeds and four cents worth of canvas," replied Perrine.

" They *are* beautiful."

The success she had made of her shoes decided her to undertake another task. She had thought several times of doing it, but it was much more difficult, or so she thought, and might mean too much expense. She wanted to make a chemise to replace the only one which she possessed. For it was very inconvenient to take off this only garment to wash it and then wait until it was dry to put it on again. She needed two yards of calico, and she wondered how much it would cost. And how would she cut the goods when she had them? These were very difficult questions to answer. She certainly had something to think about.

She wondered if it would not be wiser to begin by making a print dress to replace her waist and skirt, which was worn more than ever now, as she had to sleep in it. It could last a very little while longer. When it was finished, how would she go out? For her daily bread, as much as for the success of her future plans, she must continue to be admitted to the factory.

Yet on the Saturday evening when she had the three francs in her hand which she had earned for the week's work, she could not resist the temptation of a chemise. She still considered a waist and skirt of the utmost utility, but then a chemise also was indispensable, and besides there were many arguments in favor of the chemise — cleanliness in which she had been brought up, self-respect. Finally the chemise won the day. She would mend her waist and skirt; as the material had formerly been very strong, it would still hold a few more darns.

Every day at the luncheon hour she went to Mother Francoise's house to ask news of Rosalie. Sometimes news was given to her, sometimes not, according to whether it was the grandmother or the aunt whom she saw.

On her way to inquire for Rosalie she passed a little store which was divided into two sections. On one side newspapers, pictures and songs were sold, and on the other linens, calicos and prints. Perrine had often looked in this store. How nice it would be to go in and have them cut off as much material as she wished! Sometimes, when she had been looking in the window, pretending to look at the newspapers or a song, she had seen girls from the factory enter and come out shortly after with parcels carefully wrapped up, which they held clasped tightly to them. She had thought then that such pleasure was not for her . . . at least not then.

Now she could enter the store if she wished, for she had three silver coins in her hand. She went in.

"What is it you want, mademoiselle?" asked a little old woman politely, with a pleasant smile.

"Will you please tell me what is the price of calico the yard . . . the cheapest?" asked Perrine timidly.

"I have it at forty centimes the yard," said the old woman.

Perrine gave a sigh of relief.

"Will you cut me two yards, please?" she said.

"It won't wear very well . . . but the sixty centimes . . ."

"The forty centime one will do, thank you," said little Perrine.

"As you like," said the old woman. "I wouldn't like you to come back after and say . . . ."

SHE HAD SOME TIME AGO DECIDED ON THE SHAPE.

" Oh, I wouldn't do that," interrupted Perrine hastily.

The old woman cut off two yards, and Perrine noticed that it was not white nor shiny like the one she had admired in the window.

" Any more? " asked the shopkeeper when she had torn the calico with a sharp, dry rip.

" I want some thread also," said Perrine; " a spool of white, number forty."

Now it was Perrine's turn to leave the store with her little newspaper parcel hugged tightly to her heart. Out of her three francs (sixty centimes) she had spent eighteen, so there still remained forty-two until the following Saturday. She would have to spend twenty sous for bread, so that left her fourteen sous for extras.

She ran back all the way to her little island. When she reached her cabin she was out of breath, but that did not prevent her from beginning her work at once. She had some time ago decided upon the shape she would give her chemise. She would make it quite straight, first, because that was the simplest and the easiest way for one who had never cut out anything before and who had no scissors, and secondly, because she could use the string that was in her old one for this new one.

Everything went very well; to begin with, there was no cutting in the straight piece. Perhaps there was nothing to admire in her work but at any rate she did not have to do it over again. But when the time came for shaping the openings for the head and arms then she experienced difficulties! She had only a knife to do the cutting and she was so afraid that she would tear the calico. With a trembling hand she took the risk. At last it was finished, and on Tuesday morning she would be able to go to the factory wearing a chemise earned by her own work, cut and sewn by her own hands.

That day when she went to Mother Francoise's; it was Rosalie who came to meet her with her arm in a sling.

" Are you better? " asked Perrine.

" No, but they let me get up and they said that I could come out in the yard," replied Rosalie.

Perrine was very pleased to see her friend again and asked all kinds of questions, but Rosalie seemed rather reserved. Perrine could not understand this attitude.

" Where are you living now? " asked Rosalie.

Fearing to say where, Perrine evaded a direct answer to this question.

" It was too expensive for me here," she said, " and I had so little money left for food and other things."

" Well, did you find anything cheaper elsewhere? "

" I don't have to pay."

" Oh! . . ."

She looked narrowly at Perrine, then her curiosity got the better of her.

" Who are you with? " she asked.

Again Perrine could not give a direct answer.

"I'll tell you that later," she said.

"Oh, when you like," replied Rosalie carelessly, "only let me tell you this, if you see Aunt Zenobie in the yard or at the door you had better not come in. She doesn't want to see you here. If you come it is better to come in the evening, then she . . . she is busy."

Perrine went to the factory very saddened by this welcome. What had she done that she could not go into the house? All day long she remained under the impression that she had offended them. When evening came and she found herself alone in the cabin having nothing to do for the first time in eight days, she was even more depressed. Then she thought that she would go and walk in the fields that surrounded her little island, for she had not yet had time to do this.

It was a beautiful evening. She wandered around the pond, walking in the high grass that had not been trodden by anyone. She looked across the water at her little home which seemed almost hidden amongst the trees. The birds and beasts could not suspect that it was the work of man behind which he could lie in ambush with his gun.

At that moment she heard a noise at her feet which frightened her and a water hen jumped into the water, terrified. Then looking about her she saw a nest made of grass and feathers in which were ten white eggs, dirty little eggs with small dark spots.

Instead of being placed on the ground amongst the grass the nest was floating on the water. She examined it but without touching it, and noticed that it was made in a way to go up and down according to the flow of the water, and was so surrounded with reeds that neither the current nor the wind could carry it away.

The mother hen, anxious, took up her position at a distance and stayed there. Perrine hid herself in the high grass and waited to see if she would come back to her nest.

As she did not return, she went on with her walk, and again and again the rustling of her dress frightened other birds. The water hens, so lissom in their escape, ran to the floating leaves of the water lilies without going under. She saw birds everywhere.

When an hour later she returned to her little home the hut was hidden half in the shadows of night. It was so quiet and pretty she thought, and how pleased she was that she had shown as much intelligence as these birds . . . to make her nest here.

With Perrine, as with many little children, it was the events of the day which shaped her dreams by night. The unhappiness through which she had passed the last few months had often colored her dreams, and many times since her troubles had commenced, she had awakened in the night with the perspiration pouring off her. Her sleep was disturbed with nightmares caused by the miseries she had experienced in the day.

Now since she had been at Maraucourt and had new hopes and was at work, the nightmares had been less frequent and so she was not so sad.

Now she thought of what she was going to do at the factory the next day, of the skirt and waist that she would make, of her underwear.

Now on this particular evening after she had wandered over the fields surrounding her home and had entered her little nest to go to sleep, strange visions passed before her sleepy eyes. She thought that she was walking about the field exploring, and came upon a great big kitchen, a wonderful kitchen like in castles, and there were a number of little dwarfs of the most diabolical shapes, sitting around a big table before a blazing fire; some of them were breaking eggs, others were beating them up until they were white and frothy; and some of these eggs were as large as melons and others were as small as a little pea, and the dwarfs made the most extraordinary dishes from them. They seemed to know the every kind of dish that could be made with eggs,— boiled eggs with cheese and butter; with tomatoes; poached; fried eggs; various omelettes with ham and kidney, jam or rum; the rum set afire and flaming with sparkling lights. And then there were more important dishes still which only the head cooks were handling . . . pastries and delicious creams.

Now and again she half woke and she tried to

banish the stupid dream but it came again and the elfs still went on doing their fantastic work, so that when the factory whistle sounded she was still watching them prepare some chocolate creams which she could almost taste in her mouth.

Then she knew that what had impressed her most during her walk was not the beauty of the night but simply those eggs which she had seen in the nest, which had told her stomach that for fourteen days she had eaten only bread and water. These eggs had made her dream of the elfs and all those delicious things that they were making; she was hungry for good things and she had found it out through her dream.

Why had she not taken those eggs, or at least some of them, they did not belong to anyone for the duck was wild? Of course as she had no saucepan or frying pan or any kitchen utensils whatever, she could not prepare any of the dishes that she had seen made before her dream eyes. But there, that was the best about eggs, they could be used without any very skillful preparation; a lighted match put to a little heap of dry wood and then she could cook them hard or soft, how she liked, in the hot ashes. And she would buy a saucepan or a pan as soon as possible.

Several times this idea came to her while she was at work that day until finally she decided to buy a box of matches and a cent's worth of salt. As soon as she had made her purchases she ran back to her hut.

She had been too interested in the place where she had discovered the nest not to be able to find it again. The mother was not occupying the nest but she had been there during the day because Perrine saw now that instead of ten eggs there were eleven, which proved that she had not finished laying.

Here was a good chance for her to help herself. In the first place the eggs were fresh, and then if she only took five or six, the duck, who did not know how to count, would not notice that any one had been there.

A short time ago Perrine would not have had any scruples and she would have quickly emptied the nest, without a thought, but the sorrows that she had experienced had made her very thoughtful for the griefs of others; in this same manner her love for Palikare had made her feel an affection for all animals that she had not known in her early childhood.

After she had taken the eggs she wondered where she could cook them; naturally this could not be done in the cabin for the slightest wreath of smoke which would emerge from it would indicate to anyone who saw it that someone was living there.

There was a gypsy camp quite near which she passed by to get to her island, and a little smoke coming from there would attract no attention.

She quickly got together some wood and lighted it; soon she had a fire in the ashes of which she cooked one of her eggs. She lacked an egg cup but what did that matter? A little hole made in a piece of bread could hold the egg. In a few minutes she had the satisfaction of dipping a piece of bread in her egg, which was cooked to perfection. It seemed to her as she took the first mouthful that she had never eaten anything so good.

When she had finished her supper she wondered how she should use the remainder of her eggs. She would have to use them sparingly for she might not be able to get any more for a long time. A hot soup with an egg broken into it would be very good.

As the idea of having some soup came into her head, it was almost immediately followed by the regret that she could not have it. The success of her canvas shoes and her underwear had inspired her with a certain amount of confidence. She had proved that one can do a great deal if one perseveres, but she had not enough confidence to imagine that she could ever make a saucepan for her soup or a metal or wooden spoon, and if she waited until she had the money required to buy these utensils, she would have to content herself with the smell of the soup that came to her as she passed by the open doors.

She was telling herself this as she went to work, but just before she reached the village she saw a heap of rubbish by the side of the road and amongst the debris she noticed some tin cans which had been used for potted meat, fish and vegetables. There were different shapes, some large, some small, some high, some low.

Noticing how shiny they were on the surface,

she instinctively stopped; she had not a moment's hesitation. The saucepans, dishes, forks, spoons which she lacked were all here; she could have a whole array of kitchen utensils; she had only to make her choice. With a bound she was across the road; quickly picking out four cans she ran back and hid them behind a hedge so that when evening came she would be able to find them.

When evening came she found her treasures and made for her home.

She did not wish to make a noise on her island any more than she wished smoke to be seen, so at the end of her day's work she went to her gypsy's camp hoping that she might find a tool or something that would serve her for a hammer with which to flatten the tins that were to be used for plates, saucepans, spoons, etc.

She found that it was a very difficult task to make a spoon. It took her no less than three days to do so, and when it was done, she was not at all sure that if she had shown it to anyone, he would have recognized it for a spoon. But she had made something that served her purpose, that was enough; besides, she ate alone and there would be no one to notice her utensils.

Now for the soup for which she longed! All she wanted was butter and sorrel. She would have to buy butter and naturally as she couldn't make milk she would have to buy that also.

The sorrel she would find wild in the fields and she could also find wild carrots and oyster plants.

They were not so good as the cultivated vegetables but they would suit her very well indeed.

She not only had eggs and vegetables for her dinner, and her pots and pans, but there were fish in the pond and if she were sharp enough to catch them she would have fish too.

She needed a line and some worms. She had a long piece of string left over from the piece she had bought for her shoes and she had only to spend one sou for some hooks, then with a piece of horse hair she could pick up outside the blacksmith's door, she would have a line good enough to catch several kinds of fish; if the best in the pond passed disdainfully before her simple bait then she would have to be satisfied with little ones.

CHAPTER XIV

A BANQUET IN THE HUT

PERRINE was so busy of an evening that she let an entire week pass before she again went to see Rosalie. However, one of the girls at the factory who lodged with Mother Francoise had brought her news of her friend. Perrine, as well as being busy, had been afraid that she might see that terrible Aunt Zenobie and so she had let the days pass.

Then one evening after work she thought that she would not return at once to her little island. She had no supper to prepare. The night before she had caught some fish and cooked it, and she intended to have it cold for her supper that evening.

Rosalie was alone in the garden sitting under an apple tree. When she saw Perrine she came to the gate, half pleased, half annoyed.

"I thought that you were not coming any more," she said.

"I've been very busy."

"What with?"

Perrine showed Rosalie her shoes. Then she told her how she had made herself a chemise and the trouble she had had in cutting it.

"Couldn't you borrow a pair of scissors from

the people in your house?" asked Rosalie in astonishment.

"There is no one in my house who could lend me scissors," replied Perrine.

"Everybody has scissors!"

Perrine wondered if she ought to keep her abode a secret any longer. She was afraid that if she did so she might offend Rosalie, so she decided to tell her.

"Nobody lives in my house," she said smiling.

"Whatever do you mean?" asked Rosalie with round eyes.

"That's so, and that's why, as I wasn't able to borrow a saucepan to cook my soup in and a spoon to eat it with, I had to make them and I can tell you that it was harder for me to make my spoon than to make my shoes."

"You're joking!"

"No, really."

Then she told her everything, how she had taken possession of the cabin, and made her own cooking utensils, and about her search for eggs, and how she fished and cooked in the gypsy's camping ground.

Rosalie's eyes opened wider still in wonder and delight. She seemed to be listening to a wonderful story.

When Perrine told her how she made her first sorrel soup, she clapped her hands.

"Oh, how delicious! How you must have enjoyed it!" she cried. "What fun!"

"Yes, everything is great fun when things ge

right," said Perrine; " but when things won't go!
I worked three days for my spoon.   I couldn't
scoop it out properly.   I spoiled two large pieces of
tin and had only one left.   And my! how I banged
my fingers with the stones that I had to use in place
of a hammer!"

" But your soup, that's what I'm thinking of,"
said Rosalie.

" Yes, it was good."

" You know," said Perrine, " there's sorrel and
carrots, watercress, onions, parsnips, turnips, and
ever so many things to eat that one can find in the
fields.   They are not quite the same as the cultivated vegetables, but they are good!"

" One ought to know that!"

" It was my father who taught me to know them."

Rosalie was silent for a moment, then she said:

" Would you like me to come and see you?"

" I should love to have you if you'll promise not
to tell anyone where I live," said Perrine, delightedly.

" I promise," said Rosalie, solemnly.

" Well, when will you come?"

" On Sunday I am going to see one of my aunts
at Saint-Pipoy; on my way back in the afternoon
I can stop . . . "

Perrine hesitated for a moment, then she said
amiably:

" Do better than just call; stay to dinner with
me."

Rosalie, like the real peasant that she was, began

to reply vaguely in a ceremonious fashion, neither saying yes nor no; but it was quite plain to see that she wished very much to accept the invitation. Perrine insisted.

"Do come; I shall be so pleased," she said. "I am so lonesome."

"Well, really . . . " began Rosalie.

"Yes, dine with me; that is settled," said Perrine, brightly; "but you must bring your own spoon, because I shall not have the time nor the tin to make another one."

"Shall I bring my bread also? I can . . . "

"I wish you would. I'll wait for you in the gypsies' ground. You'll find me doing my cooking."

Perrine was very pleased at the thought of receiving a guest in her own home . . . there was a menu to compose, provisions to find . . . what an affair! She felt quite important. Who would have said a few days before that she would be able to offer dinner to a friend!

But there was a serious side. Suppose she could not find any eggs or catch a fish! Her menu then would be reduced to sorrel soup only. What a dinner!

But fortune favored her. On Friday evening she found some eggs. True, they were only waterhen's eggs, and not so large as the duck's eggs, but then she must not be too particular. And she was just as lucky with her fishing. With a red worm on the end of her line, she managed to catch a fine perch, which was quite sufficient to satisfy hers

and Rosalie's appetite.   Yet, however, she wanted
a dessert, and some gooseberries growing under a
weeping willow furnished it.   True, they were not
quite ripe, but the merit of this fruit is that you
can eat it green.

When, late Sunday afternoon, Rosalie arrived at
the gypsy camping ground, she found Perrine seated
before her fire upon which the soup was boiling.

" I waited for you to mix the yolk of an egg in
the soup," said Perrine.   " You have only to turn
it with your free hand while I gently pour the soup
over it; the bread is soaked."

Although Rosalie had dressed herself specially for
this dinner, she was not afraid to help.   This was
play, and it all seemed very amusing to her.

Soon the soup was ready, and it only had to be
carried across to the island.   This Perrine did.

The cabin door was open, and Rosalie could see
before she entered that the place was filled with
flowers.   In each corner were grouped, in artistic
showers, wild roses, yellow iris, cornflowers, and
poppies, and the floor was entirely covered with a
beautiful soft green moss.

Rosalie's exclamations of delight amply repaid
Perrine for all the trouble she had taken.

" How beautiful!   Oh, isn't it pretty!" she exclaimed.

On a bed of fresh ferns two large flat leaves were
placed opposite each other; these were to serve for
plates; and on a very much larger leaf, long and
narrow, which is as it should be for a dish, the perch

was placed, garnished with a border of watercress. Another leaf, but very small, served as a salt-cellar, also another holding the dessert. Between each dish was a white anemone, its pure whiteness standing out dazzlingly against the fresh verdure.

" If you will sit down . . . " said Perrine, extending her hand. And when they had taken their seats opposite one another the dinner commenced.

" How sorry I should have been if I hadn't have come," said Rosalie, speaking with her mouth full; " it is so pretty and so good."

" Why shouldn't you have come? "

" Because they wanted to send me to Picquigny for Mr. Bendit; he is ill."

" What's the matter with him? "

" He's got typhoid fever. He's very ill. Since yesterday he hasn't known what he's been talking about, and he doesn't know anybody. And I had an idea about you . . . "

" Me! What about me? "

" Something you can do . . . "

" If there is anything I can do for Mr. Bendit I'd be only too willing. He was kind to me; but I'm only a poor girl; I don't understand."

" Give me a little more fish and some more watercress, and I'll explain," said Rosalie. " You know that Mr. Bendit has charge of the foreign correspondence; he translates the English and German letters. Naturally, as he is off his head now, he can't translate. They wanted to get somebody else to replace him, but as this other man might take his

place after he is better (that is, if he does get
better), M. Fabry and M. Mombleux have taken
charge of the work, so that he will be sure to have
his job when he's up again.   But now M. Fabry
has been sent away to Scotland and M. Mombleux
is in a fix, because, although he can read German
all right, he's not much on English.   If the writing
isn't very clear he can't make out the letters at all.
I heard him saying so at the table when I was waiting on them.   So I thought I'd tell him that you can
speak English just as good as you can French."

"I spoke French with my father, and English
with my mother," said Perrine, " and when we were
all three talking together we spoke sometimes one,
sometimes the other, mixing two languages without
paying attention."

"I wasn't sure whether I should say anything
about you or not, but now I will, if you like."

"Why, yes; do, if you think a poor girl like me
could be of any use to them."

"'Tain't a question of being a poor girl or a young
lady; it's a question of knowing English," said
Rosalie.

"I speak it, but to translate a business letter is
another thing," said Perrine, doubtfully.

"It'll be all right with M. Mombleux; he knows
the business part."

"Well, then, tell him I shall be very pleased if I
can do anything for M. Bendit."

"I'll tell him."

The perch, although a large one, had all been

eaten, and all the watercress had disappeared. It was now time for the dessert. Perrine got up and replacel the fish plates with smaller leaf plates in the shape of a cup; she had picked the prettiest, with variegated shades, and marked as exquisitely as enameled ware. Then she offered her guest the gooseberries.

"Let me offer you some fruit from my own garden," she said, laughing, as though she were playing at keeping doll's house.

"Where is your garden?"

"Over your head. There is a gooseberry bush growing in the branches of this willow tree which holds up the cabin, so it seems."

"You know you won't be able to live in here much longer," said Rosalie.

"Until the winter, I think."

"Until winter! Why, the bird catchers will need this place pretty soon; that I'm sure."

"Oh! . . . Oh, dear . . . Oh, dear!"

The day, which had begun so brightly for Perrine, ended sadly. That night was certainly the worst Perrine had passed since she had been on her little island.

Where should she go?

And all her utensils that she had taken such trouble to make; what should she do with them?

CHAPTER XV.

I F ROSALIE had not spoken to Perrine of the near opening of the shooting season for water fowl, Perrine would have stayed on in her cabin unaware of the danger that might come to her. Although this news came as a blow to her, what Rosalie had said about M. Bendit and the translations she might do for M. Mombleux gave her something else to think about.

Yes, her island was charming, and it would be a great grief for her to leave it. And yet here was an opportunity where she could be useful to two valued employés at the factory, and this step would lead to other steps, and it would open doors perhaps through which she could pass later. This was something that she should consider above all else, even above the sorrow of being dispossessed of her little kingdom. It was not for this game — robbing nests, catching fish, picking flowers, listening to the birds sing — that she had endured all the misery and fatigue of her long journey. She had an object in view. She must remember what her mother told her to do, and do it.

She had told Rosalie that she would call at Mother Francoise's house on Monday to see if Mombleux

had need of her services. Rosalie came to meet her
and said that as no letters had come from England
that Monday, there would not be any translations
to make that day, but perhaps there would be something for the next day. This was at the luncheon
hour, so Perrine returned to the factory. It had
just struck two when Ninepin hopped up to her on
his wooden leg and told her that she was wanted at
the offices at once.

"What for?" she asked in amazement.

"What's that to do with me? They just sent
word for you to go to the office . . . go on," he said,
roughly.

She hurried off. She could not understand. If
it was a matter of helping Mombleux with a translation, why should she have to go to the office, where
everyone could see her and know that he had had to
ask for her help?

She quickly went up the steps, where she saw
Talouel standing outside waiting for her.

" Are you the girl who speaks English?" he asked.
" Now, no lies, 'cause you speak French without an
accent."

"My mother was English and my father was
French," replied Perrine, "so I speak both languages."

"Good. You are to go to Saint-Pipoy. Monsieur
Paindavoine wants you."

She was so surprised at this news that she stood
staring at the manager in amazement.

"Well, stupid?" he said.

As though to excuse herself, she said:

" I was taken aback.   I'm a stranger here and I don't know where Saint-Pipoy is."

" You won't be lost; you are to go in the carriage," said the manager.   " Here, William . . ."

M. Paindavoine's horse and carriage, which had been standing in the shade, now drew up.

" Here's the girl," said the manager to a young man.   " Take her to M. Paindavoine quickly."

Perrine was already down the steps, and was about to take her seat beside William when he stopped her with a sign of his hand.

" Not here; take the back seat," he said.

There was a narrow seat for one person at the back.   She got up into it and they started off at a brisk trot.

When they had left the village behind William, slacking the horse's speed, turned round to Perrine.

" You're going to have a chance to please the boss," he said.

" How so? " asked Perrine.

"He's got some English mechanics come over to put a machine together, and they can't understand each other.   He's got M. Mombleux there, who says he can speak English, but if he does it isn't the same English as these Englishmen speak.   They keep on jabbering, but don't seem to understand, and the boss is mad.   It makes you split your sides to hear 'em.   At last M. Mombleux couldn't go on any longer, and to calm the boss he said that he knew of a girl named Aurelie in the factory who spoke

English, and the boss made me come off at once for you."

There was a moment's silence; then he turned round again to Perrine.

" If you speak English like M. Mombleux," he said mockingly, " perhaps it'd be better if you didn't go any farther.

" Shall I put you down? " he added with a grin.

" You can go on," said Perrine, quietly.

" Well, I was just thinking for you; that's all," he said.

"Thank you; but I wish to go on, please."

Yet in spite of her apparent coolness, little Perrine was very nervous, because, although she was sure of her English, she did not know what sort of English the engineer spoke. As William had said mockingly, it was not the same that M. Mombleux understood. And she fully realized that there would be many technical words that she would not be able to translate. She would not understand, and she would hesitate, and then probably M. Paindavoine would be angry with her, the same as he had been with M. Mombleux.

Above the tops of the poplars she could already see the great smoking chimneys of the factories of Saint-Pipoy. She knew that spinning and weaving were done here, the same as at Maraucourt, and, besides that, it was here that they manufactured red rope and string. But whether she knew that or not, it was nothing that would help her in the task before her.

They turned the bend of the road. With a sweeping glance she could take in all the great buildings, and although these works were not so large as those of Maraucourt, they were nevertheless of considerable importance.

The carriage passed through the great iron gates and soon stopped before the main office.

" Come with me," said William.

He led her into an office where M. Paindavoine was seated talking to the manager of the Saint-Pipoy works.

" Here's the girl, sir," said William, holding his hat in his hand.

" Very well; you can go," said his master.

Without speaking to Perrine, M. Paindavoine made a sign to his manager to come nearer to him. Then he spoke to him in a low voice. The manager also dropped his voice to answer. But Perrine's hearing was keen, and she understood that they were speaking of her. She heard the manager reply : " A young girl, about twelve or thirteen, who looks intelligent."

"Come here, my child," said M. Paindavoine, in the same tone that she had already heard him use to Rosalie, and which was very different from that which he used for his employés.

She felt encouraged and went up to him.

" What is your name? " he asked.

" Aurelie."

" Where are your father and mother? "

" They are both dead."

"How long have you been in my employ?"

"For three weeks."

"Where do you come from?"

"I have just come from Paris."

"You speak English?"

"My mother was English, and I can speak in conversation, and I understand, but . . . "

"There are no 'buts'; you know or you do not know."

"I don't know the words used in various trades, because they use words that I have never heard, and I don't know the meaning of them," said Perrine.

"You see, Benoist," said M. Paindavoine quickly; "what this little girl says is so; that shows she is not stupid."

"She looks anything but that," answered Benoist.

"Well, perhaps we shall be able to manage somehow," said M. Vulfran. He got up, and placing one arm on the manager, he leaned on his cane with the other.

"Follow us, little girl," he said.

Perrine usually had her eyes about her and noticed everything that happened, but she took no heed where she was going. As she followed in her grandfather's footsteps, she was plunged in thought. What would be the result of this interview with the English mechanics?

They came to a big red brick building. Here she saw Mombleux walking back and forth, evidently in a bad humor, and it seemed to her that he threw her anything but a friendly look.

They went in and were taken up to the first floor. Here in a big hall stood a number of wooden crates bearing a firm's name, " Morton and Pratt, Manchester." On one of the crates the Englishmen were sitting, waiting. Perrine noticed that from their dress they had every appearance of being gentlemen, and she hoped that she would be able better to understand them than if they had been rough workingmen. When M. Vulfran entered they rose.

" Tell them that you can speak English and that they can explain to you," said M. Vulfran.

She did what she was told, and at the first words she had the satisfaction of seeing the Englishmen's faces brighten. It is true she only spoke a few words to begin the conversation, but the pleasant smile they gave her banished all her nervousness.

" They understand her perfectly," said the manager.

" Well, then, ask them," said M. Vulfran, " why they have come a week earlier than the date arranged for their coming, because it so happens that the engineer who was to direct them in their work, and who speaks English, is away for a few days."

Perrine translated the phrase accurately, and one of the men answered at once.

" They say," she said, " that they have been to Cambrai and put up some machinery, and they got through with their work quicker than they thought they would, so they came here direct instead of going back to England and returning again."

" Whose machinery were they working on at Cambrai? " asked M. Vulfran.

" It was for the M. M. and E. Aveline and Company."

" What were the machines? "

The question was put and the reply was given in English, but Perrine hesitated.

" Why do you hesitate? " asked M. Vulfran, impatiently.

" Because it's a word used in the business that I don't know," answered Perrine, timidly.

" Say the word in English."

" Hydraulic mangle."

" That's all right," said M. Vulfran. He repeated the word in English, but with quite a different accent from the English mechanics, which explains why he had not understood them when they had spoken the words.

" You see that Aveline and Company are ahead of us," he said, turning to his manager. " We have no time to lose. I am going to cable to Fabry to return at once; but while waiting we must persuade these young men to get to work. Ask them what they are standing there for, little girl."

She translated the question, and the one who seemed to be the chief gave her a long answer.

" Well? " asked M. Vulfran.

" They are saying some things that are very difficult for me to understand."

" However, try and explain to me."

" They say that the floor is not strong enough to hold their machine, which weighs . . . "

She stopped to question the workmen in English, who told her the weight.

" Ah, that is it, is it? " said M. Vulfran.

" And when the machine is started going its weight will break the flooring," she continued, turning to M. Vulfran.

" The beams are sixty centimetres in width."

She told the men what M. Vulfran said, listened to their reply, then continued:

" They say that they have examined the flooring, and that it is not safe for this machine. They want a thorough test made and strong supports placed under the floor."

" The supports can be placed there at once, and when Fabry returns a thorough examination will be made. Tell them that. Let them get to work without losing a moment. They can have all the workmen they need . . . carpenters and masons, millwrights. They have only to tell you. You have to be at their service, and then you tell Monsieur Benoist what they require."

She translated these instructions to the men, who appeared satisfied when she told them that she was to stay and interpret for them.

" You will stay here," continued M. Vulfran. " Your food will be given to you and also a lodging at the inn. You will have nothing to pay there. And if we are pleased with you you will receive something extra when Monsieur Fabry returns."

CHAPTER XVI

SHE was an interpreter; that was far better than pushing trucks. When the day's work was over, acting in the capacity of interpreter, she escorted the two Englishmen to the village inn and engaged a room for them and one for herself, not a miserable garret where she would have to sleep with several others, but a real bedroom all to herself. As they could not speak one word of French, the two Englishmen asked her if she would not take her dinner with them. They ordered a dinner that would have been enough for ten men.

That night she slept in a real bed and between real sheets, yet it was a very long time before she could get to sleep. Even when her eyelids grew too heavy to keep open her excitement was so great that every now and then she would start up in bed. She tried to force herself to be calm. She told herself that things would have to take their course, without her wondering all the time if she were going to be happy or not. That was the only sensible thing to do. Things seemed to be taking such a favorable turn she must wait. But the best arguments when

addressed to oneself have never made anyone go to
sleep, and the better the argument the more likely,
one is to keep awake.

The next morning, when the factory whistle blew,
she went to the door of the room occupied by the
two machinists and knocked, and told them it was
time to get up.

They paid no heed to the whistle, however, and it
was not until they had taken a bath and made an
elaborate *toilette,* something unknown to the villagers in those parts, and partaken of a hearty
breakfast, consisting of a thick, juicy steak, plenty
of buttered toast and several cups of tea, that they
showed any readiness to get to their work.

Perrine, who had discreetly waited for them outside, wondered if they would ever be ready. When
at last they came out, and she tripped behind them
to the factory, her one thought was that her grandfather would surely be there ahead of them.

However, it was not until the afternoon that M.
Vulfran arrived. He was accompanied by his
youngest nephew, Casimir.

The youth looked disdainfully at the work the
machinists had done, which in truth was merely in
preparation.

"These fellows won't do much before Fabry returns," he said. "That's not surprising consider-
ing the supervision you have given them, uncle."

He said this jeeringly, but instead of taking his
words lightly, his uncle reprimanded him severely:
"If you had been able to attend to this matter, I

should not have been forced to have called in this little girl, who until now has only pushed trucks."

Perrine saw Casimir bite his lip in anger, but he controlled himself and said lightly: " If I had foreseen that I should have to give up a government position for a commercial one, I should certainly have learned English in preference to German."

" It is never to late to learn," replied his uncle in a tone that brooked no further parley.

The quick words on both sides had been spoken in evident displeasure.

Perrine had made herself as small as possible. She had not dared move, but Casimir did not even turn his eyes in her direction, and almost at once he went out, giving his arm to his uncle.   Then she was able to give free rein to her thoughts.   How severe M. Vulfran was with his nephew, but what a disagreeable, horrid youth was that nephew!   If they had any affection for one another it certainly was not apparent.   Why was it?   Why wasn't this nephew kind to his old uncle, who was blind and broken down with sorrow?   And why was the old man so hard with a nephew who was taking the place of his own son?

While she was pondering these questions M. Vulfran returned, this time being led in by the manager, who, having placed him in a seat, began to explain to him the work that the machinists were now engaged upon.

Some minutes later she heard M. Benoist calling: " Aurelie! Aurelie! "

She did not move, for she had forgotten that Aurelie was the name that she had given to herself.

The third time he called: " Aurelie! "

She jumped up with a start as she realized that that was the name by which they knew her. She hurried over to them.

" Are you deaf? " demanded Monsieur Benoist.

" No, sir; I was listening to the machinists."

" You can leave me now," said M. Vulfran to his manager.

When the manager had gone he turned to Perrine, who had remained standing before him.

" Can you read, my child? "

" Yes, sir."

" English as well as French? "

" Yes, both the same."

" But while reading English can you turn it into French? "

" When the phrases are not too difficult; yes, sir."

" The daily news from the papers, do you think you could do that? "

" I have never tried that, because if I read an English paper there is no need for me to translate it for myself, because I understand what it says."

" Well, we will try. Tell the machinists that when they want you they can call you, and then come and read from an English paper some articles that I wish to have read to me in French. Go and tell the men and then come back and sit down here beside me."

When she had done what she was told, she sat

down beside M. Vulfran and took the newspaper that he handed her, "The Dundee News."

"What shall I read?" she asked as she unfolded it.

"Look for the commercial column."

The long black and white columns bewildered poor little Perrine. She was so nervous and her hands trembled so she wondered if she would ever be able to accomplish what she was asked to do. She gazed from the top of one page to the bottom of another, and still could not find what she was seeking. She began to fear that her employer would get impatient with her for being so slow and awkward.

But instead of getting impatient he told her to take her time. With that keen hearing so subtle with the blind, he had divined what a state of emotion she was in. He could tell that from the rustling of the newspaper she held in her hand.

"We have plenty of time," he said, encouragingly; "besides I don't suppose you have ever read a trade journal before."

"No, sir; I have not," she replied.

She continued to scan the sheets, then suddenly she gave a little cry of pleasure.

"Have you found it?"

"Yes, I think so."

"Now look for these words," he said in English: "Linen, Hemp, Jute, Sacks, Twine."

"But, sir, you know English," she cried, involuntarily.

"Five or six words of the trade; that is all, unfortunately," he replied.

When she had found what he required she commenced her translation, but she was so hopelessly slow, hesitating and confused, that in a few moments the beads of perspiration stood out on her forehead and hands from sheer agony, despite the fact that from time to time he encouraged her.

"That will do. I understand that . . . go on," he said.

And she continued, raising her voice when the hammering blows from the workmen became too loud.

At last she came to the end of the column.

"Now see if there is any news from Calcutta," said her employer.

She scanned the sheets again.

"Yes, here it is," she said, after a moment; "From our special correspondent."

"That's it. Read!"

"The news that we are receiving from Dacca . . ."

Her voice shook so as she said this name that Monsieur Vulfran's attention was attracted.

"What's the matter?" he said. "Why are you trembling?"

"I don't know," she said, timidly; "perhaps I am nervous."

"I told you not to mind," he chided. "You are doing very much better than I thought."

She read the cables from Dacca which mentioned

a gathering of jute along the shores of the Brahma-putra. Then he told her to look and see if there was a cable from Saint Helena.

Her eyes ran up and down the columns until the words " Saint Helena " caught her eye.

" On the 23d, the English steamer ' Alma ' sailed from Calcutta for Dundee; on the 24th, the Norwe-gian steamer ' Grundloven ' sailed from Naraing-audj for Boulogne."

He appeared satisfied.

" That is very good," he said. " I am quite pleased with you."

She wanted to reply, but afraid that her voice would betray her joy, she kept silent.

" I can see that until poor Bendit is better I can make good use of you," he continued.

After receiving an account of the work that the men had done, and telling them to be as quick as possible, he told Perrine to lead him to the man-ager's office.

" Have I to give you my hand? " she asked, tim-idly.

" Why, yes, my child," he replied. " How do you think you can guide me otherwise?   And warn me when there is anything in the way, and above all don't be absent-minded."

" Oh, I assure you, sir, you can place every con-fidence in me," she said with emotion.

" You see that I already have confidence," he replied.

She took him gently by the left hand, whilst with

his right he held his cane, feeling ahead of him cautiously as he went forward.

They had scarcely left the workshops before they came to the railway tracks, and she thought that she ought to warn him.

"Here are the rails, just here," she said. "Please . . . "

But he interrupted her.

"That you need not tell me," he said. "I know every bit of the ground round about the works; my head knows it and my feet know it, but it's the unexpected obstacles that we might find on the road that you must tell me about, something that's in the path that should not be. All the ground I know thoroughly."

It was not only his grounds that he knew, but he knew his people also. When he went through the yards his men greeted him. They not only took their hats off as though he saw them, but they said his name.

"Good morning, sir! . . . Good morning, Monsieur Vulfran!"

And to a great number he was able to reply by their names: "Good morning, Jacque!" . . . "Good morning, Pascal!" He knew the voices of all those who had long been in his employ. When he hesitated, which was rarely, for he knew almost all, he would stop and say: "It's you, is it not?" mentioning the speaker's name.

If he made a mistake he explained why he had done so.

Walking thus, it was a slow walk from the factories to the offices. She led him to his armchair; then he dismissed her.

"Until tomorrow," he said; "I shall want you then."

CHAPTER XVII

HARD QUESTIONS

THE next morning, at the same hour as on the previous day, Monsieur Paindavoine entered the workshops, guided by the manager. Perrine wanted to go and meet him, but she could not at this moment as she was busy transmitting orders from the chief machinist to the men who were working for him — masons, carpenters, smiths, mechanics. Clearly and without repetition, she explained to each one what orders were given to him; then she interpreted for the chief machinist the questions or objections which the French workmen desired to address to him.

Perrine's grandfather had drawn near. The voices stopped as the tap of his cane announced his approach, but he made a sign for them to continue the same as though he were not there.

And while Perrine, obeying him, went on talking with the men, he said quietly to the manager, though not low enough but that Perrine heard:

" Do you know, that little girl would make a fine engineer! "

" Yes," said the manager; " it's astonishing how decided and confident she is with the men."

" Yes, and she can do something else. Yesterday

she translated the 'Dundee News' more intelligently than Bendit. And it was the first time that she had read trade journal stuff."

" Does anyone know who her parents were? " asked the manager.

" Perhaps Talouel does; I do not," said Vulfran.

" She is in a very miserable and pitiful condition," said the manager.

" I gave her five francs for her food and lodging."

" I am speaking of her clothes. Her waist is worn to threads; I have never seen such a skirt on anybody but a beggar, and she certainly must have made the shoes she is wearing herself."

" And her face, what is she like, Benoist? "

" Very intelligent and very pretty."

" Hard looking or any signs of vice? "

" No; quite the contrary. She has a very frank, honest look. She has great eyes that look as though they could pierce a wall, and yet at the same time they have a soft, trusting look."

" Where in the world does she come from? "

" Not from these parts, that's a sure thing."

" She told me that her mother was English."

" And yet she does not look English. She seems to belong to quite another race, but she is very pretty; even with the old rags that she is wearing the girl seems to have a strange sort of beauty. She must have a strong character or some power, or why is it that these workmen pay such attention to such a poor little ragged thing? "

And as Benoist never missed a chance to flatter

his employer, he added: "Undoubtedly without having even seen her you have guessed all that I have told you."

"Her accent struck me as being very cultured," replied Monsieur Vulfran.

Although Perrine had not heard all that the two men had said, she had caught a few words, which had thrown her into a state of great agitation. She tried to recover her self-control, for it would never do to listen to what was being said behind her when the machinists and workmen were talking to her at the same time. What would her employer think if in giving her explanations in French he saw that she had not been paying attention to her task.

However, everything was explained to them in a manner satisfactory to both sides. When she had finished, Monsieur Vulfran called to her: "Aurelie!"

This time she took care to reply quickly to the name which in the future was to be hers.

As on the previous day, he made her sit down beside him and gave her a paper to translate for him into French. This time it was not the "Dundee News," but the "Dundee Trade Report Association," which is an official bulletin published on the commerce of jute. So without having to search for any particular article, she read it to him from beginning to end. Then, when the reading was over, as before, he asked her to lead him through the grounds, but this time he began to question her about herself.

"You told me that you had lost your mother. How long ago was that?" he asked.

"Five weeks," she replied.

"In Paris?"

"Yes, in Paris."

"And your father?"

"Father died six months before mother," she said in a low voice.

As he held her hand in his he could feel it tremble, and he knew what anguish she felt as he evoked the memory of her dead parents, but he did not change the subject; he gently continued to question her.

"What did your parents do?"

"We sold things," she replied.

"In Paris? Round about Paris?"

"We traveled; we had a wagon and we were sometimes in one part of the country, sometimes in another."

"And when your mother died you left Paris?"

"Yes, sir."

"Why?"

"Because mother made me promise not to stay in Paris after she had gone, but to go North where my father's people live."

"Then why did you come here?"

"When my mother died we had to sell our wagon and our donkey and the few things we had, and all this money was spent during her illness.   When I left the cemetery after she was buried all the money I had was five francs thirty-five centimes, which was not enough for me to take the train. So I decided to make the journey on foot."

Monsieur Vulfran's fingers tightened over hers. She did not understand this movement.

"Oh, forgive me; I am boring you," she said. "I am telling you things perhaps that are of no interest."

"You are not boring me, Aurelie," said the blind man. "On the contrary, I am pleased to know what an honest little girl you are. I like people who have courage, will, and determination, and who do not easily give up. If I like finding such qualities in men, how much more pleasure does it give me to find them in a girl of your age! So . . . you started with five francs thirty-five centimes in your pocket? . . . "

"A knife, a piece of soap," continued little Perrine, "a thimble, two needles, some thread and a map of the roads, that was all."

"Could you understand the map?"

"Yes, I had to know, because we used to travel all over the country. That was the only thing that I kept of our belongings."

The blind man stopped his little guide.

"Isn't there a big tree here on the left?" he asked.

"Yes, with a seat all around it," she replied.

"Come along then; we'll be better sitting down."

When they were seated she went on with her story. She had no occasion to shorten it, for she saw that her employer was greatly interested.

" You never thought of begging? " he asked, when she came to the time when she had left the woods after being overtaken by the terrible storm.

" No, sir; never."

" But what did you count upon when you saw that you could not get any work? "

" I didn't count on anything. I thought that if I kept on as long as I had the strength I might find something. It was only when I was so hungry and so tired that I had to give up. If I had dropped one hour sooner all would have been over."

Then she told him how her donkey, licking her face, had brought her back to consciousness, and how the ragpicker had saved her from starvation. Then passing quickly over the days she had spent with La Rouquerie, she came to the day when she had made Rosalie's acquaintance.

" And Rosalie told me," she said, " that anyone who wants work can get it in your factories. I came and they employed me at once."

" When are you going on to your relations? "

Perrine was embarrassed. She did not expect this question.

" I am not going any further," she replied, after a moment's hesitation. " I don't know if they want me, for they were angry with father. I was going to try and be near them because I have no one else, but I don't know if I shall be welcomed. Now that I have found work, it seems to me that it would be better for me to stay here. What will become of me if they turn me away? I know I shall not starve

here, and I am too afraid to go on the road again.
I shall not let them know that I am here unless
some piece of luck comes my way."

"Didn't your relatives ever try to find out about
you?" asked M. Vulfran.

"No, never," replied Perrine.

"Well, then, perhaps you are right," he said.
"Yet if you don't like to take a chance and go and
see them, why don't you write them a letter? They
may not be able to give you a home, so then you
could stay here where you'd be sure of earning your
living. On the other hand, they may be very glad
to have you, and you would have love and protec-
tion, which you would not have here. You've
learned already that life is very hard for a young
girl of your age, and in your position . . . and
very sad."

"Yes, sir; I know it is very sad," said little Perrine, lifting her beautiful eyes to the sightless eyes
of her grandfather. "Every day I think how sad
it is, and I know if they would hold out their arms
to welcome me I would run into them so quickly!
But suppose they were just as cold and hard to me
as they were with my father . . . "

"Had these relations any serious cause to be
angry with your father? Did he do anything very
bad?"

"I cannot think," said little Perrine, "that my
father, who was always so good and kind, and who
loved me and mother so much, could have ever been
bad. He could not have done anything very wrong,

and yet his people must have had, in their opinion, serious reasons for being angry with him, it seems to me."

"Yes, evidently," said the blind man. "But what they have against him they could not hold against you. The sins of the father should not fall upon the children."

"If that could be true!"

She said these words in a voice that trembled so with emotion that the blind man was surprised at the depths of this little girl's feelings.

"You see," he said, "how in the depths of your heart how much you want their love and affection."

"Yes, but how I dread being turned away," she replied.

"But why should you be?" he asked. "Have your grandparents any other children beside your father?"

"No."

"Why shouldn't they be glad that you should come and take the place of the son they have lost? You don't know what it is to be alone in the world."

"Yes, I do . . . I know only too well what it is," replied Perrine.

"Youth who has a future ahead is not like old age, which has nothing before it but Death."

She looked at him. She did not take her eyes from his face, for he could not see her. What did his words mean? From the expression of his face little Perrine tried to read the inmost thoughts that stirred this old man's heart.

"Well," he said, after waiting a moment, "what do you think you will do?"

"I hesitate because I feel so bad about it," she said.   "If I could only believe that they would be glad to have me and would not turn me away . . . "

"You know nothing of life, poor little girl," said the old gentleman.   "Age should not be alone any more than youth."

"Do you think all old people feel like that?" asked Perrine.

"They may not think that it is so, but they feel it."

"You think so?" she said, trembling, her eyes still fixed on his face.

He did not reply directly, but speaking softly as though to himself, he said:

"Yes, yes; they feel it . . . "

Then getting up from his seat abruptly, as though to drive away thoughts that made him feel sad, he said in a tone of authority: "Come across to the offices.   I wish to go there."

CHAPTER XVIII

WHEN would Fabry, the engineer, return?
That was the question that Perrine anxiously asked herself, for on that day her rôle of interpreter to the English machinists would terminate.

That of translator of newspaper articles to M. Vulfran, would that continue until M. Bendit had recovered from his illness? Here was another question that made her even still more anxious.

It was on Thursday, when she reached the factories with the two machinists, that she found Monsieur Fabry in the workshop busy inspecting the work that had already been done. Discreetly she waited at a distance, not taking part in any of the explanations that were being made, but all the same the chief machinist drew her into the conversation.

"Without this little girl's help," he said, "we should have stood here waiting with our arms folded."

Monsieur Fabry then looked at her, but he said nothing, and she on her side did not dare ask him what she had to do now, whether she was to stay at Saint-Pipoy or return to Maraucourt.

She stood there undecided, thinking that as it was

184

M. Vulfran who had sent for her, it would be he who would send her away or keep her.

He came at his usual hour, led by the manager, who gave him an account of the orders that the engineer had given and the observations that he had made.   But it appeared that he was not completely satisfied.

" It is a pity that the little girl is not here," he said in annoyance.

" But she is here," replied the manager, making a sign to Perrine to approach.

" Why was it you did not go back to Maraucourt, girl? " he asked.

" I thought that I ought not to leave here until you told me to go back," she replied.

" That was quite right," he said.   " You must be here waiting for me when I come . . . "

He stopped for a second, then went on: " And I shall also need you at Maraucourt.   You can go back this evening, and tomorrow be at the office. I will tell you what you will have to do."

When she had interpreted the orders which he wished to give to the machinists, he left, and that day she was not required to read the newspapers.

But what did that matter?   Hadn't her grandfather said that on the morrow he would need her at Maraucourt?

" I shall need you at Maraucourt! "   She kept repeating these words over and over again as she tramped along the roads over which William had driven her in the trap.

How was she going to be employed? She imagined all sorts of ways, but she could not feel certain of anything, except that she was not to be sent back to push trucks. That was a sure thing; for the rest she would have to wait. But she need not wait in a state of feverish anxiety, for from her grandfather's manner she might hope for the best. If she, a poor little girl, could only have enough wisdom to follow the course that her mother had mapped out for her before dying, slowly and carefully, without trying to hasten events, her life, which she held in her own hands, would be what she herself made it. She must remember this always, in everything she said, every time she had to make a resolution, every time she took a step forward, and each time she took this step she must take it without asking advice of anyone.

On her way back to Maraucourt she turned all this over in her little head. She walked slowly, stopping when she wanted to pick a flower that grew beneath the hedge, or when, in looking over a fence, she could see a pretty one that seemed to be beckoning to her from the meadow. Now and again she got rather excited; then she would quicken her step; then she slowed up again, telling herself that there was no occasion for her to hurry. Here was one thing she had to do — she must make it a rule, make it a habit, not to give way to an impulse. Oh, she would have to be very wise. Her pretty face was very grave as she walked along, her hands full of lovely wild flowers.

She found her island the same as she had left it, each thing in its place. The birds had even shown respect for the berries beneath the willow tree which had ripened in her absence. Here was something for her supper. She had not counted upon having berries.

She had returned at an earlier hour than when she had left the factory, so she did not feel inclined to go to bed as soon as her supper was over. She sat by the pond in the quiet of the evening, watching the night slowly fall.

Although she had been away only a short time, something seemed to have occurred to disturb the quietness of her little shelter. In the fields there was no longer the solemn silence of the night which had struck her on the first days that she had installed herself on the island. Previously, all she could hear in the entire valley, on the pond, in the big trees and the foliage, was the mysterious rustling of the birds as they returned to the nests for the night. Now the silence was disturbed by all kinds of noises — the blow of the forge, the grind of the axle, the swish of a whip, and the murmur of voices.

As she had tramped along the roads from Saint-Pipoy she had noticed that the harvest had commenced in the fields that were most exposed, and soon the mowers would come as far as her little nook, which was shaded by the big trees.

She would certainly have to leave her tiny home; it would not be possible for her to live there longer.

Whether she had to leave on account of the harvest-
ers or the bird catchers, it was the same thing, just
a matter of days.

Although for the last few days she had got used
to having sheets on her bed, and a room with a
window, and closed doors, she slept that night on
her bed of ferns as though she had never left it, and
it was only when the sun rose in the heavens that
she awoke.

When she reached the factory, instead of following her companions to where the trucks stood, she
made her way to the general offices, wondering what
she should do — go in, or wait outside.

She decided to do the latter.   If they saw her
standing outside the doors, some one would see her
and call her in.

She waited there for almost an hour.   Finally
she saw Talouel, who asked her roughly what she
was doing there.

"Monsieur Vulfran told me to come this morning
to the office to see him," she said.

"Outside there, is not the office," he said.

"I was waiting to be called in," she replied.

"Come up then."

She went up the steps, following him in.

"What did you do at Saint-Pipoy?" he asked,
turning to look at her.

She told him in what capacity M. Vulfran had
employed her.

"Monsieur Fabry then had been messing up
things?"

" I don't know."

" What do you mean — you don't know?   Are you a silly? "

" Maybe I am."

" You're not, and you know it; and if you don't reply it's because you don't want to.   Don't forget who is talking to you; do you know what I am here? "

" Yes, the foreman."

" That means the master.   And as your master you do as I tell you.   I am going to know all. Those who don't obey I fire!   Remember that! "

This was indeed the man whom she had heard the factory girls talking about when she had slept in that terrible room at Mother Francoise's.   The tyrant who wanted to be everything in the works, not only at Maraucourt, but at Saint-Pipoy, at Bacourt, at Flexelles, everywhere, and who would employ any means to uphold his authority, even disputing it with that of Monsieur Vulfran's.

" I ask you what Monsieur Fabry has been doing? " he asked, lowering his voice.

" I cannot tell you because I do not know myself. But I can tell you what observations Monsieur Vulfran had me interpret for the machinists."

She repeated what she had had to tell the men without omitting a single thing.

" Is that all? "

" That is all."

" Did Monsieur Vulfran make you translate his letters? "

" No, he did not. I only read some articles from
the ' Dundee News ' and a little paper all through;
it was called the ' Dundee Trades Report Association.' "

" You know if you don't tell me the truth, all the
truth, I'll get it pretty quick, and then . . . Ouste!
off you go."

" Why should I not speak the truth? " asked
Perrine.

" It's up to you to do so," he retorted. " I've
warned you . . . remember."

" I'll remember," said Perrine, " I assure you."

" Very good. Now go and sit down on that bench
over there. If the boss really needs you he'll remember that he told you to come here this morning.
He is busy talking to some of his men now."

She sat on the bench for almost an hour, not daring to move so long as Talouel was near. What a
dreadful man! How afraid she was of him! But
it would never do to let him see that she was afraid.
He wanted her to spy on her employer, and then tell
him what was in the letters that she translated for
him!

This indeed might well scare her, yet there was
something to be pleased about. Talouel evidently
thought that she would have the letters to translate;
that meant that her grandfather would have her
with him all the time that M. Bendit was ill.

While she sat there waiting she caught sight of
William several times. When he was not fulfilling
the duties of coachman he acted as useful man to

M. Vulfran.   Each time that he appeared on the scene Perrine thought that he had come to fetch her, but he passed without saying a word to her. He seemed always in a hurry.

Finally some workingmen came out of M. Vulfran's office with a very dissatisfied expression on their faces.   Then William came and beckoned to her and showed her into M. Vulfran's office.   She found her grandfather seated at a large table covered with ledgers, at the side of which were paper weights stamped with large letters in relief.   In this way the blind man was able to find what his eyes could not see.

Without announcing her, William had pushed Perrine inside the room and closed the door after her.   She waited a moment, then she thought that she had better let M. Vulfran know that she was there.

"Monsieur," she said, "I am here . . . Aurelie."

"Yes," he said, "I recognized your step.   Come nearer and listen to me.   I am interested in you. You have told me your troubles and I think you have been very courageous.   From the translations that you have made for me, and the manner in which you have acted as interpreter for the machinists, I see that you are intelligent.   Now that I am blind, I need someone to see for me, to tell me about things I wish to know, and also about things that strike them also.   I had hoped that William would have been able to do this for me, but unfortunately he drinks too much and I can't keep him.

" Now, would you like to take the position that he has been unable to hold? To commence with, you will have ninety francs a month. If I am pleased with you I may do more for you."

Overwhelmed with joy, Perrine stood before the blind man unable to say a word.

" Why don't you speak? " he said at last.

" I can't . . . I don't know what to say . . . to thank you," she said. Her voice broke. " I feel so . . . "

" Yes, yes," he said. " I know how you feel. Your voice tells me that. I am pleased. That is as good as a promise that you will do all you can to give me satisfaction. Now let us change the subject. Have you written to your grandparents? "

" No," said Perrine, hesitatingly; " I . . . I did not have any paper."

" Oh, very well. You will be able to find all you need in Monsieur Bendit's office. When you write tell them exactly what position you occupy in my employ. If they have anything better to offer you, they will send for you; if not, they will let you remain here."

" Oh, certainly . . . I am sure I shall stay . . . "

" Yes, I think so. I think it will be best for you. As you will be in the offices, you will be in communication with my employés; you can take my orders to them, and you will also have to go out with me, so in that case you cannot wear your factory clothes, which Monsieur Benoist tells me are rather shabby."

" They are in rags," said Perrine; " but I assure

you, sir, it is not because I am lazy or that I don't care . . . "

" I am sure of that," replied M. Vulfran.   " Now, as all that will be changed, you go to the cashier in the counting house, and he will give you a money order.   You can go then to Madame Lachaise in the village and get some clothes, some linen, hats and shoes; what you need . . . "

Perrine was listening as though it were not an old blind man with a grave face that was speaking, but a beautiful fairy who was holding over her her magic wand.

She was silent.   Then his voice recalled her to the reality.

" You are free to choose what you like, but bear in mind the choice you make will guide me in acquiring a knowledge of your character.   Now you can go and see about your things at once.   I shall not need you until tomorrow."

CHAPTER XIX

SUSPICION AND CONFIDENCE

SHE went to the counting house, and after the chief cashier and his clerks had eyed her from head to foot, she was handed the order which M. Vulfran had said was to be given to her. She left the factory wondering where she would find Madame Lachaise's shop.

She hoped that it was the woman who had sold her the calico, because as she knew her already, it would be less embarrassing to ask her advice as to what she should buy, than it would be to ask a perfect stranger. And so much hung on the choice she would make; her anxiety increased as she thought of her employer's last words: " the choice you make will guide me in acquiring a knowledge of your character."

She did not need this warning to keep her from making extravagant purchases, but then on the other hand, what she thought would be the right things for herself, would her employer consider suitable? In her fancy she had worn beautiful clothes, and when she was quite a little girl she had been very proud to display her pretty things,

194

but of course dresses on this order would not be fitting for her now. The simplest that she could find would be better.

Who would have thought that the unexpected present of new clothes could have filled her with so much anxiety and embarrassment. She knew that she ought to be filled with joy and yet here she was greatly worried and hesitating.

Just near the church she found Mme. Lachaise's shop. It was by far the best shop in Maraucourt. In the window there was a fine display of materials, ribbons, lingerie, hats, jewels, perfumes, which aroused the envy and tempted the greed of all the frivolous girls throughout the surrounding villages. It was here where they spent their small earnings, the same as their fathers and husbands spent theirs at the taverns.

When Perrine saw this display of finery she was still more perplexed and embarrassed. She entered the shop and stood in the middle of the floor, for neither the mistress of the establishment nor the milliners who were working behind the counter seemed to think that the ragged little girl required any attention. Finally Perrine decided to hold out the envelope containing the order that she held in her hand.

" What is it you want, little girl? " demanded Madame Lachaise.

As she still held out the envelope the mistress of the store caught sight of the words Maraucourt Factories, Vulfran Paindavoine in one of the corners. The expression of her face changed at once, her smile was very pleasant now.

" What do you wish Madamoiselle? " she asked, leaving her desk and drawing forward a chair for Perrine. Perrine told her that she wanted a dress, some underlinen, a pair of shoes and a hat.

" We can supply you with all those," said Madame Lachaise, " and with goods of the very best quality. Would you like to commence with the dress? Yes. Very well then, I will show you some materials."

But it was not materials that Perrine wished to see; she wanted a ready-made dress. Something that she could put on at once, or at least something that would be ready for her to wear the next day when she went out with Monsieur Paindavoine.

" Ah, you are going out with Monsieur Vulfran? " said Madame Lachaise quickly; her curiosity was strung to its highest pitch at this statement. She wondered what the all powerful master of Marau-court could have to do with this ragged little girl and she did not hesitate to ask.

But instead of replying to her question Perrine continued to explain that she wanted to see some black dresses as she was in mourning.

" You want a dress so as to be able to attend a funeral then? "

" No, it is not for a funeral, said Perrine.

" Well, you understand, Madamoiselle, if I know what you require the dress for I shall be able to know what style, material, and price it should be.

" I want the plainest style," said little Perrine timidly, " and the lightest but best wearing material, and the lowest price."

"Very good, very good," replied Madame Lachaise, " they will show you something. Virginie, attend to Madamoiselle."

How her tone had changed! her manner also. With great dignity Madame Lachaise went back to her seat at the desk, disdaining to busy herself with a customer who had such small desires. She was probably one of the servant's daughters, for whom Monsieur Vulfran was going to buy a mourning outfit; but which servant?

However as Virginie brought forward a cashmere dress trimmed with passementerie and jet, she thought fit to interfere.

" No, no, not that, she said. " That would be beyond the price. Show her that black challis dress with the little dots. The skirt will be a trifle too long and the waist too large, but it can easily be made to fit her, besides we have nothing else in black."

Here was a reason that dispensed with all others, but even though it was too large, Perrine found the skirt and waist that went with it very pretty, and the saleslady assured her that with a little alteration is would suit her beautifully, and of course she had to believe her.

The choice for the stockings and undergarments was easier because she wanted the least expensive, but when she stated that she only wanted to pur-

chase two pairs of stockings and two chemises, Mlle.
Virginie became just as disdainful as her employer,
and it was as though she was conferring a favor
that she condescended to try some shoes on Perrine,
and the black straw hat which completed the wardrobe of this little simpleton.

Could anyone believe that a girl would be such
an idiot! She had been given an order to buy
what she wanted and she asked for two pairs of
stockings and two chemises. And when Perrine
asked for some handkerchiefs, which for a long time
had been the object of her desires, this new pur-
chase, which was limited to three handkerchiefs,
did not help to change the shopkeeper's or the saleslady's contempt for her.

" She's nothing at all," they murmured.

" And now shall we send you these things? "
asked Mme. Lachaise.

" No, thank you," said Perrine, " I will call this
evening and fetch them when the alterations are
made."

" Well, then, don't come before eight o'clock or
after nine," she was told.

Perrine had a very good reason for not wishing
to have the things sent to her. She was not sure
where she was going to sleep that night. Her
little island was not to be thought of. Those who
possess nothing can dispense with doors and locks,
but when one has riches . . . for despite the
condescension of the shopkeeper and her assistant,
these were riches to Perrine and needed to be

guarded. So that night she would have to take a lodging and quite naturally she thought of going to Rosalie's grandmother. When she left Madame Lachaise's shop, she went on her way to Mother Francoise's to see if she could accommodate her and give her what she desired; that was a tiny little room that would not cost much.

As she reached the gate she met Rosalie coming out, walking quickly.

"You're going out?" cried Perrine.

"Yes, and you . . . so you are free then?"

In a few hurried words they explained.

Rosalie, who was going on an important errand to Picquigny, could not return to her grandmother's at once, as she would have liked, so as to make the best arrangements that she could for Perrine; but as Perrine had nothing to do for that day, why shouldn't she go with her to Picquigny; and they would come back together; it would be a pleasure trip then.

They went off gaily, and Rosalie accomplished her errand quickly, then their pleasure trip commenced. They walked through the fields, chatting and laughing, picked flowers, then rested in the heat of the day under the shadows of the great trees. It was not until night that they arrived back in Maraucourt. Not until Rosalie reached her grandmother's gate did she realize what time it was.

"What will Aunt Zenobie say?" she said half afraid.

"Oh well . . ." began Perrine.

"Oh well, I don't care," said Rosalie defiantly, "I've enjoyed myself . . . and you?"

"Well, if you who have people to talk to every day have enjoyed yourself, how much more have I who never have anybody to talk to," said Perrine ruefully.

"I've had a lovely time," she sighed.

"Well, then we don't care what anybody says," said Rosalie bravely.

Fortunately, Aunt Zenobie was busy waiting on the boarders, so the arrangements for the room was made with Mother Francoise, who did not drive too hard a bargain and that was done quickly and promptly. Fifty francs a month for two meals a day; twelve francs for a little room decorated with a little mirror, a window, and a dressing table.

At eight o'clock Perrine dined alone in the general dining room, a table napkin on her lap. At eighty-thirty she went to Madame Lachaise's establishment to fetch her dress and other things which were quite ready for her. At nine o'clock, in her tiny room, the door of which she locked, she went to bed, a little worried, a little excited, a little hesitating, but, in her heart of hearts full of hope.

Now we should see.

What she did see the next morning when she was called into M. Vulfran's office after he had given his orders to his principal employés, was such a severe expression on his face that she was thoroughly disconcerted; although the eyes that turned towards her as she entered his room were devoid of look, she could not mistake the expression on this face that she had studied so much.

Certainly it was not the kind look of a benefactor, but quite the reverse: it was an expression of displeasure and anger that she saw.

What had she done wrong that he should be angry with her?

She put this question to herself but she could find no reply to it; perhaps she had spent too much at Madame Lachaise's and her employer had judged her character from these purchases. And in her selection she had tried to be so modest and economical. What should she have bought then? or rather what should she not have bought?

But she had no more time to wonder, for her employer was speaking to her in a severe tone:

"Why did you not tell me the truth?" he said.

"In what have I not told the truth?" she asked in a frightened voice.

"In regard to your conduct since you came to this village."

"But I assure you, Monsieur, I have told you the truth."

"You told me that you lodged at Mother Francoise's house. And when you left there where did you go? I may as well tell you that yesterday Zenobie, that is Francoise's daughter, was asked to give some information, some references of you, and she said that you only spent one night in her mother's house, then you disappeared, and no one knew what you did from that night until now."

Perrine had listened to the commencement of this cross examination in afright, but as Monsieur Vulfran went on she grew braver.

"There is some one who knows what I did after I left the room I used at Mother Francoise's," she said quietly.

"Who?"

"Rosalie, her grand-daughter, knows. She will tell you that what I am now going to tell you, sir, is the truth. That is, if you think my doings are worth knowing about."

"The position that you are to hold in my service demands that I know what you are," said Monsieur Vulfran.

"Well, Monsieur, I will tell you," said little Perrine. "When you know you can send for Rosalie and question her without me seeing her, and then you will have the proof that I have not deceived you."

"Yes, that can be done," he said in a softened voice, "now go on . . ."

She told her story, dwelling on the horror of that night in that miserable room, her disgust, how she was almost suffocated, and how she crept outside at the break of dawn too sick to stay in that terrible garret one moment longer.

"Cannot you bear what the other girls could?" asked her employer.

"The others perhaps have not lived in the open air as I have," said Perrine, her beautiful eyes fixed on her grandfather's face, "I assure you I am not hard to please. We were so poor that we endured great misery. But I could not stay in that room. I should have died, and I don't think it was wrong of me to try to escape death. I could not live if I had to sleep there."

"Why! can that room be so unhealthy, so unwholesome as that?" mused Monsieur Vulfran.

"Oh, sir," cried Perrine, "if you could see it you would never permit your work girls to live there, never, never."

"Go on with your story," he said abruptly.

She told him how she had discovered the tiny island and how the idea had come to her to take possession of the cabin.

"You were not afraid?" he asked.

"I am not accustomed to being afraid," she said, with a wan little smile flitting across her beautiful face.

"You are speaking of that cabin in the valley there a little to the side of the road to Saint-Pipoy, on the left, are you not?" asked Monsieur Vulfran.

"Yes, Monsieur."

"That belongs to me and my nephews use it. Was it there that you slept?"

"I not only slept there, but I worked there and I ate there, and I even gave a dinner to Rosalie, and she can tell you about it," said little Perrine eagerly, for now that she had told him her story she wanted him to know everything. "I did not leave the cabin until you sent for me to go to Saint-Pipoy, and then you told me to stay there so as to be on hand to interpret for the machinists. And now tonight I have taken a lodging again at Mother Francoise's, but now I can pay for a room all to myself."

" Were you rich then, that you were able to invite a friend to dinner? " asked the blind man.

" If I only dare tell you," said Perrine timidly.

" You can tell me everything," said the blind man.

" I may take up your time just to tell you a story about two little girls? " asked little Perrine.

" Now that I cannot use my time as I should like," said the blind man sadly, " it is often very long, very long . . . and empty."

A shade passed over her grandfather's face. He had so much; there were men who envied him — and yet how sad and barren was his life. When he said that his days were " empty " Perrine's heart went out to him. She also, since the death of her father and mother, knew what it was for the days to be long and empty, nothing to fill them but the anxiety, the fatigue, and the misery of the moment. No one to share them with you, none to uphold you, or cheer you. He had not known bodily fatigue, privations and poverty. But they are not the only trials to be borne, there are other sorrows in this world from which one suffers. And it was those other sorrows that had made him say those few words in such a sad, sad tone; the memory of which made this old blind man bend his head while the tears sprang into his sightless eyes. But no tears fell. Perrine's eyes had not left his face; if she

had seen that her story did not interest him, she
would have stopped at once, but she knew that he
was not bored. He interrupted her several times
and said:

"And you did that!"

Then he questioned her, asking her to tell him
in detail what she had omitted for fear of tiring
him. He put questions to her which showed that
he wished to have an exact account, not only of
her work, but above all to know what means she had
employed to replace all that she had been lacking.

"And that's what you did?" he asked again and
again.

When she had finished her story, he placed his
hand on her head: "You are a brave little girl,"
he said, "and I am pleased to see that one can do
something with you. Now go into your office and
spend the time as you like; at three o'clock we will
go out."

CHAPTER XX

THE SCHEMERS

M R. BENDIT'S office which Perrine occupied was a tiny place whose sole furniture consisted of a table and two chairs, a bookcase in blackwood, and a map of the world.

Yet with its polished pine floor, and a window with its red and white shade, it appeared very bright to Perrine. Not only was the office assigned to her cheerful, but she found that by leaving the door open she could see and occasionally hear what was going on in the other offices.

Monsieur Vulfran's nephews, Theodore and Casimir, had their rooms on the right and on the left of his; after theirs came the counting house, then lastly, there was Fabry, the engineer's, office. This one was opposite hers. Fabry's office was a large room where several draughtsmen were standing up before their drawings, arranged on high inclined desks.

Having nothing to do and not liking to take M. Bendit's chair, Perrine took a seat by the door. She opened one of the dictionaries which were the only kind of books the office contained. She would have preferred anything else but she had to be contented with what was there.

The hours passed slowly, but at last the bell rang for luncheon. Perrine was one of the first to go out. On the way she was joined by Fabry and Mombleux. They also were going to Mother Francoise's house.

" So then you are a comrade of ours, Madamoiselle," said Mombleux, who had not forgotten his humiliation at Saint-Pipoy, and he wanted to make the one who was the cause of it pay for it.

She felt the sarcasm of his words and for a moment she was disconcerted, but she recovered herself quickly.

" No, Monsieur," she said quietly," not of yours but of William's."

The tone of her reply evidently pleased the engineer, for turning to Perrine he gave her an encouraging smile.

" But if you are replacing Mr. Bendit? " said Mombleux obstinately.

" Say that Madamoiselle is keeping his job for him," retorted Fabry.

" It's the same thing," answered Mombleux.

" Not at all, for in a week or two, when he'll be better, he'll come back in his old place. He certainly would not have had it if Madamoiselle had not been here to keep it for him."

" It seems to me that you and I also have helped to keep it for him," said Mombleux.

" Yes, but this little girl has done her share; he'll have to be grateful to all three of us," said Fabry, smiling again at Perrine.

If she had misunderstood the sense of Mombleux's words, the way in which she was treated at Mother Francoise's would have enlightened her. Her place was not set at the boarders' table as it would have been if she had been considered their equal, but at a little table at the side. And she was served after everyone else had taken from the dishes what they required.

But that did not hurt her; what did it matter to her if she were served first or last, and if the best pieces had already been taken. What interested her was that she was placed near enough to them to hear their conversation. She hoped that what she heard might guide her as to how she should act in the midst of the difficulties which confronted her.

These men knew the habits of M. Vulfran, his nephews, and Talouel, of whom she stood so much in fear; a word from them would enlighten her and she might be shown a danger which she did not even suspect, and if she was aware of it she could avoid it. She would not spy upon them. She would not listen at doors. When they were speaking they knew that they were not alone. So she need have no scruples but could profit by their remarks.

Unfortunately on that particular morning they said nothing that interested her; their talk was on insignificant matters. As soon as she had finished her meal she hurried to Rosalie, for she wanted to know how M. Vulfran had discovered that she had only slept one night at her grandmother's house.

"It was that Skinny who came here while you were at Picquigny," said Rosalie, "and he got Aunt Zenobie to talk about you; and you bet it isn't hard to make Aunt Zenobie talk especially when she gets something for doing so. She told him that you had spent only one night here and all sorts of other things besides."

"What other things?"

"I don't know because I was not there, but you can imagine the worst, but fortunately it has not turned out badly for you."

"No, on the contrary it has turned out very well, because M. Vulfran was amused and interested when I told him my story."

"I'll tell Aunt Zenobie, that'll make her mad."

"Oh, don't put her against me."

"Put her against you; oh, there's no danger of that now. She knows the position that M. Vulfran has given you, you won't have a better friend . . . seemingly. You'll see tomorrow. Only if you don't want that Skinny to know your business, don't tell anything to her."

"That I won't."

"Oh, she's sly enough."

"Yes, but now you've warned me . . ."

At three o'clock as arranged, M. Vulfran rang for Perrine and they drove off in the pheaton to make the customary round of the factories, for he did not let a single day pass without visiting the different buildings.

Although he could not see he could at least be seen, and when he gave his orders it was difficult to believe that he was blind; he seemed to know everything that was going on.

That day they began at the village of Flexelles. They stayed some time in the building and when they came out William was not to be seen. The horse was tied to a tree and William, the coachman, had disappeared. As soon as his employer had gone into his factories, William of course, as usual, had hurried to the nearest wine shop . . . meeting a boon companion there he had forgotten the hour.

M. Vulfran sent one of his men off to search for his recalcitrant coachman. After waiting several minutes, the blind man became very angry. Finally William, with head held high, came staggering along.

" I can tell by the sound of his footsteps that he is drunk, Benoist," said M. Vulfran, addressing his manager, who stood beside him. " I am right, am I not? "

" Yes, sir . . . nothing can be hidden from you. He is drunk . . . "

William began to apologize.

" I've just come from . . ." he began, but his employer cut him short.

" That is enough," said M. Vulfran, sternly. " I can tell by your breath and the way you walk that you are drunk."

" I was just going to say, sir," began William

again, as he untied the horse, but at that moment
he dropped the whip and stooping down, he tried
three times to grasp it. The manager looked grave.

"I think it would be better if I drove you to
Maraucourt," he said. "I am afraid you would
not be safe with William."

"Why so?" demanded William insolently.

"Silence," commanded M. Vulfran, in a tone that
admitted of no reply. "From this moment you can
consider yourself dismissed from my service."

"But, sir, I was going to say . . ."

With an uplifted motion of his hand M. Vulfran
stopped him and turned to his manager.

"Thank you, Benoist," he said, "but I think this
little girl can drive me home. Coco is as quiet as
a lamb, and she can well replace this drunken
creature."

He was assisted into the carriage, and Perrine
took her place beside him. She was very grave, for
she felt the responsibility of her position.

"Not too quickly," said M. Vulfran, when she
touched Coco with the end of her whip.

"Oh, please, sir, I don't want to go quickly, I
assure you," she said, nervously.

"That's a good thing; let her just trot."

There was a great surprise in the streets of Maraucourt when the villagers saw the head of the firm
seated beside a little girl wearing a hat of black
straw and a black dress, who was gravely driving
old Coco at a straight trot instead of the zigzag
course that William forced the old animal to take

in spite of herself. What was happening? Where was this little girl going? They questioned one another as they stood at the doors, for few people in the village knew of her and of the position that M. Vulfran had given her.

When they arrived at Mother Francoise's house, Aunt Zenobie was leaning over the gate talking to two women. When she caught sight of Perrine she stared in amazement, but her look of astonishment was quickly followed by her best smile, the smile of a real friend.

" Good day, Monsieur Vulfran! Good day, Mademoiselle Aurelie!" she called out.

As soon as the carriage had passed she told her neighbors how she had procured the fine position for the young girl who had been their boarder. She had recommended her so highly to Skinny.

" She's a nice girl, though," she added, " and she'll not forget what she owes us. She owes it all to us."

If the villagers had been surprised to see Perrine driving M. Vulfran, Talouel was absolutely stunned.

" Where is William? " he cried, hurrying down the steps of the veranda to meet his employer.

" Sent off for continual drunkenness," said M. Vulfran, smiling.

" I had supposed that you would take this step eventually," said Talouel.

" Exactly," replied his employer briefly.

Talouel had established his power in the house by these two words, " I suppose." His aim was to persuade his chief that he was so devoted to his interests that he was able to foresee every wish that he might have. So he usually began with these words, " I suppose that you want . . . "

He had the subtlety of the peasant, always on the alert, and his quality for spying made him stop at nothing to get the information he desired. M. Vulfran usually made the same reply when Talouel had " supposed " something.

" Exactly," the blind man would say.

" And I suppose you find," continued Talouel, as he helped his employer to get down, " that the one who has replaced him deserves your trust? "

" Exactly," said the blind man again.

" I'm not astonished," added the crafty Talouel. " The day when Rosalie brought her here I thought there was something in her, and I was sure you would soon find that out."

As he spoke he looked at Perrine, and his look plainly said: " You see what I've done for you. Don't forget it, and be ready to do me a service."

A demand of payment on this order was not long in coming.

A little later, stopping before the door of the office in which Perrine sat, he said in a low voice from the doorway:

" Tell me what happened with William."

Perrine thought that if she frankly replied to his question she would not be revealing any serious matter, so she related exactly what had occurred.

" Ah, good," he said, more at ease. " Now, if he

should come to me and ask to be taken back I'll
settle with him."

Later on Fabry and Mombleux put the same
question to her, for everyone now knew that little
Perrine had had to drive the chief home because his
coachman had been too drunk to hold the reins.

"It's a miracle that he hasn't upset the boss a
dozen times," said Fabry, "for he drives like a
crazy creature when he's drunk.   He should have
been sent off long ago."

"Yes, and he would have been," said Mombleux,
smiling, "if certain ones who wanted his help had
not done all they could to keep him."

Perrine became all attention.

"They'll make a face when they see that he's
gone, but I'll give William his due: he didn't know
that he was spying."

They were silent while Zenobie came in to change
the plates.   They had not thought that the pretty
little girl in the corner was listening to their conversation.   After Zenobie had left the room they
went on with their talk.

"But what if the son returns?" asked Mombleux.

"Well, most of us want him back, for the old
man's getting old," said Fabry; "but perhaps he's
dead."

"That might be," agreed Mombleux.   "Talouel's
so ambitious he'd stop at nothing.   He wants to
own the place, and he'll get it if he can."

"Yes, and who knows?   Maybe he had a hand
in keeping M. Edmond away.   Neither of us were

here at the time, but you might be sure that Talouel would work out things to his own interests."

" I hadn't thought of that."

" Yes, and at that time he didn't know that they'd be others to take the place of M. Edmond. I'm not sure what he's scheming to get, but it's something big."

" Yes, and he's doing some dirty work for sure, and only think, when he was twenty years old he couldn't write his own name."

Rosalie came into the room at this moment and asked Perrine if she would like to go on an errand with her. Perrine could not refuse. She had finished her dinner some time ago, and if she remained in her corner she would soon awaken their suspicions.

It was a quiet evening. The people sat at their street doors chatting. After Rosalie had finished her errand she wanted to go from one door to another to gossip, but Perrine had no desire for this, and she excused herself on the plea of being tired. She did not want to go to bed. She just wanted to be alone, to think, in her little room, with the door closed. She wanted to take a clear account of the situation in which she now found herself.

When she heard Fabry and Mombleux speaking of the manager she realized how much she had to fear this man. He had given her to understand that he was the master, and as such it was his right to be informed of all that happened. But all that was nothing compared with what had been revealed to her in the conversation that she had just heard.

She knew that he wished to exercise his authority over everyone. But she had not known that his ambition was to take her grandfather's place some day. This man was scheming to replace the all-powerful master of the Maraucourt factories; for years he had plotted with this object in view. All this she had just learned. The two men whose conversation she had overheard were in a position to know the facts. And this terrible man, now that she had replaced William, intended that she should spy upon his employer.

What should she do? She was only a little girl, almost a child, and there was no one to protect her. What should she do?

She had asked herself this question before, but under different circumstances. It was impossible for her to lie down, so nervous and excited was she at what she had heard.

Perhaps this dreadful man had schemed to keep her dear dead father away from his home, and he was still working in an underhanded way for what? Was he trying to get out of the way the two nephews who would replace his master? If he had the power to do this, what might he not do to her if she refused to spy for him.

She spent the greater part of the night turning these questions over in her little head. At last, tired out with the difficulties which confronted her, she dropped her curly head on the pillow and slept.

CHAPTER XXI

LETTERS FROM DACCA

THE first thing that M. Vulfran did upon reaching his office in the morning was to open his mail. Domestic letters were arranged in one pile and foreign letters in another. Since he had gone blind his nephews or Talouel read the French mail aloud to him; the English letters were given to Fabry and the German to Mombleux.

The day following the conversation between Fabry and Mombleux which had caused Perrine so much anxiety, M. Vulfran, his nephews and the manager were occupied with the morning's mail. Suddenly Theodore exclaimed:

" A letter from Dacca, dated May 29."

" In French? " demanded M. Vulfran.

" No, in English."

" What signature? "

" It's not very clear . . . looks like Field. Fildes . . . preceded by a word that I can't make out. There are four pages. Your name occurs in several places, uncle.   Shall I give it to Fabry? "

Simultaneously, Theodore and Talouel cast a quick look at M. Vulfran, but catching each other in this act, which betrayed that each was intensely curious, they both assumed an indifferent air.

" I'm putting the letter on your table, uncle," said Theodore.

" Give it to me," replied M. Vulfran.

When the stenographer had gone off with the replies to the various letters, M. Vulfran dismissed his manager and his two nephews and rang for Perrine. She appeared immediately.

" What's in the letter? " he asked·

She took the letter that he handed to her and glanced at it.   If he could have seen her he would have noticed that she had turned very pale and that her hands trembled.

" It is an English letter, dated May 29, from Dacca," she replied.

" From whom? "

" From Father Fields."

" What does it say? "

" May I read a few lines first, please . . . before I tell you? "

" Yes, but do it quickly."

She tried to do as she was told, but her emotion increased as she read . . . the words dancing before her eyes.

" Well? " demanded M. Vulfran, impatiently.

" It is difficult to read," she murmured, " and difficult to understand; the sentences are very long."

" Don't translate literally; just tell me what it is about."

There was another long pause; at last she said:

" Father Fields says that Father Leclerc, to whom you wrote, is dead, and that before dying he asked

SHE TRIED TO DO AS SHE WAS TOLD, BUT HER EMOTION
INCREASED AS SHE READ.

him to send this reply to you. He was unable to communicate with you before, as he had some difficulty in getting together the facts that you desired. He excuses himself for writing in English, as his knowledge of French is very slight."

"What information does he send?" asked the blind man.

"I have not come to that yet, sir," replied Perrine.

Although little Perrine gave this reply in a very gentle voice, the blind man knew that he would gain nothing by hurrying her.

"You are right," he said; "not being in French, you must understand it thoroughly before you can explain it to me. You'd better take the letter and go into Bendit's office; translate it as accurately as you can, writing it out so that you can read it to me. Don't lose a minute. I'm anxious to know what it contains."

He called her back as she was leaving.

"This letter relates to a personal matter," he said, "and I do not wish anyone to know about it . . . understand . . . no one. If anyone dares question you about it, you must say nothing, nor give them any inkling of what it is about. You see what confidence I place in you. I hope that you will prove yourself worthy of my trust. If you serve me faithfully, you may be sure that you will be taken care of."

"I promise you, sir, that I'll deserve your trust," said Perrine, earnestly.

"Very well; now hurry."

But hurry she could not.   She read the letter
from beginning to end, then re-read it.   Finally she
took a large sheet of paper and commenced to write:

" Dacca, May 29.

" Honored Sir:

" It is with great grief that I inform you that we
have lost our Reverend Father Leclerc, to whom you
wrote for certain important information.   When
dying he asked me to send a reply to your letter,
and I regret that it could not have been sent earlier,
but after a lapse of twelve years I have had some
difficulty in getting the facts that you desire, and I
must ask pardon for sending the information I now
have in English, as my knowledge of French is very
slight . . . "

Perrine, who had only read this far to M. Vulfran,
now stopped to read and correct what she had done.
She was giving all her attention to her translation
when the office door was opened by Theodore Paindavoine.   He came into the room, closing the door
after him, and asked for a French and English
dictionary.

This dictionary was opened before her.   She
closed it and handed it to him.

" Are you not using it? " he asked, coming close
to her.

" Yes, but I can manage without it," she replied.

" How's that? "

" I really only need it to spell the French words

correctly," she said, " and a French dictionary will
do as well."

She knew that he was standing just at the back
of her, and although she could not see his eyes,
being afraid to turn round, she felt that he was
reading over her shoulder.

" Ah, you're translating that letter from Dacca? "
he said.

She was surprised that he knew about this letter
which was to be kept a secret.   Then she realized
that he was questioning her, and that his request
for a dictionary was only a pretext.   Why did he
need an English dictionary if he could not understand a word of English?

" Yes, monsieur," she said.

" Is the translation coming along all right? " he
asked.

She felt that he was bending over her, that his
eyes were fixed on what she had translated. Quickly
she moved her paper, turning it so that he could
only see it sideways.

" Oh, please, sir," she exclaimed; " don't read it.
It is not correct . . . it is all confused.   I was just
trying."

" Oh, never mind that."

" Oh, but I do mind.   I should be ashamed to let
you see this."

He wanted to take the sheet of paper, but she put
both her small hands over it.   She determined to
hold her own even with one of the heads of the
house.

Until then he had spoken pleasantly to her.

"Now give it to me," he said briefly. "I'm not playing schoolmaster with a pretty little girl like you."

"But, sir, it is impossible; I can't let you see it," she said obstinately.

Laughingly he tried to take it from her, but she resisted him.

"No, I will not let you have it," she said with determination.

"Oh, this is a joke!" replied Theodore.

"It is not a joke; I am very serious," said little Perrine. "Monsieur Vulfran forbade me to let anyone see this letter. I am obeying him."

"It was I who opened it."

"The letter in English is not the translation."

"Oh, my uncle will show me this wonderful translation presently," he replied.

"If your uncle shows it, very well; but that won't be me showing it. He gave me his orders and I must obey him."

He saw by her resolute attitude that if he wanted the paper he would have to take it from her by force. But then, if he did so, she would probably call out. He did not dare go as far as that.

"I am delighted to see how faithfully you carry out my uncle's orders, even in trivial things," he said, sarcastically, leaving the room.

When he had gone and closed the door Perrine tried to go on with her work, but she was so upset she found it impossible to do so. She knew that

Theodore was not delighted, as he had said, but furious. If he intended to make her pay for thwarting his will, how could she defend herself against such a powerful enemy. He could crush her with the first blow and she would have to leave.

The door was again opened and Talouel, with gliding step, came into the room. His eyes fell at once on the letter.

"Well, how is the translation of that letter from Dacca coming along?" he asked.

"I have only just commenced it," replied Perrine timidly.

"M. Theodore interrupted you just now. What did he want?"

"A French and English dictionary."

"What for? He doesn't know English."

"He did not tell me why he wanted it."

"Did he want to know what was in the letter?" asked Talouel.

"I had only commenced the first phrase," said Perrine, evasively.

"You don't ask me to believe that you have not read it?"

"I have not yet translated it."

"I ask you if you have read it."

"I cannot reply to that."

"Why not?"

"Because M. Vulfran has forbidden me to speak of this letter."

"You know very well that M. Vulfran and I are as one. All of his orders pass by me; all favors that he bestows are also passed by me. I have to know all that concerns him."

" Even his personal affairs? "

" Does that letter relate to personal affairs then? " asked Talouel.

She realized that she had let herself be caught.

" I did not say that," she said. " I said that in case it was a personal letter, ought I to let you know the contents? "

" I certainly should know," said Talouel, " if it relates to personal affairs. Do you know that he is ill from worrying over matters which might kill him? If he now received some news that might cause him great sorrow or great joy, it might prove fatal to him. He must not be told anything suddenly. That is why I ought to know beforehand anything that concerns him, so as to prepare him. I could not do that if you read your translation straight off to him."

He said this in a suave, insinuating voice, very different from his ordinary rough tones.

She was silent, looking up at him with an emotion which made her very pale.

" I hope that you are intelligent enough to understand what I am telling you," he continued. " It is important for us, for the entire town, who depend upon M. Vulfran for a livelihood, to consider his health. See what a good job you have now with him; in time it will be much better. We, every one of us, must work for his good. He looks strong, but he is not so strong as he appears, so much sorrow has undermined his health; and then the loss of his sight depresses him terribly. He places every confidence in me, and I must see that nothing hurts him."

If Perrine had not known Talouel she might have been won by his words; but after what she had heard the factory girls say about him, and the talk that she had overheard between Fabry and Mombleux, who were men able to judge character, she felt that she could not believe in him. He was not sincere. He wanted to make her talk, and he would attempt any deceit and hypocrisy to gain his object.

M. Vulfran had told her that if she were questioned she must not let anyone know the contents of the letter. Evidently he had foreseen what might happen. She must obey him.

Talouel, leaning on her desk, fixed his eyes on her face. She needed all her courage; it seemed as though he were trying to hypnotize her. In a hoarse voice which betrayed her emotion, but which did not tremble, however, she said:

"Monsieur Vulfran forbade me to speak of this letter to anyone."

Her determined attitude made him furious, but controlling himself, he leaned over her again and said gently, but firmly: "Yes, of course; but then I'm not anyone. I am his other self."

She did not reply·

"Are you a fool?" he cried at last in a stifled voice.

"Perhaps I am," she said.

"Well, then, understand," he said, roughly, "you'd better show some intelligence if you want to hold this job that M. Vulfran has given you. If you haven't any intelligence you can't hold the job, and instead of protecting you, as I intended, it will be my duty to pack you off . . . fire you! Understand?"

"Yes, sir."

"Well, think about it; think what your position is today and think what it will be tomorrow, turned out in the streets; then let me know what you decide to do. Tell me this evening."

Then as she showed no signs of weakening, he went out of the room with the same gliding step with which he had entered.

CHAPTER XXII

A CABLE TO DACCA

M. VULFRAN was waiting for her. She had no time to think over what Talouel had threatened. She went on with her translation, hoping that her emotion would die down and leave her in a state better able to come to a decision as to what she should do. She continued to write:

" So much time has elapsed since the marriage of your son, M. Edmond Paindavoine, that I have had some difficulty in getting together the facts. It was our own Father Leclerc who performed this marriage.

" The lady who became your son's wife was endowed with the finest womanly qualities. She was upright, kind, charming; added to these qualities, she was gifted with remarkable personal charms. The time is past when all the knowledge the Hindu woman possessed consisted in the art of being graceful and the science of etiquette of their social world. Today the Hindu woman's mind is cultivated to a remarkable degree. Your son's wife was a highly educated girl. Her father and mother were of the Brahmin faith, but Father Leclerc had the joy of converting them to our own religion. Unfortunately, when a Hindu is converted to our religion

227

he loses his caste, his rank, his standing in social life. This was the case with the family whose daughter married your son. By becoming Christians, they became to a certain extent outcasts.

"So you will quite understand that being cast off by the all-powerful Hindu world, this charming girl, who was now a Christian, should turn and take her place in European society. Her father went into partnership with a well-known French exporter, and the firm was known as Doressany (Hindu) & Bercher (French).

"It was in the home of Madame Bercher that your son met Marie Doressany and fell in love with her. Everybody spoke in the highest praise of this young lady. I did not know her, for I came to Dacca after she left. Why there should have been any obstacle to this union I cannot say. That is a matter I must not discuss. Although there were, however, objections, the marriage took place and in our own Chapel. The Reverend Father Leclerc bestowed the nuptial blessing upon the marriage of your son and Marie Doressany. This marriage was recorded in our registers, and a copy of it can be sent to you if you wish.

"For four years your son Edmond lived at the home of his wife's parents. There a little girl was born to the young couple. Everyone who remembers them speaks of them as a model couple, and like all young people, they took part in the social pleasures of their world.

"For some time the firm of Doressany & Bercher

prospered, then hard times came, and after several bad seasons the firm was ruined. M. and Mme. Doressany died at some months' interval, and Monsieur Bercher with his family returned to France. Your son then traveled to Dalhousie as collector of plants and antiquities for various English houses. He took with him his young wife and his little girl, who was about three years old.

" He did not return to Dacca, but I learn from one of his friends to whom he has written several times, and from Father Leclerc, who wrote regularly to Mme. Paindavoine, that they had a villa at Dehra. They selected this spot to live in as it was the center of his voyages; he traveled between the Thiberian frontier and the Himalayas.

" I do not know Dehra, but we have a mission in this town, and if you think it might help in our researches I shall be pleased to send you a letter for one of the Fathers whose help might be useful in this matter . . . "

At last the letter was finished. The moment she had translated the last word, without even waiting to write the polite ending, she gathered up her sheets and went quickly to M. Vulfran's office. She found him walking back and forth the length of the room, counting his steps as much to avoid bumping against the wall as to curb his impatience.

" You have been very slow," he said.

" The letter was long and difficult," she replied.

" And you were interrupted, were you not? I heard the door of your office open and close twice."

Since he put the question to her, she thought that she ought to reply truthfully.   It would solve the problem that had caused her so much anxiety.

" Monsieur Theodore and Monsieur Talouel came into the office," she said.

" Ah! . . . "

He seemed as though he wanted to say more, but refrained.

" Give me the letter first," he said, " and we'll see to the other matter after.   Sit down beside me and read slowly.   Don't raise your voice."

She read.   Her voice was somewhat weak.

As she read the blind man murmured to himself from time to time: " Model couple " . . . " social pleasures " . . . " English houses " . . . " which? " . . . " One of his friends " . . . " Which friend? "

When she had finished there was a silence. Finally M. Vulfran spoke:

" Can you translate into English as well as you translate English into French? " he asked.

" I can do it if the phrases are not too difficult," she replied.

" A cable? "

" Yes, I think so."

" Well, sit down at that little table and write." He dictated in French:

" Father Fields' Mission, Dacca:

" Thanks for letter.   Please send by cable, reply prepaid, twenty words . . . name of friend who received last news, date of letter.   Send also name

of the Reverend Father at Dehra. Inform him that
I shall write him immediately. Paindavoine."

"Translate that into English and make it shorter
rather than longer, if possible. At one franc sixty
centimes a word, we must not waste words. Write
very clearly."

The translation was quickly made.

"How many words?" he asked.

"In English . . . thirty-seven."

He made the calculation for the message and for
the return answer.

"Now," he said to Perrine, giving her the money,
"take it yourself to the telegraph office, hand it in
and see that no mistakes are made by the receiver."

As she crossed the veranda she saw Talouel, who,
with his hands thrust in his pockets, was strolling
about as though on the lookout for all that passed in
the yards as well as in the offices.

"Where are you going?" he demanded.

"To the cable office with a message," replied
Perrine. She held the paper in one hand and the
money in the other. He took the paper from her,
snatching it so roughly that if she had not let it go
he would have torn it. He hastily opened it. His
face flushed with anger when he saw that the message was written in English.

"You know that you've got to talk with me later
on, eh?" he said.

"Yes, sir."

She did not see M. Vulfran again before three

o'clock, when he rang for her to go out. She had wondered who would replace William, and she was very surprised when M. Vulfran told her to take her seat beside him, after having sent away the coachman who had brought old Coco around.

"As you drove him so well yesterday, there is no reason why you should not drive him well today," said M. Vulfran. "Besides, I want to talk to you, and it is better for us to be alone like this."

It was not until they had left behind the village, where their appearance excited the same curiosity as the evening before, and were going at a gentle trot along the lanes, that M. Vulfran began to talk. Perrine would like to have put off this moment; she was very nervous.

"You told me that M. Theodore and Talouel came into your office?" said the blind man.

"Yes, sir."

"What did they want?"

She hesitated. Her little face wore a very worried look.

"Why do you hesitate?" asked the blind man. "Don't you think that you ought to tell me everything?"

"Yes, indeed," said Perrine, fervently. Was this not the best way to solve her difficulties? She told what had happened when Theodore had come into the office.

"Was that all?" asked M. Vulfran, when she stopped.

"Yes, sir; that was all."

" And Talouel? "

Again she told exactly what had occurred, only
omitting to tell him that Talouel had said that a
sudden announcement of news, good or bad, might
prove fatal to him. She then told him what had
passed regarding the cable; and also that Talouel
said he was going to talk with her after work that
same day.

As she talked she had let old Coco go at her own
will, and the old horse, taking advantage of her
freedom, shambled along calmly from one side of
the road to the other, sniffing the odor of the warm
hay that the breeze wafted to his nostrils.

When Perrine stopped talking her grandfather
remained silent for some time. Knowing that he
could not see her, she fixed her eyes on his face and
she read in his expression as much sadness as annoyance.

" No harm shall come to you," he said at last.
" I shall not mention what you have told me, and if
anyone wants to take revenge on you for opposing
their attempts I shall be near to protect you. I
thought something like this would happen, but it
will not occur a second time. In the future you
will sit at the little table that is in my office. I
hardly think that they'll try to question you before
me. But as they might try to do so after you leave
off work, over at Mother Francoise's where you eat,
I shall take you to my home to live with me. You
will have a room in the chateau, and you will eat
at my table. As I am expecting to have some cor

respondence with persons in India, and I shall receive letters in English and cables, you alone will know about them. I must take every precaution, for they will do their utmost to make you talk. I shall be able to protect you if you are by my side; besides, this will be my reply to those who try to force you to speak, as well as a warning if they still try to tempt you. Then, also, it will be a reward for you."

Perrine, who had been trembling with anxiety when M. Vulfran commenced to speak, was now so overcome with joy that she could find no words with which to reply.

"I had faith in you, child," continued the old man, "from the moment I knew what struggle you had made against poverty. When one is as brave as you, one is honest. You have proved to me that I have not made a mistake, and that I can be proud of you. It is as though I have known you for years. I am a very lonely and unhappy man. What is my wealth to me? It is a heavy burden if you have not the health to enjoy it. And yet there are those who envy me. There are seven thousand men and women who depend upon me for a living. If I failed there would be misery and hunger and perhaps death for many. I must keep up for them. I must uphold the honor of this house which I have built up, little by little. It is my joy, my pride . . . and yet . . . I am blind!"

The last words were said with such bitterness that Perrine's eyes filled with tears. The blind man continued: "You ought to know from village talk and from the letter that you translated that I have a son. My son and I disagreed. We parted; there were many reasons for us doing so. He then married against my wishes and our separation was complete. But with all this my affection for him has not changed. I love him after all these years of absence as though he were still the little boy I brought up, and when I think of him, which is day and night, it is the little boy that I see with my sightless eyes. My son preferred that woman to his own father. Instead of coming back to me he preferred to live with her because I would not, or could not, receive her. I hoped that he would give in, but he thought probably that I in time would give in. We have both the same characters. I have had no news from him. After my illness, of which I am sure he knew, for I have every reason to believe that he has been kept informed of all that happens here, I thought that he would come back to me, but he has not returned. That wretched woman evidently holds him back. She is not content with having taken him from me, she keeps him . . . the wretch . . . "

The blind man stopped. Perrine, who had been hanging on his words, had scarcely breathed, but at the last words she spoke.

"The letter from Father Fields said that she was a lady, honorable and upright. He does not speak of her as a wretch."

"What the letter says cannot go against facts,"

said the blind man, obstinately. " The main fact
which has made me hate her is that she keeps my son
from me. A creature of her kind should efface herself and let him return and take up again the life
which is his. It is through her that we are parted.
I have tried to find him, but I cannot. He must
come back and take his place. You may not understand all I tell you, my child, but when I die my
whole fortune must go to my son. He is my heir.
When I die who will take my place if he is not here?
Can you understand what I am saying, little girl? "
said the old man, almost entreatingly.

" I think so, sir," said Perrine gently.

" But there, I don't wish you to understand entirely. There are those around me who ought to
help me. There are certain ones who do not want
my boy to return; it is to their interest that he
should not come back, so they try to think that he is
dead. My boy dead! Could he be? Could God
strike me such a terrible blow? They try to believe
it, but I will not. No, I will not! It can't be!
Oh, what should I do if my boy was dead! "

Perrine's eyes were no longer fixed on the blind
man's face; she had turned her face from him as
though he could see her own.

" I talk to you frankly, little girl," continued the
old man, " because I need your help. They are
going to try and tempt you again to spy for them.
I have warned you; that is all that I can do."

They could now see the factory chimneys of Fer-
cheux. Still a few more rods and they came to the

village.   Perrine, who was trembling, could only
find words to say in a broken voice: "Monsieur
Vulfran, you may trust me.   I will serve you faithfully with all my heart."

CHAPTER XXIII

THAT evening, when the tour of the factories was over, instead of returning to his office as was his custom, M. Vulfran told Perrine to drive straight to the chateau.

For the first time she passed through the magnificent iron gates, a masterpiece of skill that a king had coveted, so it was said, these wonderful iron gates which one of France's richest merchants had bought for his chateau.

"Follow the main driveway," said M. Vulfran.

For the first time also she saw close to the beautiful flowers and the velvety lawns which until then she had only seen from a distance. The beautiful blossoms, red and pink masses, seemed like great splashes on the verdure. Accustomed to take this road, old Coco trotted along calmly, and as there was no occasion to guide her, Perrine was able to gaze right and left of her and admire the flowers, plants and shrubs in all their beauty. Although their master could not see them as formerly, the same attention and skill was showered upon them.

Of her own accord, Coco stopped before the wide steps where an old servant, warned by the lodge-keeper's bell, stood waiting.

238

"Are you there, Bastien?" asked M. Vulfran, without getting down.

"Yes, sir."

"Then take this young girl to the butterfly room, which is to be hers in the future. See that everything is given to her that she needs. Set her plate opposite to mine at table. Now send Felix to me. I want him to drive me to the office."

Perrine thought that she was dreaming.

"We dine at eight o'clock," said M. Vulfran. "Until then you are free to do as you like."

She got out of the carriage quickly and followed the old butler. She was so dazed that it was as though she had suddenly been set down in an enchanted palace.

And was not this beautiful chateau like a palace? The monumental hall, from which rose a wonderful stairway of white marble, up which ran a crimson carpet, was a delight to the eyes. On each landing exquisite flowers and plants were grouped artistically in pots and jardinieres. Their perfume filled the air.

Bastien took her to the second floor, and without entering opened the door of a room for her.

"I'll send the chambermaid to you," he said, leaving her.

She passed through a somber little hall, then found herself in a very large room draped with ivory colored cretonne patterned with butterflies in vivid shades. The furniture was ivory colored wood, and the carpet gray, with clusters of wild flowers, primrose, poppies, cornflowers and butter-cups.

How pretty and dainty it was!

She was still in a dream, pushing her feet into the soft carpet, when the maid entered.

" Bastien told me that I was to be at your service, mademoiselle," she said.

Here stood a chambermaid in a clean light dress and a muslin cap at her service . . . she who only a few days before had slept in a hut on a bed of ferns with rats and frogs scampering about her.

" Thank you," she said at last, collecting her wits, " but I do not need anything . . . at least I think not."

" If you like I will show you the apartment," said the maid.

What she meant by " show the apartment " was to throw open the doors of a big wardrobe with glass doors, and a closet, then to pull out the drawers of the dressing table in which were brushes, scissors, soaps and bottles, etc. That done, she showed Perrine two knobs on the wall.

" This one is for the lights," she said, flashing on the electric light, " and this one is the bell if you need anything.

" If you need Bastien," she explained, " you have to ring once, and if you need me, ring twice."

How much had happened in a few hours! Who would have thought when she took her stand against Theodore and Talouel that the wind was going to blow so favorably in her direction. How amusing it was . . . their ill feeling towards her had itself brought her this good luck.

" I suppose that young girl did something foolish? " said Talouel, meeting his employer at the foot of the steps. " I see she has not returned with you."

" Oh, no; she did not," replied M. Vulfran.

" But if Felix drove you back . . . ? "

" As I passed the chateau I dropped her there so that she would have time to get ready for dinner."

" Dinner? Oh, I suppose . . . "

He was gasping with amazement, and for once he could not say what he did suppose.

" You do nothing but ' suppose '," said M. Vulfran, tartly. " I may as well tell you that for a long time I have wanted someone intelligent to be near me, one who is discreet and whom I can trust. This young girl seems to have these qualities. I am sure that she is intelligent, and I have already had the proof that I can trust her."

M. Vulfran's tone was significant. Talouel could not misunderstand the sense of his words.

" I am taking her to live with me," continued M. Vulfran, " because I know that there are those who are trying to tempt her. She is not one to yield, but I do not intend that she should run any risk at their hands."

These words were said with even greater significance.

" She will stay with me altogether now," continued M. Vulfran. " She will work here in my office; during the day she will accompany me; she will eat at my table. I shall not be so lonesome at my meals, for her chatter will entertain me."

" I suppose she will give you all the satisfaction that you expect," remarked Talouel suavely.

" I suppose so also," replied his employer, very drily.

Meanwhile Perrine, leaning with her elbows on the window sill, looked out dreamily over the beautiful garden, at the factories beyond the village with its houses and church, the meadows in which the silvery water glistened in the oblique rays of the setting sun; and then her eyes turned in the opposite direction, to the woods where she had sat down the day she had come, and where in the evening breeze she had seemed to hear the soft voice of her mother murmuring, " I know you will be happy."

Her dear mother had foreseen the future, and the big daisies had also spoken true. Yes, she was beginning to be happy. She must be patient and all would come right in time. She need not hurry matters now. There was no poverty, no hunger or thirst, in this beautiful chateau where she had entered so quickly.

When the factory whistle announced the closing hour she was still standing at her window, deep in thought. The piercing whistle recalled her from the future to the present.

Along the white roads between the fields she saw a black swarm of workers, first a great compact mass, then gradually it grew smaller, as they dwindled off in different directions in groups towards their homes.

Old Coco's gentle trot was soon heard on the drive, and Perrine saw her blind grandfather returning to his home.

She gave herself a real wash with eau de Cologne as well as soap, a delicious perfume soap. It was not until the clock on the mantle shelf struck eight that she went down.

She wondered how she would find the dining room. She did not have to look for it, however. A footman in a black coat, who was standing in the hall, showed her the way. Almost immediately M. Vulfran came in. No one guided him. He seemed to have no difficulty in finding his way to his seat.

A bowl of beautiful orchids stood in the middle of the table, which was covered with massive silver and cut glass, which gleamed in the lights that fell from the crystal chandelier.

For a moment she stood behind her chair, not knowing what to do. M. Vulfran seemed to sense her attitude.

" Sit down," he said.

The dinner was served at once. The servant who had shown her the way to the dining room put a plate of soup before her, while Bastien brought another to his master which was full to the brim.

If she had been dining there alone with M. Vulfran she would have been quite at her ease, but the inquisitive glances the servants cast at her made her feel deeply embarrassed. Probably they were wondering how a little tramp like her would eat.

Fortunately, however, she made no mistakes.

The dinner was very simple — soup, roast lamb, green peas and salad — but there was abundance of dessert . . . two or three raised stands of delicious fruit and cakes.

" Tomorrow, if you like, you may go and see the hot houses where these fruits are grown," said M. Vulfran.

Perrine thanked him and said she would like to.

She had commenced by helping herself discreetly to some cherries. M. Vulfran wished her also to take some apricots, peaches and grapes.

" Take all you want," he said. " At your age I should have eaten all the fruit that is on the table . . . if it had been offered to me."

Bastien selected an apricot and peach and placed them before Perrine as he might have done for an intelligent monkey, just to see how the " little animal " would eat.

But despite the delicious fruit, Perrine was very pleased when the dinner came to an end. She hoped that the next day the servants would not stare so much.

" Now you are free until tomorrow," said M. Vulfran, rising from his seat. " It is moonlight, and you can go for a stroll in the garden, or read in the library, or take a book up to your own room."

She was embarrassed, wondering if she ought not

to tell M. Vulfran that she would do as he wished.
While she stood hesitating she saw Bastien making
signs to her which at first she did not understand.
He held an imaginary book in one hand and appeared to be turning the pages with the other, then
glanced at M. Vulfran and moved his lips as though
he were reading. Suddenly Perrine understood.
She was to ask if she might read to him.

" But don't you need me, sir? " she said, timidly.
" Would you not like me to read to you? "

Bastien nodded his head in approval. He seemed
delighted that she had guessed what he had tried to
explain.

" Oh, you need some time to yourself," replied
M. Vulfran.

" I assure you that I am not at all tired," said
Perrine.

" Very well, then," said the blind man; " follow
me into the study."

The library was a big somber room separated
from the dining room by the hall. There was a
strip of carpet laid from one room to the other,
which was a guide for the blind man. He now
walked direct to the room opposite.

Perrine had wondered how he spent his time when
he was alone, as he could not read. From the appearance of the room one could not guess, for the
large table was covered with papers and magazines.
Before the window stood a large Voltaire chair, up-
holstered in tapestry. The chair was rather worn.
This seemed to indicate that the blind man sat for

long hours face to face with the sky, the clouds of
which he could never see.

"What could you read to me?" he asked Perrine.

"A newspaper," she said, "if you wish. There
are some on the table."

"The less time one gives to the newspapers the
better," he replied. "Do you like books on
travels?"

"Yes, sir; I do," she said.

"I do, too," he said. "They amuse one as well
as instruct one."

Then, as though speaking to himself, as though
unaware of her presence, he said softly: "Get away
from yourself. Get interested in another life than
your own."

"We'll read from 'Around the World'," he said.
He led her to a bookcase which contained several
volumes on travels and told her to look in the index.

"What shall I look for?" she asked.

"Look in the I's . . . for the word India."

Thus he was following his own thoughts. How
could he live the life of another? His one thought
was of his son. He now wanted to read about the
country where his boy lived.

"Tell me what you find," he said.

She read aloud the various headings concerning
India. He told her which volume to take. As she
was about to take it she stood as though transfixed,
gazing at a portrait hanging over the fireplace which
her eyes, gradually becoming accustomed to the dim
light, had not seen before.

" Why are you silent? " he asked.

" I am looking at the portrait over the mantel shelf," she said, in a trembling voice.

" That was my son when he was twenty," said the old gentleman; " but you can't see it very well. I'll light up."

He touched the electric knob and the room was flooded with light.   Perrine, who had taken a few steps nearer, uttered a cry and let the book of travels fall to the floor.

" What is the matter? " he asked.

She did not reply, but stood there with her eyes fixed on the picture of a fair young man dressed in a hunting suit leaning with one hand on a gun and the other stroking the head of a black spaniel.

There was silence in the room, then the blind man heard a little sob.

" Why are you crying? " he asked.

Perrine did not reply for a moment.   With an effort she tried to control her emotion.

" It is the picture . . . your son . . . you are his father? " she stammered.

At first he did not understand, then in a voice that was strangely sympathetic he said:

" And you . . . you were thinking of your father, perhaps? "

" Yes, yes, sir; I was."

" Poor little girl," he murmured.

CHAPTER XXIV

GETTING AN EDUCATION

THE next morning, when Theodore and Casimir entered their uncle's office to attend to the correspondence, they were amazed to see Perrine installed at her table as though she were a fixture there.

Talouel had taken care not to tell them, but he had contrived to be present when they entered so as to witness their discomfiture. The sight of their amazement gave him considerable enjoyment. Although he was furious at the way this little beggar girl had imposed, as he thought, upon the senile weakness of an old man, it was at least some compensation to know that the two nephews felt the same astonishment and indignation that he had.

Evidently they did not understand her presence in this sacred office, where they themselves only remained just the time necessary to report on the business of which they were in charge.

Theodore and Casimir looked in dismay at one another, but they did not dare ask questions. Talouel left the room the same time as they.

" You were surprised to see that girl in the boss' office, eh? " he said, when they got outside.

They did not deign to reply.

" If you had not come in late this morning, I should have let you know that she was there, and then you would not have looked so taken back. She noticed how surprised you were."

He had managed to give them two little knocks: First, there was a gentle scolding for them being late; secondly, he had let them see that he, a foreman, had noticed that they had been unable to hide their disconfiture and that the girl had noticed it, too. And they were M. Vulfran's nephews! Ah! ha!

" M. Vulfran told me yesterday that he had taken that girl to live at the chateau with him, and that in the future she would work in his office."

" But who is the girl? "

" That's what I'd like to know.   I don't think your uncle knows either.   He told me he wanted someone to be with him whom he could trust."

" Hasn't he got us? " asked Casimir.

" That is just what I said to him.   I mentioned you both, and do you know what he replied? "

He wanted to pause to give more effect to his words, but he was afraid that they would turn their backs upon him before he had said what he wanted.

" ' Oh, my nephews,' he said, ' and what are they? ' From the tone in which he said those few words I thought it better not to reply," continued Talouel. " He told me then that he intended to have that girl up at the chateau with him because there was someone trying to tempt her to tell something that she should not tell. He said he knew that she could be trusted, but he said he didn't like others that he could not trust to put the girl in such a position. He said she had already proved to him that she could be trusted. I wonder who he meant had tried to tempt her?

"I thought it my duty to tell you this, because while M. Edmond is away you two take his place," added Talouel.

He had given them several thrusts, but he wanted to give them one last sharp knock.

"Of course, M. Edmond might return at any moment," he said. "I believe that your uncle is on the right track at last. He has been making inquiries, and from the looks of things I think we shall have him back soon."

"What have you heard? Anything?" asked Theodore, who could not restrain his curiosity.

"Oh, I keep my eyes open," said Talouel, "and I can tell you that that girl is doing a lot of translating in the way of letters and cables that come from India."

At that moment he looked from a window and saw a telegraph boy strolling up to the office.

"Here is another cable coming," he said. "This is a reply to one that has been sent to Dacca. It must be very annoying for you not to be able to speak English. You could be the first to announce to the boss that your cousin will be coming back. Now that little tramp will be the one to do it."

Talouel hurried forward to meet the telegraph boy.

"Say, you don't hurry yourself, do you?" he cried.

"Do you want me to kill myself?" asked the boy, insolently.

He hurried with the message to M. Vulfran's office.

"Shall I open it, sir?" he asked eagerly.

"Yes, do," said M. Vulfran.

"Oh, it is in English," replied Talouel, as he looked at the missive.

"Then Aurelie must attend to it," said M. Vulfran, and with a wave of his hand dismissed the manager.

As soon as the door had closed Perrine translated the cable.

It read: "Friend Leserre, a French merchant. Last news from Dehra five years. Wrote Father Makerness according to your wish."

"Five years," cried M. Vulfran. Then, as he was not the sort of man to waste time in regrets, he said to Perrine: "Write two cables, one to M. Leserre in French and one to Father Makerness in English."

She quickly wrote the cable that she had to translate into English, but she asked if she could get a dictionary from Bendit's office before she did the one in French.

"Are you not sure of your spelling?" asked M. Vulfran.

"No, I am not at all sure," she replied, "and I should not like them at the office to make fun of any message that is sent by you."

"Then you would not be able to write a letter without making mistakes?"

"No, I know I should make a lot of mistakes. I can spell French words all right at the commencement, but the endings I find very difficult. I find it much easier to write in English, and I think I ought to tell you so now."

"Have you never been to school?"

"No, never. I only know what my father and mother taught me. When we stopped on the roads they used to make me study, but I never studied very much."

"You are a good girl to tell me so frankly. We must see to that, but for the moment let us attend to what we have on hand."

It was not until the afternoon, when they were driving out, that he again referred to her spelling.

"Have you written to your relations yet?" he asked.

"No, sir."

"Why not?"

"Because I would like nothing better than to stay here with you, who are so kind to me," she said.

"Then you don't want to leave me?" asked the blind man.

"No, I want to help you all I can," said Perrine softly.

" Very well, then you must study so as to be able
to act as a little secretary for me. Would you like
to be educated? "

" Indeed I would! And I will work so hard,"
said Perrine.

" Well, the matter can be arranged without de-
priving myself of your services," said M. Vulfran;
" there is a very good teacher here and I will ask
her to give you lessons from six to eight in the
evenings. She is a very nice woman; there are only
two things against her; they are her height and
her name; she is taller than I am, and her shoulders
are much broader than mine. Her name is Madamoiselle Belhomme. She is indeed a *bel homme*, for
although she is only forty her shoulders and figure
are more massive than any man's I know . . . I
must add that she has not a beard."

Perrine smiled at this description of the teacher
that she was to have.

After they had made a tour of the factories they
stopped before a girl's school and Mlle. Belhomme
ran out to greet M. Vulfran. He expressed a wish
to get down and go into the school and speak with
her. Perrine, who followed in their footsteps, was
able to examine her. She was indeed a giant, but
her manner seemed very womanly and dignified.
At times her manner was almost timid and did not
accord at all with her appearance.

Naturally she could not refuse anything the all-
powerful master of Maraucourt asked, but even if
she had had any reasons to refuse M. Vulfran's

request the little girl with the beautiful eyes and hair pleased her very much.

"Yes," she said to M. Vulfran, "we will make her an educated girl. Do you know she has eyes like a gazelle. I have never seen a gazelle, but I should imagine their great brown eyes are like hers. They are wonderful . . ."

The next day when M. Vulfran returned to his home at the dinner hour he asked the governess what she thought of her new pupil. Mlle. Belhomme was most enthusiastic in her praise of Perrine.

"Does she show any intelligence?" asked M. Vulfran.

"Why she is wonderfully intelligent," replied Mlle. Belhomme; "it would have been such a calamity if she had remained without an education . . ."

M. Vulfran smiled at Mlle. Belhomme's words.

"What about her spelling?" he asked.

"Oh, that is very poor but she'll do better. Her writing is fairly good but, of course, she needs to study hard. She is so intelligent it is extraordinary. So as to know exactly what she knew in writing and spelling I asked her to write me an account of Maraucourt. In twenty to a hundred lines I asked her to describe the village to me. She sat down and wrote. Her pen flew over the paper; she did not hesitate for words; she wrote four long pages; she described the factories, the scenery, every thing clearly and in detail. She wrote about the birds

and the fishes over near the pond, and about the
morning mists that cover the fields and the water.
Then of the calm, quiet evenings. Had I not seen
her writing it I should have thought that she had
copied it from some good author. Unfortunately
the spelling and writing is very poor but, as I said,
that does not matter. That is merely a matter of
a few months, whilst all the lessons in the world
would not teach her how to write if she had not
been gifted with the sense of feeling and seeing in
such a remarkable manner; that she can convey to
others what she feels and sees. If you have time
to let me read it to you, you will see that I have
not exaggerated."

The governess read Perrine's narrative to him.
He was delighted. He had wondered once or twice
if he had been wise in so promptly befriending this
little girl and giving her a place in his home. It
had appeared to him strange the sudden fancy that
he had taken to her.

He told Mlle. Belhomme how her little pupil had
lived in a cabin in one of the fields, and how, with
nothing except what she found on hand, she contrived to make kitchen utensils and shoes, and how
she had made her meals of the fish, herbs and fruit
that she found.

Mlle. Belhomme's kind face beamed as the blind
man talked. She was greatly interested in what he
told her. When M. Vulfran stopped the governess
remained silent, thinking.

"Don't you think," she said at last, "that to

know how to create the necessities that one needs
is a master quality to be desired above all?"

"I certainly do, and it was precisely because that
child could do that that I first took an interest in
her. Ask her some time to tell you her story and
you will see that it required some energy and courage for her to arrive where she is now."

"Well, she has received her reward since she has
been able to interest you."

"Yes, I am interested, and already attached to
her. I am glad that you like her, and I hope that
you will do all that you can with her."

Perrine made great progress with her studies.
She was interested in everything her governess had
to tell her, but her beautiful eyes betrayed the greatest interest when Mlle. Belhomme talked of her
grandfather. Many times Perrine had spoken of
M. Vulfran's illness to Rosalie, but she had only
received vague replies to her queries; now, from her
governess, she learned all the details regarding his
affliction.

Like everyone at Maraucourt, Mlle. Belhomme
was concerned with M. Vulfran's health, and she
had often spoken with Dr. Ruchon so she was
in a position to satisfy Perrine's curiosity better
than Rosalie could.

Her grandfather had a double cataract. It was
not incurable; if he were operated upon he might
recover his sight. The operation had not yet been
attempted because his health would not allow
it . . . . He was suffering from bronchial trouble,

and if the operation was to be a success he would
have to be in a perfect state of health. But M. Vulfran was imprudent. He was not careful enough
in following the doctor's orders. How could he
remain calm, as Dr. Ruchon recommended, when
he was always worked up to a fever of anxiety over
the continued absence of his son. So long as he
was not sure of his son's fate, there was no chance
for the operation and it was put off. But . . . .
would it be possible to have it later? That the
oculists could not decide. They were uncertain,
so long as the blind man's health continued in this
precarious state.

But when Mlle. Belhomme saw that Perrine was
also anxious to talk about Talouel and the two
nephews and their hopes regarding the business
she was not so communicative. It was quite natural
that the girl should show an interest in her benefactor, but that she should be interested in the village gossip was not permissible. Certainly it was
not a conversation for a governess and her
pupil . . . It was not with talks of this kind
that one should mould the character of a young
girl.

Perrine would have had to renounce all hope of
getting any information from her governess if Casimir's mother, Madame Bretoneux, had not decided
to come to the chateau on a visit. This coming visit
opened the lips of Mlle. Belhomme, which otherwise would certainly have remained closed.

As soon as the governess heard that Mme. Bretoneux was coming she had a very serious talk with her little pupil.

"My dear child," she said, lowering her voice, "I must give you some advice; I want you to be very reserved with this lady who is coming here tomorrow."

"Reserved, about what?" asked Perrine in surprise.

"Monsieur Vulfran did not only ask me to take charge of your education but to take a personal interest in you; that is why I give you this advice."

"Please, Madamoiselle, explain to me what I ought to do," said Perrine; "I don't understand at all what this advice means, and I am very nervous."

"Although you have not been very long at Maraucourt," said Mlle. Belhomme, "you must know that M. Vulfran's illness and the continued absence of his son is a cause of anxiety to all this part of the country."

"Yes, I have heard that," answered Perrine.

"What would become of all those employed in the works, seven thousand, and all those who are dependent on these seven thousand if Monsieur Vulfran should die and his son not return? Will he leave his fortune and works to his nephews, of which he has no more confidence in one than the other, or to one who for twenty years has been his right hand and who, having managed the works with him is, perhaps more than anyone else, in a position to keep his hold on them?

"When M. Vulfran took his nephew Theodore

into the business everyone thought that he intended
to make him his heir.   But later, when Monsieur
Casimir left college and his uncle sent for him, they
saw that they had made a mistake and that M. Vulfran had not decided to leave his business to these
two boys.   His only wish was to have his son back
for, although they had been parted for ten years,
he still loved him.   Now no one knew whether the
son was dead or alive.   But there were those who
wished that he was dead so that they themselves
could take M. Vulfran's place when he died.

"Now, my dear child," said the governess, "you
understand you live here in the home of M. Vulfran
and you must be very discreet in this matter and
not talk about it to Casimir's mother.   She is working all she can for her son's interest and she will
push anyone aside who stands in his way.   Now,
if you were on too good terms with her you would
be on bad terms with Theodore's mother, and the
other way about.   Then, on the other hand, should
you gain the good graces of both of them you would
perhaps have reason to fear one from another direction.   That is why I give you this little advice.   Talk
as little as possible.   And if you are questioned, be
careful to make replies as vague as possible.   It is
better sometimes to be looked upon rather as too
stupid than too intelligent.   This is so in your
case . . . the less intelligent you appear the more
intelligent you will really be."

CHAPTER XXV

MEDDLING RELATIVES

THIS advice, given with every kindness, did not tend to lessen Perrine's anxiety. She was dreading Madame Bretoneux's visit on the morrow.

Her governess had not exaggerated the situation. The two mothers were struggling and scheming in every possible way, each to have her son alone inherit one day or another the great works of Maraucourt and the fortune which it was rumored would be more than a hundred million francs.

The one, Mme. Stanislaus Paindavoine, was the wife of M. Vulfran's eldest brother, a big linen merchant. Her husband had not been able to give her the position in society which she believed to be hers, and now she hoped that, through her son inheriting his uncle's great fortune, she would at last be able to take the place in the Parisian world which she knew she could grace.

The other, Madame Bretoneux was M. Vulfran's married sister who had married a Boulogne merchant, who in turn had been a cement and coal merchant, insurance agent and maritime agent, but with all his trades had never acquired riches. She wanted her brother's wealth as much for love of the money as to get it away from her sister-in-law, whom she hated.

While their brother and his only son had lived on good terms, they had had to content themselves with borrowing all they could from him in loans which they never intended to pay back; but the day when Edmond had been packed off to India, ostensibly to buy jute but in reality as a punishment for being too extravagant and getting into debt, the two women had schemed to take advantage of the situation. On each side they had made every preparation so that each could have her son alone, at any moment, take the place of the exile.

In spite of all their endeavors the uncle had never consented to let the boys live with him at the chateau. There was room enough for them all and he was sad and lonely, but he had made a firm stand against having them with him in his home.

" I don't want any quarrels or jealousy around me," he had always replied to the suggestions made.

He had then given Theodore the house he had lived in before he built the chateau and another to Casimir that had belonged to the late head of the counting house whom Mombleux had replaced.

So their surprise and indignation had been intense when a stranger, a poor girl, almost a child, had been installed in the chateau where they themselves had only been admitted as guests.

What did it mean?

Who was this little girl?

What had they to fear from her?

Madame Bretoneux had put these questions to her son but his replies had not satisfied her. She decided to find out for herself, hence her visit.

Very uneasy, when she arrived, it was not long before she felt quite at ease again so well did Perrine play the part that mademoiselle had advised her.

Although M. Vulfran had no wish to have his nephews living with him he was very hospitable and cordial to their parents when they came to visit him. On these occasions the beautiful mansion put on its most festive appearance; fires were lighted everywhere; the servants put on their best liveries; the best carriages and horses were brought from the stables, and in the evening the villagers could see the great chateau lighted up from ground floor to roof.

The victoria, with the coachman and footman, had met Mme. Bretoneux at the railway station. Upon her getting out of the carriage Bastien had been on hand to show her to the apartment which was also reserved for her on the first floor.

M. Vulfran never made any change in his habits when his relations came to Maraucourt. He saw them at meal times, spent the evenings with them, but no more of his time did he give them. With him business came before everything; his nephew, the son of whichever one happened to be visiting there, came to luncheon and dinner and remained the evening as late as he wished, but that was all.

M. Vulfran spent his hours at the office just the

same and Perrine was always with him, so Madame Bretoneux was not able to follow up her investigations on the " little tramp " as she had wished.

She had questioned Bastien and the maids; she had made a call on Mother Francoise and had questioned her carefully, also Aunt Zenobie and Rosalie, and she had obtained all the information that they could give her; that is, all they knew from the moment of her arrival in the village until she went to live in the great house as a companion to the millionaire. All this, it seemed, was due exclusively to her knowledge of English.

She found it a difficult matter, however, to talk to Perrine alone, who never left M. Vulfran's side unless it was to go to her own room. Madame Bretoneux was in a fever of anxiety to see what was in the girl and discover some reason for her sudden success.

At table Perrine said absolutely nothing. In the morning she went off with M. Vulfran; after she had finished luncheon she went at once to her own room. When they returned from the tour of the factories she went at once to her lessons with her governess; in the evening, upon leaving the table, she went up again to her own room. Madame Bretoneux could not get the girl alone to talk with her. Finally, on the eve of her departure, she decided to go to Perrine's own room. Perrine, who thought that she had got rid of her, was sleeping peacefully.

A few knocks on the door awoke her. She sat up in bed and listened. Another knock.

She got up and went to the door.

" Who is there? " she asked, without opening it.

" Open the door, it is I . . . Madame Bretoneux," said a voice.

Perrine turned the lock. Madame Bretoneux slipped into the room while Perrine turned on the light.

" Get into bed again," said Madame Bretoneux, " we can talk just as well."

She took a chair and sat at the foot of the bed so that she was full face with Perrine.

" I want to talk with you about my brother," she began. " You have taken William's place and I want to tell you a few things that you should do; for William, in spite of his faults, was very careful of his master's health. You seem a nice little girl and very willing, and I am sure if you wish you could do as much as William. I assure you that we shall appreciate it."

At the first words Perrine was reassured; if it was only of M. Vulfran's health that she wanted to speak she had nothing to fear.

" I think you are a very intelligent girl," said Mme. Bretoneux with a flattering, ingratiating smile.

At these words and the look which accompanied them Perrine's suspicions were aroused at once.

" Thank you," she said, exaggerating her simple child-like smile, " all I ask is to give as good service as William."

"Ah, I was sure we could count on you," said Mme. Bretoneux.

" You have only to say what you wish, Madame," said little Perrine, looking up at the intruder with her big innocent eyes.

" First of all you must be very attentive about his health; you must watch him carefully and see that he does not take cold. A cold might be fateful; he would have pulmonary congestion and that would aggravate his bronchitis. Do you know if they could cure him of his bronchial trouble they could operate upon him and give him back his sight? Think what happiness that would be for all of us."

" I also would be happy," replied Perrine.

" Those words prove that you are grateful for what he has done for you, but, then, you are not of the family."

Perrine assumed her most innocent air.

" Yes, but that does not prevent me from being attached to M. Vulfran," she said, " believe me, I am."

" Of course," answered Mme. Bretoneux, " and you can prove your devotion by giving him the care which I am telling you to give him. My brother must not only be protected from catching cold, but he must be guarded against sudden emotions which might, in his state of health, kill him. He is trying to find our dear Edmond, his only son. He is making inquiries in India . . ."

She paused, but Perrine made no reply.

" I am told," she went on, " that my brother gets

you to translate the letters and cables that he receives from India. Well, it is most important that if there be bad news that my son should be informed first. Then he will send me a telegram, and as it is not far from here to Boulogne I will come at once to comfort my poor brother. The sympathy of a sister is deeper than that of a sister-in-law, you understand."

" Certainly, Madame, I understand; at least I think so," said Perrine.

" Then we can count on you? "

Perrine hesitated for a moment, but as she was forced to give a reply she said:

" I shall do all that I can for M. Vulfran."

" Yes, and what you do for him will be for us," continued Mme. Bretoneux, " the same as what you do for us will be for him. And I am going to show you that I am not ungrateful. What would you say if I gave you a very nice dress? "

Perrine did not want to say anything, but as she had to make some reply to the question she put it into a smile.

"A very beautiful dress to wear in the evening," said Mme. Bretoneux.

" But I am in mourning," answered Perrine.

" But being in black does not prevent you from wearing a lovely dress. You are not dressed well enough to dine at my brother's table. You are very badly dressed — dressed up like a clever little dog."

Perrine replied that she knew she was not well dressed but she was somewhat humiliated to be compared with a clever little dog, and the way the comparison was made was an evident intention to lower her.

"I took what I could find at Mme. Lachaise's shop," she said in self-defense.

"It was all right for Mme. Lachaise to dress you when you were a little factory girl, but now, that it pleases my brother to have you sit at the table with him, we do not wish to blush for you. You must not mind us making fun of you, but you have no idea how you amused us in that dreadful waist you have been wearing . . ."

Mme. Bretoneux smiled as though she could still see Perrine in the hideous waist.

"But there," she said brightly, "all that can be remedied; you are a beautiful girl, there is no denying that, and I shall see that you have a dinner dress to set off your beauty and a smart little tailored costume to wear in the carriage, and when you see yourself in it you will remember who gave it you. I expect your underwear is no better than your waist. Let me see it . . ."

Thereupon, with an air of authority, she opened first one drawer, then another, then shut them again disdainfully with a shrug of her shoulders.

"I thought so," she said, "it is dreadful; not good enough for you."

Perrine felt suffocated; she could not speak.

"It's lucky," continued Mme. Bretoneux, "that I came here, for I intend to look after you."

Perrine wanted to refuse everything and tell this

woman that she did not wish her to take care of her, but remembered the part she had to play. After all, Mme. Bretoneux's intentions were most generous; it was her words, her manner, that seemed so hard.

"I'll tell my brother," she continued, "that he must order from a dressmaker at Amiens, whose address I will give him, the dinner dress and the tailor suit which is absolutely necessary, and in addition some good underwear. In fact, a whole outfit. Trust in me and you shall have some pretty things, and I hope that they'll remind you of me all the time. Now don't forget what I have told you."

CHAPTER XXVI

PAINFUL ARGUMENTS

A FTER the talk his mother had had with Perrine, Casimir, by his looks and manner, gave her every opportunity to confide in him. But she had no intention of telling him about the researches that his uncle was having made both in India and in England. True, they had no positive news of the exile; it was all vague and contradictory, but the blind man still hoped on. He left no stone unturned to find his beloved son.

Mme. Bretoneux's advice had some good effect. Until then Perrine had not taken the liberty of having the hood of the phaeton pulled up, if she thought the day was chilly, nor had she dared advise M. Vulfran to put on an overcoat nor suggest that he have a scarf around his neck; neither did she dare close the window in the study if the evening was too cool, but from the moment that Mme. Bretoneux had warned her that the damp mists and rain would be bad for him she put aside all timidity.

Now, no matter what the weather was like, she never got into the carriage without looking to see that his overcoat was in its place and a silk scarf in the pocket; if a slight breeze came up she put the scarf around his neck or helped him into his coat. If a drop of rain began to fall she stopped at once and put up the hood. When she first walked out with him, she had gone her usual pace and he had followed without a word of complaint. But now that she realized that a brisk walk hurt him and usually made him cough or breathe with difficulty, she walked slowly; in every way she devised means of going about their usual day's routine so that he should feel the least fatigue possible.

Day by day the blind man's affection for little Perrine grew. He was never effusive, but one day while she was carefully attending to his wants he told her that she was like a little daughter to him. She was touched. She took his hand and kissed it.

"Yes," he said, "you are a good girl." Putting his hand on her head, he added: "Even when my son returns you shall not leave us; he will be grateful to you for what you are to me."

"I am so little, and I want to be so much," she said.

"I will tell him what you have been," said the blind man, "and besides he will see for himself; for my son has a good kind heart."

Often he would speak in these terms, and Perrine always wanted to ask him how, if these were his sentiments, he could have been so unforgiving and severe with him, but every time she tried to speak the words would not come, for her throat was closed

HE TOLD HER THAT SHE WAS LIKE A LITTLE DAUGHTER
TO HIM.

with emotion. It was a serious matter for her to broach such a subject, but on that particular evening she felt encouraged by what had happened. There could not have been a more opportune moment; she was alone with him in his study where no one came unless summoned. She was seated near him under the lamplight. Ought she to hesitate longer?

She thought not.

"Do you mind," she said, in a little trembling voice, "if I ask you something that I do not understand? I think of it all the time, and yet I have been afraid to speak."

"Speak out," he said.

"What I cannot understand," she said timidly, "is that loving your son as you do, you could be parted from him."

"It is because you are so young you do not understand," he said, "that there is duty as well as love. As a father, it was my duty to send him away; that was to teach him a lesson. I had to show him that my will was stronger than his. That is why I sent him to India where I intended to keep him but a short while. I gave him a position befitting my son and heir. He was the representative of my house. Did I know that he would marry that miserable creature? He was mad!"

"But Father Fields said that she was not a miserable creature," insisted Perrine.

"She was or she would not have contracted a marriage that was not valid in France," retorted the blind man, " and I will not recognize her as my daughter."

He said this in a tone that made Perrine feel suddenly cold. Then he continued abruptly: " You wonder why I am trying to get my son back now if I did not want him back after he had married. Things have changed. Conditions are not the same now as then. After fourteen years of this so-called marriage my son ought to be tired of this woman and of the miserable life that he has been forced to live on account of her. Besides conditions for me have also changed. My health is not what it was, and I am blind. I cannot recover my sight unless I am operated upon and I must be in a calm state favorable to the success of this operation. When my son learns this do you think he will hesitate to leave this woman? I am willing to support her and her daughter also. I am sure many times he has thought of Maraucourt and wanted to return. If I love him I know that he also loves me. When he learns the truth he will come back at once, you will see."

" Then he would have to leave his wife and daughter? "

" He has no wife nor has he a daughter," said the old man sternly.

" Father Fields says that he was married at the Mission House by Father Leclerc," said Perrine.

" This marriage was contracted contrary to the French law," said M. Vulfran.

" But was it not lawful in India? " asked Perrine.

" I will have it annulled in Rome," said the blind man.

" But the daughter? "

" The law would not recognize that child."

" Is the law everything? "

" What do you mean? "

" I mean that it is not the law that makes one love or not love one's parents or children. It was not the law that made me love my poor father. I loved him because he was good and kind and he loved me. I was happy when he kissed me and smiled at me. I loved him and there was nothing that I liked better than to be with him. He loved me because I was his little girl and needed his affection; he loved me because he knew that I loved him with all my heart. The law had nothing to do with that. I did not ask if it was the law that made him my father. It was our love that made us so much to each other."

" What are you driving at? " asked M. Vulfran.

" I beg your pardon if I have said anything I should not say, but I speak as I think and as I feel."

"And that is why I am listening to you," said the blind man; " what you say is not quite reasonable, but you speak as a good girl would."

" Well, sir, what I am trying to say is this," said Perrine boldly; " if you love your son and want to have him back with you, he also loves his daughter and wants to have her with him."

" He should not hesitate between his father and his daughter," said the old man; " besides, if the

marriage is annulled, she will be nothing to him.
He could soon marry that woman off again with
the dowry that I would give her. Everything is
changed since he went away. My fortune is much
larger . . . . He will have riches, honor and position.
Surely it isn't a little half-caste that can keep him
back."

"Perhaps she is not so dreadful as you imagine,"
said Perrine.

"A Hindu."

"In the books that I read to you it says that the
Hindus are more beautiful than the Europeans,"
said Perrine.

"Travelers' exaggerations," said the old man
scoffingly.

"They have graceful figures, faces of pure oval,
deep eyes with a proud look. They are patient,
courageous, industrious; they are studious . . ."

"You have a memory!"

"One should always remember what one reads,
should not one?" asked Perrine. "It does not seem
that the Hindu is such a horrible creature as you
say."

"Well, what does all that matter to me as I do
not know her."

"But if you knew her you might perhaps get
interested in her and learn to love her."

"Never! I can't bear to think of her and her
mother! . . ."

"But if you knew her you might not feel so angry
towards her."

He clenched his fist as though unable to control his fury, but he did not stop her.

"I don't suppose that she is at all like you suppose," said Perrine; "Father Fields is a good priest and he would not say what was not true, and he says that her mother was good and kind and a lady . . ."

"He never knew her; it is hearsay."

"But it seems that everyone holds this opinion. If she came to your house would you not be as kind to her as you have been to me, . . . a stranger?"

"Don't say anything against yourself."

"I do not speak for or against myself, but what I ask is for justice. I know if that daughter, your granddaughter, came here she would love you with all her heart."

She clasped her hands together and looked up at him as though he could see her; her voice shook with emotion.

"Wouldn't you like to be loved by your granddaughter?" she asked pleadingly.

The blind man rose impatiently.

"I tell you she can never be anything to me," he cried. "I hate her as I hate her mother. The woman took my son from me and she keeps him from me. If she had not bewitched him he would have been back long before this. She has been everything to him while I, his father, have been nothing."

He strode back and forth, carried away with his

anger. She had never seen him like this. Suddenly
he stopped before her.

" Go to your room," he said almost harshly, " and
never speak of those creatures to me again; besides,
what right have you to mix up in this? Who told
you to speak to me in such a manner? "

For a moment she was dumbfounded, then she
said:

" Oh, no one, sir, I assure you. I just put myself
into your little granddaughter's place, that is all."

He softened somewhat, but he continued still in
a severe voice: " In the future do not speak on this
subject; you see it is painful for me and you must
not annoy me."

" I beg your pardon," she said, her voice full of
tears; " certainly I ought not to have spoken so."

CHAPTER XXVII

THE BLIND MAN'S GRIEF

MONSIEUR VULFRAN advertised in the principal newspapers of Calcutta, Dacca, Bombay and London for his son. He offered a reward of forty pounds to anyone who could furnish any information, however slight it might be, about Edmond Paindavoine. The information must, however, be authentic. Not wishing to give his own address, which might have brought to him all sorts of correspondence more or less dishonest, he put the matter into the hands of his banker at Amiens.

Numerous letters were received, but very few were serious; the greater number came from detectives who guaranteed to find the person they were searching for if the expenses for the first steps necessary could be sent them. Other letters promised everything without any foundation whatever upon which they based their promises. Others related events that had occurred five, ten, twelve years previous; no one kept to the time stated in the advertisement, that was the last three years.

Perrine read or translated all these letters for the blind man. He would not be discouraged at the meagre indications sent him.

"It is only by continued advertising that we shall

get results," he said always. Then again he advertised.

Finally, one day a letter from Bosnia gave them some information which might lead to something. It was written in bad English, and stated that if the advertiser would place the forty pounds promised with a banker at Serajevo the writer would furnish authentic information concerning M. Edmond Paindavoine going back to the month of November of the preceding year. If this proposition was acceptable, the reply was to be sent to N. 917, General Delivery, Serajevo.

This letter seemed to give M. Vulfran so much relief and joy that it was a confession of what his fears had been.

For the first time since he had commenced his investigations, he spoke of his son to his two nephews and Talouel.

"I am delighted to tell you that at last I have news of my son," he said. "He was in Bosnia last November."

There was great excitement as the news was spread through the various towns and villages. As usual under such circumstances, it was exaggerated.

"M. Edmond is coming back. He'll be home shortly," went from one to another.

"It's not possible!" cried some.

"If you don't believe it," they were told, "you've only to look at Talouel's face and M. Vulfran's nephews."

Yet there were some who would not believe that

the exile would return. The old man had been too hard on him. He had not deserved to be sent away to India because he had made a few debts. His own family had cast him aside, so he had a little family of his own out in India. Why should he come back? And then, even if he was in Bosnia or Turkey, that was not to say that he was on his way to Maraucourt. Coming from India to France, why should he have to go to Bosnia? It was not on the route.

This remark came from Bendit, who, with his English coolheadedness, looked at things only from a practical standpoint, in which sentiment played no part. He thought that just because everyone wished for the son and heir to return, it was not enough to bring him back. The French could wish a thing and believe it, but he was English, he was, and he would not believe that he was coming back until he saw him there with his own eyes!

Day by day the blind man grew more impatient to see his son. Perrine could not bear to hear him talk of his return as a certainty. Many times she tried to tell him that he might be disappointed. One day, when she could bear it no longer, she begged him in her sweet voice not to count too much upon seeing his son for fear something might still keep him away.

The blind man asked her what she meant.

"It is so terrible to hear the worst when one has been expecting the best," she said brokenly. "If I say this it is because that is just what happened to me. We had thought and hoped so much when my father was ill that he would get better, but we lost him, and poor mama and I did not know how to bear it. We would not think that he might die."

" Ah, but my boy is alive, and he will be here soon. He will come back to me very soon," said the old man in a firm voice.

The next day the banker from Amiens called at the factory. He was met at the steps by Talouel, who did all in his power to get the first information which he knew the banker was bringing. At first his attitude was very obsequious, but when he saw that his advances were repulsed, and that the visitor insisted upon seeing his employer at once, he pointed rudely in the direction of M. Vulfran's office and said:

" You will find him over there in that room," and then turned and went off with his hands in his pockets.

The banker knocked on the door indicated.

" Come in," called out M. Vulfran, in answer to his knock.

" What, you . . . you at Maraucourt!" he exclaimed when he saw his visitor.

" Yes, I had some business to attend to at Picquigny, and I came on here to bring you some news received from Bosnia."

Perrine sat at her little table. She had gone very white; she seemed like one struck dumb.

" Well?" asked M. Vulfran.

"It is not what you hoped, what we all hoped," said the banker quietly.

"You mean that that fellow who wrote just wanted to get hold of the forty pounds."

"Oh, no; he seems an honest man . . . "

"Then he knows nothing?"

"He does, but unfortunately his information is only too true."

"Unfortunately!" gasped the blind man. This was the first word of doubt that he had uttered. "You mean," he added, "that they have no more news of him since last November?"

"There is no news since then. The French Consul at Serajevo, Bosnia, has sent me this information:

"'Last November your son arrived at Serajevo practising the trade of a strolling photographer . . . ' "

"What do you mean?" exclaimed M. Vulfran. "A strolling photographer! . . . My son?"

"He had a wagon," continued the banker, "a sort of caravan in which he traveled with his wife and child. He used to take pictures on the market squares where they stopped . . . "

The banker paused and glanced at some papers he held in his hand.

"Oh, you have something to read, haven't you?" said the blind man as he heard the paper rustle. "Read, it will be quicker."

"He plied the trade of a photographer," continued the banker, consulting his notes, "and at the beginning of November he left Serajevo for Travnik, where he fell ill.   He became very ill . . . "

"My God!" cried the blind man.   "Oh, God . . ."

M. Vulfran had clasped his hands; he was trembling from head to foot, as though a vision of his son was standing before him.

"You must have courage," said the banker, gently.   "You need all your courage.   Your son . . ."

"He is dead!" said the blind man.

"That is only too true," replied the banker.   "All the papers are authentic.   I did not want to have any doubt upon the matter, and that was why I cabled to our Consul at Serajevo.   Here is his reply; it leaves no doubt."

But the old man did not appear to be listening. He sat huddled up in his big chair, his head drooped forward on his chest.   He gave no sign of life. Perrine, terrified, wondered if he were dead.

Then suddenly he pulled himself together and the tears began to run down his wrinkled cheeks.   He brushed them aside quickly and touched the electric bell which communicated with Talouel's and his nephew's offices.

The call was so imperative that they all ran to the office together.

"You are there?" asked the blind man; "Talouel, Theodore and Casimir?"

All three replied together.

"I have just learned of the death of my son," said their employer.   "Stop work in all the factories immediately. Tomorrow the funeral services will be held in the churches at Maraucourt, Saint-Pipoy and all the other villages."

" Oh, uncle! " cried both the nephews.

He stopped them with uplifted hand.

" I wish to be alone . . . leave me," was all he said.

Everyone left the room but Perrine. She alone remained.

" Aurelie, are you there? " asked the blind man.

She replied with a sob.

" Let us go home," he said.

As was his habit, he placed his hand on her shoulder, and it was like this that they passed through the crowd of workers who streamed from the factory. As they stood aside for him to pass, all who saw him wondered if he would survive this blow. He, who usually walked so upright, was bent like a tree that the storm has broken.

Could he survive this shock? Perrine asked herself this question with even greater agony, for it was she and she alone who knew how his great frame was trembling. His shaking hands grasped her shoulder convulsively, and without him uttering one word little Perrine knew how deeply her grandfather was smitten.

After she had guided him into his study he sent her away.

" Explain why I wish to be left alone. No one is to come in here. No one is to speak to me . . .

"And I refused to believe you," he murmured as she was leaving him.

"Oh, please; if you will let me . . ."

"Leave me," he said roughly.

Perrine closed the door softly.

CHAPTER XXVIII

AN UNRESPECTED FUNERAL

THERE was considerable bustle and excitement at the chateau all that evening. First M. and Mme. Stanislas Paindavoine, who had received a telegram from Theodore, arrived. Then M. and Mme. Bretoneux, sent for by Casimir, came. After that came Mme. Bretoneux's two daughters, their husbands and children. No one wished to miss the funeral service for poor dear Edmond.

Besides, this was the decisive moment for clever manoeuvring. What a disaster if this big industry should fall into the hands of one so incapable as Theodore! What a misfortune if Casimir took charge! Neither side thought that a partnership could be possible, and the two cousins share alike. Each wanted all for himself.

Both Mme. Bretoneux and Mme. Paindavoine had ignored Perrine since their arrival. They had given her to understand that they did not require her services any longer.

Sat sat in her room hoping that M. Vulfran would send for her so that she could help him into the church, as she had done every Sunday since William had gone. But she waited in vain. When the bells, which had been tolling since the evening before, announced mass, she saw him get up into his carriage leaning on his brother's arm, while his sister and sister-in-law, with the members of their families, took their places in other carriages.

She had no time to lose, for she had to walk. She hurried off.

After she had left the house over which Death had spread its shroud, she was surprised to notice as she hastened through the village that the taverns had taken on their Sunday air. The men drank and laughed and the women chatted at their doors, while the children played in the street. Perrine wondered if none of them were going to attend the service.

Upon entering the church, where she had been afraid that she would not find room, she saw that it was almost empty. The bereaved family sat in the choir; here and there was some village authority, a tradesman and the heads of the factories. Very few of the working men and women were present; they had not thought to come and join their prayers to those of their employer's.

Perrine took a seat beside Rosalie and her grandmother, who was in deep mourning.

"Alas! my poor little Edmond," murmured the old nurse, wiping her eyes. "What did M. Vulfran say?"

But Perrine was too overcome to reply. The services commenced.

As she left the church, Mlle. Belhomme came up

to her, and, like Francoise, wanted to question her about M. Vulfran. Perrine told her that he had not spoken to her since the evening before.

"As I saw him kneeling there so crushed and broken for the first time, I was pleased that he was blind," said the governess sadly.

"Why?" asked Perrine.

"Because he could not see how few people came to the church. What indifference his men have shown! If he could have seen that empty church it would have added to his grief."

"I think he must have known how few there were there," said Perrine. "His ears take the place of his eyes, and that empty silence could not deceive him."

"Poor man," murmured Mlle. Belhomme; "and yet . . ."

She paused. Then, as she was not in the habit of holding anything back, she went on: "And yet it will be a great lesson to him. You know, my child, you cannot expect others to share your sorrows if you are not willing to share theirs.

"M. Vulfran gives his men what he considers their due," she continued, in a lower voice. "He is just, but that is all. He has never been a father to his men. He is all for business, business only. What a lot of good he could have done, however, not only here, but everywhere, if he had wished, by setting an example. Had he been more to his men you may be sure that the church would not have been as empty as it was today."

Perhaps that was true, but how it hurt Perrine to hear this from the lips of her governess, of whom she was so fond.   If anyone else had said so she might not have felt it so deeply.   Yes, undoubtedly it was too true.

They had been walking as they talked, and had now reached the schools where Mlle. Belhomme lived.

"Come in and we'll have luncheon together," she said.   She was thinking that her pupil would not be allowed to take her accustomed place at the family table.

"Oh, thank you," said Perrine; "but M. Vulfran might need me."

"Well, in that case you had better go back," said Mlle. Belhomme.

When she reached the chateau she saw that M. Vulfran had no need of her, that he was not even thinking of her.   Bastien, whom she met on the stairs, told her that when he came back from the church he had gone to his own room and locked himself in, forbidding anyone to enter.

"He won't even sit down on a day like this with his family," said Bastien, "and they are all going after luncheon.   I don't think he even wants to say goodbye to them.   Lord help us!   What will become of us?   Oh, poor master!"

"What can I do?" asked Perrine.

"You can do a great deal.   The master believes in you, and he's mighty fond of you."

"Mighty fond of me?" echoed Perrine.

" Yes, and it's I as says it," said the butler.   " He likes you a whole lot."

As Bastien had said, all the family left after luncheon.   Perrine stayed in her room, but M. Vulfran did not send for her.   Just before she went to bed, Bastien came to tell her that his master wished her to accompany him the next morning at the usual hour.

" He wants to get back to work, but will he be able? " said the old butler.   " It will be better for him if he can.   Work means life for him."

The next day at the usual hour Perrinè was waiting for M. Vulfran.   With bent back he came forward, guided by Bastien.   The butler made a sign to her that his master had passed a bad night.

" Is Aurelie there? " asked the blind man in a changed voice, a voice low and weak, like that of a sick child.

Perrine went forward quickly.

" I am here, M. Vulfran," she said.

" Let us get into the carriage, Aurelie," he said.

As soon as he had taken his place beside Perrine his head drooped on his chest.   He said not a word.

At the foot of the office steps Talouel was there ready to receive him and help him to alight.

" I suppose you felt strong enough to come? " he said, in a sympathetic voice which contrasted with the flash in his eyes.

" I did not feel at all strong, but I came because I thought that I ought to come," said his employer.

" That is what I meant . . . I . . . "

M. Vulfran stopped him and told Perrine to guide him to his office.

The mail, which had accumulated in two days, was read, but the blind man made no comments on the correspondence. It was as though he were deaf or asleep. The heads of the factory then came in to discuss an important question that had to be settled that day. When the immediate business was settled Perrine was left alone with the blind man. He was silent.

Time passed; he did not move. She had often seen him sit still, but on such occasions, from the expression on his face, she had known that he was following his work as though he were watching with his eyes. He listened to the whistle of the engines, the rolling of the trucks; he was attentive to every sound and seemed to know exactly what was going on, but now he seemed as though he were turned into a statue. There was no expression in his face and he was so silent. He did not seem to be breathing. Perrine was overcome by a sort of terror. She moved uneasily in her chair; she did not dare speak to him.

Suddenly he put his two hands over his face and, as though unaware that anyone was present, he cried: "My God! my God! you have forsaken me! Oh, Lord, what have I done that you should forsake me!"

Then the heavy silence fell again. Perrine trembled when she heard his cry, although she could not grasp the depth of his despair.

Everything that this man had attempted had been a success; he had triumphed over his rivals; but now, with one blow, that which he wanted most had been snatched from him.   He had been waiting for his son; their meeting, after so many years of absence, he had pictured to himself, and then . . .

Then what?

" My God," cried the blind man again, " why have you taken him from me? "

CHAPTER XXIX

THE ANGEL OF REFORM

A S THE days passed M. Vulfran became very weak. At last he was confined to his room with a serious attack of bronchitis, and the entire management of the works was given over to Talouel, who was triumphant.

When he recovered he was in such a state of apathy that it was alarming. They could not rouse him; nothing seemed to interest him, not even his business. Previously they had feared the effect a shock would have on his system, but now the doctors desired it, for it seemed that only a great shock could drag him out of this terrible condition. What could they do?

After a time he returned to his business, but he scarcely took account of what Talouel had done during his absence. His manager, however, had been too clever and shrewd to take any steps that his employer would not have taken himself.

Every day Perrine took him to his various factories, but the drives were made in silence now. Frequently he did not reply to the remarks she made from time to time, and when he reached the works he scarcely listened to what his men had to say.

"Do what you think best," he said always.   "Arrange the matter with Talouel."

How long would this apathy last?

One afternoon, when old Coco was bringing them back to Maraucourt, they heard a bell ringing.

"Stop," he said; "I think that's the fire alarm."

Perrine stopped the horse.

"Yes, it's a fire," he said, listening.   "Do you see anything?"

"I can see a lot of black smoke over by the poplars on the left," replied Perrine.

"On the left?   That is the way to the factory."

"Yes; shall I drive that way?" asked Perrine.

"Yes," replied M. Vulfran, indifferently.

It was not until they reached the village that they knew where the fire was.

"Don't hurry, M. Vulfran," called out a peasant; "the fire ain't in your house.   It's La Tiburce's house that's on fire."

La Tiburce was a drunken creature who minded little babies who were too young to be taken to the crèche.   She lived in a miserable tumble-down house near the schools.

"Let us go there," said M. Vulfran.

They had only to follow the crowd, for the people, when they saw the flames and smoke rising, were running excitedly to the spot where the fire was. Before reaching the scene Perrine had to stop several times for fear of running someone down.   Nothing in the world would have made the people get out of their way.   Finally M. Vulfran got out of the carriage and, guided by Perrine, walked through the crowd. As they neared the entrance to the house, Fabry, wearing a helmet, for he was chief of the firemen, came up to them.

" We've got it under control," he said, " but the house is entirely burnt, and what's worse, several children, five or six, perhaps, are lost. One is buried beneath, two have been suffocated, and we don't know where the other three are."

" How did it happen? " asked M. Vulfran.

" La Tiburce was asleep, drunk. She is still in that condition. The biggest of the children were playing with the matches. When the fire began to flare up some of the children got out, and La Tiburce woke up. She is so drunk she got out herself but left the little ones in the cradle."

The sound of cries and loud talking could be heard in the yard. M. Vulfran wanted to go in.

" Don't go in there, sir," said Fabry. " The mothers whose two children were suffocated are carrying on pretty badly."

" Who are they? "

" Two women who work in your factory."

" I must speak to them."

Leaning on Perrine's shoulder, he told her to guide him. Preceded by Fabry, who made way for them, they went into the yard where the firemen were turning the hose on the house as the flames burst forth in a crackling sound.

In a far-off corner several women stood round the two mothers who were crying. Fabry brushed

aside the group.   M. Vulfran went up to the bereaved parents, who sat with their dead children on
their knees.   Then one of the women, who thought
perhaps that a supreme help had come, looked up
with a gleam of hope in her eyes.   When she recognized M. Vulfran she raised her arm to him threat-
eningly.

"Ah," she cried, "come and see for yourself what
they do to our babies while we are sweating and
killing ourselves for you.   Can you give us back
their lives?   Oh, my little boy."

She burst into sobs as she bent over her child.

M. Vulfran hesitated for a moment; then he
turned to Fabry and said:

"You are right; let us go."

They returned to the offices.   After a time Talouel
came to tell his employer that out of the six children
that they had thought were dead, three had been
found in the homes of neighbors, where they had
been carried when the fire first broke out.   The
burial for the other three tiny victims was to take
place the next day.

When Talouel had gone, Perrine, who had been
very thoughtful, decided to speak to M. Vulfran.

"Are you not going to the burial service of these
little babies?" she asked.   Her trembling voice
betrayed her emotion.

"Why should I go?" asked M. Vulfran.

"Because that would be the most dignified answer
you could give to what that poor woman said."

"Did my work people come to the burial service of my son?" asked M. Vulfran, coldly.

"They did not share your sorrow," said Perrine gravely, "but if you share theirs now they will be touched."

"You don't know how ungrateful the working-man is."

"Ungrateful! For what? The money they receive? They consider that they have a right to the money they earn. It is theirs. Would they show ingratitude if an interest was taken in them, if a little friendly help was given them? Perhaps it would not be the same, do you think so? Friend-ship creates friendship. One often loves when one knows one is loved, and it seems to me that when we are friendly to others, we make friends our-selves. It means so much to lighten the burdens of the poor, but how much more is it to lighten their sorrows . . . by helping to share them."

It seemed to her that she had still so much to say on this subject, but M. Vulfran did not reply. He did not even appear to be listening to her, and she was afraid to say more. Later she might make another attempt.

As they left the office M. Vulfran turned to Talouel, who was standing on the steps, and said:

"Tell the priest to arrange a suitable burial for the three children. It will be at my expense and I shall be there."

Talouel jumped.

"And let everyone know," continued M. Vulfran,

" that all who wish to go to the church tomorrow can take the time off.   This fire is a great misfortune."

" We are not responsible for it," said Talouel.

" Not directly . . . no," said M. Vulfran.

Perrine had another surprise the next morning. After the mail had been opened and the replies dictated, M. Vulfran detained Fabry and said: " I want you to start for Rouen.   I think you can spare the time.   I have heard that they have built a model crèche there.   It is not built by the town, but someone has had it built to the memory of one whom they have lost.   I want you to see how this is made.   Study it in all its details — the construction, heating and ventilation and the expense of keeping it up.   In three months we must have a crèche at the entrance of all my factories.   I don't want such a calamity as that which occurred yesterday to take place again.   I rely upon you and the responsibility is upon you now."

That evening Perrine told the great news to her governess, who was delighted.   While they were talking about it, M. Vulfran came into the room.

" Mademoiselle," he said, " I have come to ask a favor of you in the name of all the village.   It is a big favor.   It may mean a great sacrifice on your part.   This is it."

In a few words he outlined the request he had to make.   It was that mademoiselle should send in her resignation at the schools and take charge of the five crèches which he was going to build.   He knew of no one who was capable of taking on their shoulders such a big burden. He would donate a crèche to each village and endow it with sufficient capital to keep up its maintenance.

Although Mlle. Belhomme loved to teach, and it would be indeed a sacrifice for her to give up her school, she felt, after she had talked with the blind man, that it was here where her duty lay. It was indeed a great work that she was called upon to do, and she would enter upon her task with all the enthusiasm of which her big heart was capable.

"This is a great thing you are doing Monsieur Vulfran," she said, with tears in her eyes, "and I will do all I can to make this work a success."

"It is your pupil one must thank for it," said the blind man, "not I. Her words and suggestions have awakened something in my heart. I have stepped out on a new road. I am only at the first steps. It is nothing compared with what I intend to do."

"Oh, please," said Perrine, her eyes bright with delight and pride, "if you still want to do something . . . "

"What is it?" he asked with a smile.

"I want to take you somewhere . . . tonight."

"What do you mean? Where do you want to take me?" asked the blind man, mystified.

"To a place where your presence only for a few moments will bring about extraordinary results," said Perrine.

" Well, can't you tell me where this mysterious place is? " asked M. Vulfran.

" But if I tell you, your visit will not have the same effect. It will be a failure. It will be a fine evening and warm, and I am sure that you will not take cold. Please say you will go ! "

" I think one could have confidence in her," said Mademoiselle Belhomme, " although her request seems a little strange and childish."

" Well," said M. Vulfran, indulgently, " I'll do as you wish, Aurelie. Now at what hour are we to start on this adventure? "

" The later it is the better it will be," said Perrine.

During the evening he spoke several times of the outing they were to have, but Perrine would not explain.

" Do you know, little girl, you have aroused my curiosity? " he said at last.

" I am glad you are interested," she said gravely. " There is so much that can be done in the future. Do not look back to the past any more."

"The future is empty for me," said the blind man bitterly.

" Oh, no; it is not," said Perrine, lifting her lovely face to his. Her eyes were shining with a beautiful light. " It will not be empty if you think of others. When one is a child, and not very happy, one often thinks that if a wonderful fairy came to them, of what beautiful things they would ask. But if one is the fairy, or rather the magician one-self, and can do all the wonderful things alone, wouldn't it be splendid to use one's power . . . ? "

The evening passed. Several times the blind man asked if it were not time to start, but Perrine delayed as long as possible.

At last she said that she thought they could start. The night was warm, no breeze, no mists. The atmosphere was a trifle heavy and the sky dark.

When they reached the village it was all quiet. All seemed to sleep. Not a light shone from the windows.

The dark night made no difference to the blind man. As they walked along the road from the chateau he knew exactly where he was.

" We must be nearing Francoise's house," he said, after they had walked a little distance.

" That is just where we are going," said Perrine. " We are there now. Let me take your hand and guide you, and please don't speak. We have some stairs to go up, but they are quite easy and straight. When we get to the top of these stairs I shall open a door and we shall go into a room for just one moment."

" What do you want me to see . . . when I can't see anything? " he said.

" There will be no need for you to see," replied Perrine.

" Then why come? "

" I want you here," said Perrine earnestly. " Here are the stairs. Now step up, please."

They climbed up the stairs and Perrine opened a

door and gently drew M. Vulfran inside a room and
closed the door again.

They stood in a suffocating, evil-smelling room.

" Who is there? " asked a weary voice.

Pressing his hand, Perrine warned M. Vulfran
not to speak.

The same voice spoke:

" Get into bed, La Noyelle.   How late you are."

This time M. Vulfran clasped Perrine's hand in
a sign for them to leave the place.

She opened the door and they went down, while
a murmur of voices accompanied them.   When they
reached the street M. Vulfran spoke: " You wanted
me to know what that room was the first night when
you slept there? "

" I wanted you to know what kind of a place all
the women who work for you have to sleep in.   They
are all alike in Maraucourt and the other villages.
You have stood in one of these dreadful rooms; all
the others are like it.   Think of your women and
children, your factory hands, who are breathing that
poisoned air.   They are slowly dying.   They are
almost all weak and sick."

M. Vulfran was silent.   He did not speak again,
neither did Perrine.   When they entered the hall
he bade her good night, and guided by Bastien, he
went to his own room.

CHAPTER XXX

GRANDFATHER FINDS PERRINE

ONE year had passed since Perrine had arrived at Maraucourt on that radiant Sunday morning. What a miserable lonely little girl she had been then.

The day was just as radiant now, but what a change in Perrine, and, be it said, in the whole village also. She was now a lovely girl of fifteen. She knew she was loved and loved for herself, and this is what gave the deep look of happiness to her eyes.

And the village! No one would have recognized it now. There were new buildings, pretty cottages, and a hospital commanding a view of the surrounding country. Near the factories were two handsome red brick buildings. These were the crèches where the little children, whose mothers were working in the factories, were kept. All the little children had their meals there, and many of them slept there. It was a home for them.

M. Vulfran had bought up all the old houses, the tumble-down hovels and huts, and had built new cottages in their places. There was a large restaurant built where the men and women could get a

302

dinner for eleven cents, the meal consisting of a soup, stew or roast, bread and cider.

Every little cottage, for which the tenant paid one hundred francs a year, had its own tiny garden in which to grow vegetables for the family.

In the road leading to the chateau there was now a fine recreation ground, which was greatly patronized after the factories had closed. There were merry-go-rounds, swings, bowling alleys and a stand for the musicians who played every Saturday and Sunday, and of course on every holiday. This public park of amusement was used by the people of all five villages. Monsieur Vulfran had thought it better to have one place of reunion and recreation. If his people all met together to enjoy their leisure hours, it would establish good relations and a bond of friendship between them. At the end of the grounds there was a fine library with a reading and writing room.

M. Vulfran's relations thought that he had gone mad. Did he intend to ruin himself? That is to say, ruin them? Some steps ought to be taken to prevent him from spending his fortune in this manner. His fondness for that girl was a proof that he was losing his mind. That girl did not know what she was doing! All their animosity was centered on her. What did it matter to her that his fortune was being thrown away? But if Perrine had all the relations against her, she knew that she had M. Vulfran's friendship, and the family doctor, Doctor Ruchon, Mlle. Belhomme and Fabry all

adored her. Since the doctor had seen that it was
the "little girl" who had been the means of his
patient exerting this wonderful moral and intellec-
tual energy, his attitude to her expressed the greatest respect and affection. In the doctor's eyes, Perrine was a wonderful little girl.

"She can do a great deal more than I can," he
said, shaking his gray head.

And Mlle. Belhomme, how proud she was of her
pupil! As to Fabry, he was on the best of terms
with her. He had been so closely connected with
her in the good work that had been done, for Fabry
had superintended everything.

It was half-past twelve. Fabry had not yet arrived. M. Vulfran, usually so calm, was getting
impatient. Luncheon was over and he had gone
into his study with Perrine; every now and again
he walked to the window and listened.

"The train must be late," he murmured.

Perrine wanted to keep him away from the window, for there were many things going on outside
in the park about which she did not wish him to
know. With unusual activity, the gardeners were
putting great pots of flowers on the steps and in
front of the house. Flags were flying from the
recreation grounds, which could be seen from the
windows.

At last the wheels of a carriage were heard on the
drive.

"There's Fabry," said M. Vulfran. His voice
expressed anxiety, but pleasure at the same time.

Fabry came in quickly. He also appeared to be in a somewhat excited state. He gave a look at Perrine which made her feel uneasy without knowing why.

"I got your telegram," said M. Vulfran, "but it was so vague. I want to be sure. Speak out."

"Shall I speak before mademoiselle?" asked Fabry, glancing at Perrine.

"Yes, if it is as you say."

It was the first time that Fabry had asked if he could speak before Perrine. In the state of mind in which she was suddenly thrown, this precaution only made her the more anxious.

"The person whom we had lost trace of," said Fabry, without looking at Perrine, "came on to Paris. There she died. Here is a copy of the death certificate. It is in the name of Marie Doressany, widow of Edmond Vulfran Paindavoine."

With trembling hands the blind man took the paper.

"Shall I read it to you?" asked Fabry.

"No, if you have verified the names we will attend to that later. Go on."

"I not only got the certificate; I wanted to question the man whom they call Grain-of-Salt. She died in a room in his house. Then I saw all those who were present at the poor woman's funeral. There was a street singer called the Baroness and an old shoemaker called Carp. It was the miserable existence which she had been forced to live that had finally killed her. I even saw the doctor who attended her, Dr. Cendrier. He wanted her to go to the hospital, but she would not be parted from her daughter. Finally, to complete my investigations, they sent me to a woman who buys rags and bones. Her name is La Rouquerie. I could not see her until yesterday, as she had been out in the country."

Fabry paused. Then for the first time he turned to Perrine and bowed respectfully.

"I saw Palikare, mademoiselle," he said. "He is looking very well."

Perrine had risen to her feet. For some moments she stood listening, dazed. Then her eyes filled with tears.

"I then had to find out what had become of the little daughter," continued Fabry. "This ragpicker told me that she had met her in the Chantilly woods and that she was dying of hunger. It was her own donkey that she sold to the ragpicker who found her."

"Tell me," cried M. Vulfran, turning his sightless eyes towards Perrine, who was trembling from head to foot, "why this little girl did not say who she was? You understand how deeply a little girl can feel, so can you explain this?"

Perrine took a few steps towards him.

"Tell me why she does not come into my arms . . . her grandfather's arms."

"Oh, grandpapa," cried Perrine, throwing her arms about his neck.

CHAPTER XXXI

THE GRATEFUL PEOPLE

FABRY had left the room, leaving the grand-father and his granddaughter together. For a long time the old man and the girl sat with their arms about each other. They only spoke now and again, just to exchange a word of affection.

"My little granddaughter . . . my boy's little girl," murmured the blind man, stroking her curls.

"My grandpapa," murmured Perrine, rubbing her soft cheek against his.

"Why didn't you tell me who you were?" he asked at last.

"But didn't I try several times?" replied Perrine. "Do you remember what you said to me the last time I spoke of dear mother and myself. You said: 'Understand, never speak to me again of those wretched creatures.'"

"But could I guess that you were my grand-daughter?" he said.

"If I had come straight to you, don't you think you would have driven me away and not have listened to me?" asked Perrine.

"Ah," said the blind man, sadly, "who knows what I would have done!"

"I thought so," said Perrine, "and I thought it

307

best not to let you know me until, like mama said, 'you would get to love me.'"

"And you have waited so long, and you had so many proofs of my affection."

"But was it the affection of a grandfather? I did not dare think so," said Perrine.

"When I began to suspect that you were my son's child, I then quickly got positive proofs, and I gave you every chance to tell me that you were. Finally I employed Fabry, who, with his investigations, forced you to throw yourself into my arms. If you had spoken sooner, my little darling, you would have spared me many doubts."

"Yes," said Perrine sweetly, "but we are so happy now, and doesn't that prove that what I did was all for the best?"

"Well, all is well. We will leave it at that. Now tell me all about your father . . . my boy."

"I cannot speak to you of my father without speaking of my mother," said Perrine gravely. "They both loved me so much, and I loved them just the same."

"My little girl," said the blind man, "what Fabry has just told me of her has touched me deeply. She refused to go to the hospital where she might have been cured because she would not leave you alone in Paris . . ."

"Oh, yes; you would have loved her," cried Perrine; "my darling mother."

"Talk to me about her," said the old man, "about them both."

" Yes," said Perrine; " I will make you know her and then you will love her."

Perrine told about their life before they lost all their money; then about their travels through the various countries and the wanderings over the mountains; then of her father's illness and his death, and how she and her sick mother journeyed through France with the hope that they could reach Maraucourt in time before the sick woman died.

While they were talking they could hear vague sounds outside in the garden.

" What is the matter out there? " asked M. Vulfran.   Perrine went to the window.   The lawns and drive were black with a crowd of men, women and children.   They were dressed in their Sunday clothes; many of them carried banners and flags. This crowd, between six and seven thousand people, reached outside the grounds to the public park, and the murmur of their voices had reached the ears of the blind man and had turned his attention from Perrine's story, great though it was.

" What is it? " he asked.

" It is your birthday today," said Perrine, smiling, " and all your men are here to celebrate it and to thank you for all you have done for them and their families."

" Oh! . . . "

The blind man walked to the window as though he could see them.   He was recognized and a murmur ran through the crowd.

"*Mon Dieu,*" he murmured, "how terrible they
would be if they were against us." For the first
time he realized the strength of the masses which
he controlled.

"Yes," said Perrine, "but they are with us because we are with them."

"Yes, little girl, and it is all due to you," he replied. "This is very different from the day when
the service for your dear father was held in that
empty church."

"Yes, they are all here now," said Perrine, "and
this is the Order of the Day, grandpapa dear: I am
to guide you to the steps exactly at two o'clock.
From there everyone will be able to see you. A man
representing each village where you have your factories will come up the steps, and fatherly old
Gathoye in the name of all is to make a speech."

At this moment the clock struck two.

"Now give me your hand, grandpapa, dear," said
Perrine.

They reached the top of the steps and a great
cheer broke out. Then the dear old Gathoye, who
was the oldest employé, came forward alone. He
was followed by the five delegates. Ten times the
old man had been made to go over his speech that
morning.

"Monsieur Vulfran, sir," he began, " it is to wish
you . . . it is to congratulate you . . . to congratulate you on . . . "

Here he stopped short and began gesticulating
with his hands, and the crowd, who saw his eloquent

gestures, thought that he making an elaborate speech.

After some vain efforts, during which he scratched his head several times, he said: "This is how it is: I had a fine speech all ready, but I've gone and forgot all I got to say. I had to congratulate you and thank you in the name of all from the bottom of our hearts . . . "

He raised his hand solemnly.

"I swear that's so on the faith of your oldest employé, Gathoye."

Although the speech was very incoherent, nevertheless it touched M. Vulfran deeply. With his hand on Perrine's shoulder, he moved forward to the balustrade. There all could see him from below.

"My friends," he called out in a loud voice, "your sincere kind wishes give me the greatest pleasure, all the more so as you bring them to me on the happiest day of my life, the day when I have found my little granddaughter, the daughter of my only son whom I have lost. You know her; you have seen her at the factory. She will go on with the work we have already begun, and I promise you that your future, and your children's future, is in good hands."

Thereupon he leaned down towards Perrine and before she could protest he lifted her up in his arms that were still strong, and presented her to the crowd, then kissed her tenderly.

Then a deafening cheer rang out. It was continued for several minutes. Cheers came from the mouths of seven thousand men, women and children.

Then, as the Order of the Day had been previously
arranged, a line was formed and in single file they
passed before their old chief and his granddaughter.
With a bow and a hearty wish each man passed by.

" Ah, grandpapa, if you could only see their kind
faces ! " cried Perrine.

But there were some faces that were not exactly
radiant.   The two nephews certainly looked very
glum when, after the ceremony, they came up to
their cousin to offer their congratulations.

" As for me," said Talouel, who did not mean to
lose any time in paying court to the young heiress,
" I had always supposed . . . "

The excitement of the day proved too much for
M. Vulfran.   The doctor was called in.

" You can understand, doctor," said the blind man
anxiously, " how much I want to see my little granddaughter.   You must get me into a state so that I
can have this operation."

" That is just it," said the doctor cheerily, " you
must not have all this excitement.   You must be
perfectly calm.   Now that this beautiful weather
has come, you must go out, but you must keep quiet,
and I guarantee that as soon as your cough has gone
we shall be able to have a successful operation."

And the doctor's words came true.   A month
after M. Vulfran's birthday two specialists came
down from Paris to perform the operation.

When they wished to put him under an anesthetic
he refused.

" If my granddaughter will have the courage to

hold my hand," he said, " you will see that I will be brave. Is it very painful? "

They would use cocaine to alleviate the pain.

The operation was over. Then came five or six days of waiting. The patient was kept in a dark room. Then at last the grandfather was allowed to see his little granddaughter.

" Ah, if I had only had my eyes," he cried as he gazed at Perrine's beautiful little face, " I should have recognized her at the first glance. What fools' Couldn't anyone have seen the likeness to her father? This time Talouel would have been right if he had said that he ' supposed ' . . ."

They did not let him use his eyes for long. Again the bandage was put on and was kept on for thirty days. Then one of the oculists who had remained at the chateau went up to Paris to select the glasses which would enable him to read and see at a distance.

What M. Vulfran desired most, now that he had seen Perrine's sweet face, was to go out and see his works, but this needed great precaution, and the trip had to be postponed for a time, for he did not wish to be closed up in a landau with the windows up, but to use his old phaeton and be driven by Perrine and show himself with her everywhere. For that they had to wait for a warm, sunny day.

At last the day they wanted came. The sky was blue, the air soft and warm. After luncheon Perrine gave the order to Bastien for the phaeton with old Coco to be at the door.

"Yes, at once, mademoiselle," he said with a smile.

Perrine was surprised at the tone of his reply and his smile; but she paid no more attention to it, as she was busy fussing about her grandfather so that he would not take cold.

Presently Bastien came to say that the phaeton was ready. Perrine's eyes did not leave her grandfather as he walked forwards and down the steps alone. When they reached the last step a loud bray made her start. She looked up.

There stood a donkey harnessed to a phaeton! A donkey, and that donkey was like Palikare, a Palikare shiny and glossy, with polished shoes and adorned with a beautiful yellow harness with blue tassels. The donkey, with his neck stretched out, continued to bray. In spite of the groom's hold upon him he turned and tried to get to Perrine.

"Palikare!" she cried.

She flew to him and flung her arms around his neck.

"Oh, grandpapa, what a lovely surprise!" she cried, dancing around her dear Palikare.

"You don't owe it to me," said her grandfather. "Fabry bought it from that ragpicker to whom you sold it. The office staff offer it as a gift to their old comrade."

"Oh, hasn't Monsieur Fabry got a good, kind heart!" cried Perrine.

"Yes, he thought of it, but your cousins did not," said M. Vulfran. "I have ordered a pretty cart from Paris for him.   This phaeton is not the thing for him."

They got up into the carriage and Perrine took the reins delightedly.

" Where shall we go first, grandpapa? " she asked.

" Why, to the log cabin," he said.   " Don't you think I want to see the little nest where you once lived, my darling? "

He referred to the cabin on the island where she had lived for a time the preceding year.   It remained fondly in his mind. She drove on to the entrance and helped her grandfather alight at the path.

The cabin seemed just the same as when Perrine left it.

" How strange," said M. Vulfran, " that only a few steps from a great industrial center you were able to live the life of a savage here."

" In India we led a real savage life," said Perrine. " Everything around us belonged to us there, but here, I had no right to this and I was often very afraid."

After M. Vulfran had inspected the little log hut he wanted to see the crèche at Maraucourt.

He thought that he would easily recognize it, as he had so often discussed the plans with Fabry, but when he found himself at the entrance, and was able to see at a glance all the other rooms, the dormitory where the little babies were asleep in their rose and blue cribs according to the sex, the playroom where those who could walk were playing, the kitchen, the lavatory, he was surprised and delighted.

Using large glass doors, the architect had cleverly made his plans so that from the first room the mothers could see all that went on in the other rooms where they were not allowed to enter.

In the nursery the children sprang forward and jumped upon Perrine, showing her the playthings that they had in their hands.

" I see that you are known here," said M. Vulfran.

"Known!" replied Mlle. Belhomme, greeting them. " She is loved by all; she is a little mother to them, and no one can play like she can."

M. Vulfran put his arms affectionately around his daughter as they went on to the carriage.

They returned home slowly as evening fell. Then as they passed from one hill to another, they found themselves overlooking the surrounding country, where new roofs and tall chimneys could be seen everywhere.

M. Vulfran took Perrine's hand.

" All that is your work, child," he said; " I only thought of business. See what you have done. But so that this can all be continued in the years to come, we shall have to find you a husband, one who will be worthy you, who will work for us. We will not ask anything more of him. I think one day we shall find the right man and we shall all be happy . . . en famille . . ."

THE END

THE BERRY PATCH

JOSEPHINE LAWRENCE

12mo. Illustrated.   *Beautiful cloth binding, stamped in gold and jacket in colors.*

Price, $1.50 Net.

The Berry family home was called the Berry Patch because of the "cross-patch" dispositions of the children, but, at heart, they all wanted to be right, and so the clash of experiences at last brought good results. In the process of interesting events, the reform of the family brought about the reform of the community, with unhappy dispositions changed into lovable characters, that make good citizens and reach social success.

Elspeth Oliver is the girl whose energy keeps things whirling in the Berry Patch. Judge Berry was the great authority on what's what among them, and John Tabor, the school teacher, was the romantic character in the community. All the human excitements of pride and self-will enter into the various ambitions. Even generous impulses were taught restraint in the experiences of various kinds, showing that there is an appropriate time and place for everything.

The Berry Patch children did not get into mischief from any desire to make trouble, but because a surplus of energy was engaged in making discoveries. However, the greatest of all discoveries was that experience is a dear teacher, and random experiences sometimes cost many tears. Human nature in the "Berry Patch" is revealed in so many ways that it makes profitable and interesting reading for those who are troubled with household troubles.

Send for Our Free Illustrated Catalogue.

CUPPLES & LEON COMPANY, PUBLISHERS   **New York**